monsoonbooks

THE MAN WHO WORE HIS WIFE'S SARONG

Born in Malaysia, Suchen Christine Lim grew up in Malaysia and Singapore. Awarded a Fulbright grant, she is a Fellow of the International Writers' Programme at the University of Iowa, and is the first Singapore writer honoured as the university's International Writer-in-Residence. In 2012 she received the Southeast Asia Write Award. In 1992, her novel, *Fistful of Colours*, won the inaugural Singapore Literature Prize, and in 2015 it was selected by *The Sunday Times* as one of the top 10 Singapore classic novels. Another novel, *The River's Song*, was selected by *Kirkus Reviews* (USA) as one of "The 100 Best Books of 2015". Other novels include *Rice Bowl*, *Gift From The Gods*, and *A Bit of Earth*, shortlisted for the Singapore Literature Prize.

The Man who Wore his Wife's Sarong is an updated and expanded edition of *The Lies that Build a Marriage*, which was shortlisted for the Singapore Literature Prize in 2008, featuring four additional stories.

T0127573

ALSO BY SUCHEN CHRISTINE LIM

Novels
Fistful of Colours
(inaugural Singapore Literature Prize winner)

A Bit of Earth
(shortlisted for the Singapore Literature Prize)

Gift From the Gods

Ricebowl

The Lies that Build a Marriage

The River's Song

Nonfiction
Stories of the Chinese Overseas

THE MAN WHO WORE

HIS WIFE'S SARONG

STORIES OF THE UNSUNG, UNSAID
AND UNCELEBRATED IN SINGAPORE

SUCHEN CHRISTINE LIM

monsoonbooks

Published in 2017
by Monsoon Books Ltd
www.monsoonbooks.co.uk

No.1 Duke of Windsor Suite, Burrough Court,
Burrough on the Hill, Leicestershire LE14 2QS, UK

ISBN (paperback): 978-1-912049-08-0
ISBN (ebook): 978-1-912049-09-7

Cover design by Cover Kitchen.

Individual story publication history on page 288.
The Man who Wore his Wife's Sarong is an updated and
expanded edition of *The Lies that Build a Marriage*, first
published by Monsoon Books (Singapore) in 2007.

MIX
Paper from
responsible sources
FSC® C018072

Printed in Great Britain by Clays Ltd, St Ives plc
20 19 18   2 3 4 5

For those made less equal by ignorance and unjust laws,
or silenced because of their difference, work or livelihood.

CONTENTS

INTRODUCTION

by Rev Dr Yap Kim Hao
The first elected Asian Bishop of the Methodist Church
in Malaysia & Singapore
Pastoral Advisor, Free Community Church

In October 2005, I asked Suchen Christine Lim to write a story for the Christmas Day service of the Free Community Church. I wanted a story to serve the LGBT community and to help grow a more inclusive church for both gays and straights in Singapore. I did not foresee the impact that her story would make on Christmas Day. After Suchen had read out *The Morning After* to a packed congregation in the auditorium of the Arts House, there was absolute silence. Seconds later, thunderous applause broke out. The congregation rose to its feet and gave her a standing ovation. Men cried and hugged each other. The applause went on and on. This was the first time that such a story about a young man coming out to his mother and family was read out in a church service in place of the usual sermon. Suchen's story of a young man's courage and honesty, and a mother's love and confusion touched our hearts that Christmas Day.

Later, the lesbian community in the church asked her to write a story for them to celebrate International Women's Day. Suchen wrote and read to them, *My Two Mothers* – a beautiful story of the love and affection that two lesbian Chinese *amah jieh* or maids have for each other and their adopted daughter. Then Rev Kang Ho Soon, pastor of the Kampong Kapor Methodist Church asked Suchen to write a story for Mothers' Day. Again she obliged. The result was *Usha & My Third Child,* a story that touched on abortion and what motherhood means for an unmarried girl and her counsellor, an unhappily married woman.

Since then these stories have snowballed into a collection of stories of 'the unsaid, unsung and uncelebrated' that tackle difficult themes that discomfit a mainstream congregation or audience, and highlight difficult subjects that families would rather not talk about if they could help it such as my son is publicly caned in school or my son is HIV infected or my father is having an affair with my mother's tenant. The stories speak to those who know what it is like to live at the margins of society dealing with issues we do not discuss with our family members. Read the stories and talk about them.

MEI KWEI, I LOVE YOU

Potong Pasir

1

Two hours past midnight, Cha-li was sitting inside her grey Toyota, watching the corner house in Sennett Estate. There were nights when she wanted to call it quits, but she didn't because she'd given her word. Keeping her word was essential in her business. It was what drew women to her. The scarred, the abused, the cheated, the exploited, the rejects and the victims. Single or married, they came to her at the temple. They knew by word of mouth that her speciality was adultery and infidelity. Not for her—the commercial investigations or surveillance of employees or insurance fraud or missing persons. A specialist in unfaithfulness, that's what you are, a client had told her. Cha-li liked the phrase. It made her feel she was more than a private eye. She was the PI who peered into hearts seething with dark secrets and contradictions. But she was cautious about making any claims. A private investigator deals with hard facts—the what, the when and the where—not the speculative whys and wherefores. That was what she told Robina Lee, who'd come to see her two weeks ago.

Where is Charlie Wong? Robina had asked in a peremptory voice.

I am Cha-li Wong, she answered as confusion clouded the young woman's eyes. Cha-li was used to such reactions. Before meeting her in person, many people thought her Mandarin name, Cha-li (Beautiful Guard), was Charlie, because they'd expected the investigator to be a guy. Just like they'd expected a guy to take over as the medium of Lord Sun Wukong's temple. Ah well, such things no longer bothered her.

Robina Lee, the woman introduced herself. Not my married name, she added, and sat down across from Cha-li, who reckoned her age to be thirty or so. Robina was tanned, slim and looked tense. Her lips were rouged a deep pink, and her eyes had dark rings around them. Cha-li noted the smart black stilettos and expensive black leather purse, and wondered if Robina was one of those high-flying execs from the towering offices in Shenton Way. The look that Robina gave her seemed haughty at first. Seated with legs crossed and hands clenched tightly around the arms of the chair, she said in pitch-perfect Mandarin, My husband is seeing another woman. I would like to engage your services to find out who the woman is. What hold she has on him. What black magic, and here Robina switched to the Hokkien dialect and said emphatically, what *kong tau* the vixen used to ensnare him. I need a private investigator and a medium. I'm told you're both. I will pay you well above market rates if you agree to handle the case.

Taken aback, Cha-li muttered that she'd stopped conducting séances. She was more of a caretaker than a medium of the temple these days. No matter, Robina Lee said, and would not take no for an answer. She desperately needed a private investigator with knowledge of the black arts and *kong tau*. But what proof did she have that her husband had eaten *kong tau*? Cha-li asked. Robina stared at her hands, still clenched. Her husband was always distracted at home after dinner each night. At times he was glassy-eyed, distant and vague. He shot out of the house the moment his mobile rang. The family's business and reputation were suffering. But that did not necessarily prove he was bewitched, Cha-li pointed out. Robina's voice rose. Proof? You want proof? Then you tell me. Why else would a young man desert his young wife for a woman old enough to be his mother? Look at me. I am not yet thirty!

Cha-li calmed her down, agreed that it was an uncommon case. Far more common for a man to leave his old wife for a young mistress. But as a private investigator, she had to suspend judgement. Observe, listen, gather and assemble the facts, objects, people and events without adding or subtracting, explaining or interpreting. That should be the PI's objective, she explained to Robina. The temple medium, on the other hand, could go beyond the realm of fact and information to things hovering in the shadows, at the corner of one's eye.

Look, I don't care what you do. Just be discreet. I will pay you well. Those were Robina Lee's parting words.

A black cat jumped onto the bonnet of Robert Lee's white Mercedes and disappeared down the other side. Cha-li glanced at her watch. 2:38 a.m. Was he spending the night in the corner house? Could he be so bold as to leave his car parked in front of the house till morning? Cha-li rolled down her window and settled in to wait the whole night.

Butterfly Avenue was hushed, and the air was cool under the thick canopy of trees and bush. All the houses down the road had switched off their lights except the corner house at the end of the row of two-story terraces, each with a fenced-in garden, driveway and a car under the porch, the symbols that spelled *middle class* and *private property ownership*. Cha-li doubted she'd ever be able to own one of these prim-looking terraces. She was familiar with this private housing estate known as Sennett Estate in Potong Pasir, which had made history when it voted in Singapore's sole opposition MP in 1984. A teenager then, she saw how Prime Minister Lee Kuan Yew tore into and shredded the academic record of the opposition candidate, Chiam See Tong, and that had so roused the residents of Potong Pasir that they voted for the underdog. That year her heart had swelled with pride as she watched Kai-yeh, her adoptive father and medium of the Lord Sun Wukong's temple, rally the villagers to vote for Mr. Chiam. 1984 was also the year she crossed Upper Serangoon, the busy main road that separated her village from wealthy Sennett Estate, to attend Cedar Girls' School, not far from Butterfly Avenue.

Cha-li reached for the night-vision binoculars in her glove box and trained them on the house at the corner. The front door had opened and two figures had emerged. Robert Lee was with a woman silhouetted against the light from the living room. The woman was laughing and pushing him towards the gate. Cha-li's heart stopped. She couldn't breathe. Is that Rose? But Rose was dead. Died in Macau. That was what her sources had told her years ago. Were they wrong? Cha-li watched the woman in the red housecoat open the gate, push Mr. Lee out and shut it. Her eyes following the woman's retreating figure, she failed to catch the sound of a car engine starting. She didn't even see the white Mercedes drive away. Something was unravelling inside her head.

Mei kwei, Mei kwei, wo ai ni.
Rose, Rose, I love you.
A song she hadn't heard for years.

They had grown up together, she and Rose, in Lord Sun Wukong's temple in Potong Pasir village. She was the medium's adopted daughter while Rose was the unwanted mewling waif fished out of the temple's bucket latrine. Throughout their childhood, Rose was caned often, while she, Cha-li, was spoiled rotten by Kai-ma, her adoptive mother, and Kai-yeh, her adoptive father who channelled the spirit of Lord Sun Wukong, the Monkey King.

In those days, Potong Pasir was a stinking labyrinth of filthy lanes, muddy ponds, duck and vegetable farms, *attap* huts and outhouses with bucket latrines. The latrine is in your flesh! Kai-ma railed at Rose. Go and bathe, you filthy rag! But no matter how often Rose took a bath, she could never shake off the stench that seemed to seep into her clothes, her hair and under her skin. Rose cursed the mother who gave birth to her and dumped her in the temple's outhouse. The children teased her. *Sai! Sai!* they yelled in Hokkien. Even the adults called her *Ah Sai*—lump of shit. The village boys would kick open the door of the outhouse whenever Rose was crouched inside. One day, Cha-li heard a loud quacking and flapping of wings. The bullies had jumped into the duck pond splashing and yelling as they frantically washed themselves—evidently, Rose had suddenly opened the outhouse door and hurled several brown lumps at them. You are the *sai*! Not me! I am Rose the beautiful! she screeched. Cha-li laughed.

Rose ran away from the temple several times, away from the

stink and choke of joss and other incense. Away from Kai-ma's caning and the boys' taunting. But the trail of rot pursued her wherever she went. The faster she ran, darting this way and that among the huts, the more lost she felt. Sometimes Cha-li found her crying in Yee Soh's outhouse with the mangy bitch snarling outside. Sometimes Rose hid under the bushes after Kai-ma had caned her. Once Cha-li found her on Upper Serangoon Road, a wiry urchin gulping exhaust fumes from the city's buses as though they were fresh air. The fumes overwhelmed the stench in her flesh, Rose said, her eyes bright as stars. The world outside Potong Pasir was a heady mix of new smells, speed and ceaseless motion to her. She gripped Cha-li's arm. Run! she yelled, and pulled Cha-li along. Cars honked as they dashed across the busy road, dodging bicycles, motorcycles, hawkers' carts and trishaws ferrying women and children.

Once across, Rose demanded: How much you have in your pocket? Show me. Come on, you monkey. She twisted Cha-li's arm. I know you've got money in your pocket. Her nails dug into Cha-li's flesh until she cried out. Then all of a sudden she felt Rose's hand stroking her face. Don't cry, little monkey, please don't cry. A thrill shot through Cha-li's heart. It was pounding so hard against her rib cage she had to shut her eyes to stop the dizziness coursing through her, the better to savour the sensuous feel of Rose's hand on her cheek. She took out all the coins in her pocket and dropped them into Rose's hand.

I knew it! You little monkey! Forty cents! Let's go and buy *tau huey*!

Sweet bean curd was Rose's favourite dessert. She ate tubs of it in those half-forgotten days, which was why her skin was so smooth and fair, and smelled so sweet that Cha-li almost swooned when Rose held her in the kitchen the night they both turned fifteen. Prostitute! Kai-ma's broom hit them on their heads. Rose sprinted out of the kitchen, and didn't return for three days and three nights.

Cha-li sighed, and returned the binoculars to her glove box feeling as if she had crawled out of a black hole where time had warped like a rattan mat left in the sun too long. How long had she been sitting in the car lost in her own thoughts? She was ashamed. This was uncharacteristic. And worse, she'd lost her quarry. Robert Lee's white Mercedes was gone. The gate of the corner house was shut, and the woman who looked like Rose had disappeared back inside. The house stood in darkness. Butterfly Avenue was wrapped in silence at three a.m. The night air was soft and sweet, as though this avenue was not part of such a densely populated city, as though it belonged to a time when there were few cars, and migrant workers from China, India or Bangladesh hadn't yet squeezed Singaporeans out of the crowded buses and trains.

Cha-li took out her black notebook, wrote down the time, date and her observations, and then shut it. It pained her to think of what she'd tell Robina Lee the next day. The woman had phoned earlier to say that she was coming to the temple tomorrow. Cha-li had no wish to see her yet, but an operative must maintain close contact with her client just as a medium must maintain close psychic contact with the spirit she is channelling.

She got out of the car. She had to clear her head. She walked past the corner house and followed the road beyond the silent gated bungalows, their orange roofs gleaming in the ghostly night sky. There was no moon. Just banks of ominous grey clouds. Her mind returned to the woman who looked like Rose. If it was Rose, what was she doing back here? Had she moved up in the world through Robert Lee, son of a hotel chain tycoon? Was he her young lover? Was he bankrolling her?

Information was scarce at this point. Robina Lee was reluctant to tell her more. You are the investigator. You find out, she'd said at their last meeting. And let me remind you of your high fee plus expenses. In return, I expect the strictest confidence.

Cha-li grimaced at the memory of that voice. No, she didn't want to see Robina Lee tomorrow, and looked up, surprised that her feet had led her to the gate of Cedar Girls' School. She must have turned onto Cedar Avenue without thinking. This was their secondary school before Rose was expelled for what the school called 'unhealthy relationships'.

Monkey! Rose had yelled on the first day. Did you see the school toilet? No shit! No flies! No smell! So clean! You just pull the metal chain. And whooooosh! The water flushes away everything! Rose's face was glowing. The toilets aren't like those in Potong Pasir village. When I grow up I want to live in a beautiful house with a clean toilet just like this. And me? What about me? Cha-li asked. Oh, you? You will live in the temple, *lor*! You will be Lord Sun Wukong's medium. No, Cha-li protested. But it was not a very strong protest.

She turned away from the school and returned to Butterfly Avenue. A dog barked at her, strident and querulous. Cha-li crossed over to the other side of the road just so the stupid Alsatian wouldn't wake up the neighbourhood. The avenue was U-shaped, and where it curved, there was a small playground with a slide and a swing under the trees. Their shadows fell across the park where a girl's soft giggles broke the night's calm. She saw a young Rose and herself on the swing. Rose was pushing her higher and higher, and she was laughing and screaming, Stop! Stop!

What must you say? What must you say?
Mei kwei, Mei kwei, wo ai ni.
Rose, Rose, I love you.

The Alsatian's barking grew louder, joined now by the yelpings of other dogs. She quickened her pace. Just as she was about to reach her grey Toyota, a glimpse of black hair caught her attention. Near the red car. No, the black one. No. It's a mirage. An optical illusion. She must be hallucinating. Go home, Cha-li. Get some sleep!

She parked her Toyota in the wasteland next to the canal, formerly known as the Kallang River, that meandered through Potong Pasir village. Wild grass, bush and creepers grew around the old temple. The wasteland became a fairground every August during the feast of the Monkey King when an open-air stage was erected and a street opera was performed for the gods and devotees. When Kai-yeh was the medium, the entire village of Potong Pasir would gather at the temple to pray, eat and watch street opera for three days and three nights. These days, however, like the slow-flowing Kallang River that had given way to the rapid Kallang Canal, the street operas had given way to *getai* in which scantily clad women sang and danced, not for the gods but for the younger devotees who loved MTV. The wasteland had also shrunk, and the concrete blocks of housing board flats had moved closer to the temple each year.

Cha-li unlocked the side gate, collected the mail from the red letterbox and opened the door to her private quarters. Exhausted but hungry, she cooked a bowl of instant noodles and ate it while sorting through her mail.

What's this? She tore open the letter from the National Development Board. Her application to renew the temple's lease had been rejected. *We regret to inform you that the temple's site has been rezoned for public housing* ... Cha-li swore under her breath. Lord Sun Wukong's Temple had been here forever. This was her home. She must see Kai-yeh and let him know the bad news at once.

2

Outside the ward in the Goddess of Mercy Home for the Aged Sick, Mr. Singh, the night watchman, looked flummoxed. The gate, which he had padlocked the night before, was unlocked again this morning.

'The third time this week, Mr. Singh,' the staff nurse said.

'But Miss Tan, I lock the gate last night!'

'No, you didn't. The gate was open when I arrived. And you weren't at the gate.'

'I had to go to the loo.'

'We have residents here suffering from severe dementia. The gate must be locked at all times. I have to report this to the matron.'

'If you report, then I *susah-lah*!'

'If I don't report, and something happens, then how? I'm not going to be responsible, you know!'

Sitting on a chair next to the bed, arms resting on her lap, Cha-li stared out the window and pretended not to look at Kai-yeh's wizened face. Curled like a shrivelled foetus on his side, Kai-yeh was following the altercation outside his ward with avid interest. Neither of them spoke until the nurse and watchman walked away.

'Troublemaker,' Cha-li hissed. 'You did it, didn't you?'

Kai-yeh's eyes lit up. For a second, Cha-li saw the simian features pass through his wrinkled face like a wind moving across water. Then his lungs seized up. His chest heaved with the effort to draw in air. Fourth stage, the doctor had told her. The cancer had spread to his lungs. When his coughing worsened, Cha-li summoned the nurse. An oxygen mask was placed over his nostrils. Aahh ... ah, Kai-yeh dragged in each breath of air. Cha-li placed a hand on his chest. Gradually his breathing quieted. He waved off her hand, and pointed to the mask clamped over his face. Cha-li took it off.

'I ... I ... Rose. Bring ... her ... back here.'

'What? Kai-yeh. Did Rose visit you?'

He coughed again and again, and could not stop. Each explosion was worse than the one before. The young Malay nurse strode into the room and clamped the oxygen mask back on. 'You should go. The patient has to rest.'

Cha-li bent down and whispered in the old man's ear, 'Kai-yeh, you hang in there. I'll find Rose.'

His eyes remained closed; he gave no sign that he'd heard. Cha-li knew he wouldn't last long. She had to find Rose before Kai-yeh entered the eternal Peach Garden.

She drove back to Potong Pasir via Aljunied Road, past

Mount Vernon where the crematorium used to be, where the Christian cemetery and its dead slept in peace, where love had made the evening air fragrant when Rose held her hand as they walked among the tombstones and kissed in front of the dead.

She slowed as she turned onto Serangoon Road, and let the trucks and buses roar past her. New condominiums and shopping malls had replaced the black-and-white colonial bungalows. No remnants of the dairies, duck farms, vegetable gardens and *attap* houses remained. Rural disarray and abundant greenery had given way to concrete flyovers, congested roads and blocks of flats built by the Housing and Development Board. The only real village left in Potong Pasir was St. Andrew's Village, a school complex with a chapel and an artificial rugby pitch. Butterfly Avenue and Sennett Estate, on the other side of Upper Serangoon Road, were part of the Potong Pasir constituency now, although this could change in the next general election when boundaries would be redrawn, and the authorities would once again deny that such redrawing of electoral boundaries was gerrymandering.

Cha-li thought of going to see the opposition MP, but changed her mind. She doubted that the old man, Chiam, could save the temple sitting on land slated for development. The temple was famous for its support of the opposition. Since the early 1980s, Kai-yeh had invoked the spirit of Lord Sun Wukong to help Chiam See Tong win in every general election, and Chiam's success was credited to Lord Sun Wukong's benevolence to the people of Potong Pasir. Cha-li smiled. So many stories had circulated to explain how Chiam, a humble lawyer with less-than-stellar school results, had held his own against the might of the PAP in general election after general election. No, the temple was doomed.

The authorities would sooner bulldoze it to the ground than preserve it.

Cha-li parked her car and went into the temple, surprised to find Robina Lee among the women praying at the altar of the Monkey King.

'Good morning, Wong Sifu,' the women greeted her.

In their eyes, she would always be Sifu or Master Wong, who channelled the spirit of the Monkey King. That she was also a private investigator was irrelevant to them; it was just a job to fill her rice bowl. Periodically, Cha-li suffered pangs of unease. She was a fraud burdened by a sacred duty that had been imposed on her as a child. As the chosen one, selected by Kai-yeh, who had consulted the Monkey King's spirit before anointing her as his successor, she had to serve in his absence. Years of performing the rituals, the chanting and the comforting had won her scores of grateful devotees, women who respected and adored her. Some had even been her lovers when she was young, handsome, lonely and pining for Rose.

'Good morning, Sifu!' the women called out to her again.

'Good morning, good morning!' she said, laughing as she opened the door to her office. Robina followed her inside and closed the door. She was wearing a dark pantsuit and sunglasses. When she took off her glasses, Cha-li saw the wretched look in her eyes. Her face was puffy, and there was a dark bruise on her right temple.

'Did your husband do this?'

Robina shook her head, and Cha-li didn't press her.

'He slept in the baby's room last night. He didn't want me near him.' Robina's voice was flat. 'You must give me a ritual cleansing. Please.'

Shocked by the request, Cha-li tried to focus her attention on the case instead.

'I have checked out your husband's new office in Shenton Way. His clients are all Indians. Rich fat cats who are buying up our luxury condos.'

'Robert is repulsed by the sight of me.'

'He's running some kind of consultancy that includes real estate.'

'Help me, Wong Sifu,' Robina pleaded, kneeling suddenly.

'No, no, please. Please stand up.'

'Our little boy is only six months old. Robert owes people a lot of money. My father-in-law does not know it yet. I fear ... I ...'

'Wait, Robina. I know. I ran a check—'

'He's bewitched. It's that vixen. Please, Wong Sifu, help me. The family ... the ... the scandal will ruin his father. Please, Sifu!'

Cha-li sighed. She was hoping it wouldn't lead to this. 'Go into the prayer hall, Robina. I have to change.'

She did not move until the woman had left the room. Then she locked the door.

The anointed are never free. They must respond to the cries of the broken and lost—Kai-yeh had drilled this into her from a young age. They sought her, these broken hearts. She had tried to tell them that Lord Sun Wukong, the Monkey King, was a figment of an author's imagination, but all to no avail. Besides, there were the women's testimonies. *Lord Sun Wukong answered my prayers*, some claimed. *He granted me a son*, declared another. *He made my husband stop seeing that woman and come back to me.*

She sighed. The women's beliefs had tinted their perceptions and shaped their universe. Lord Sun Wukong was the godly spirit who came to their aid. If she was tempted at times to tell them to pray to a rock, which would work just as well, she restrained herself. If praying had helped these women to sit still long enough for their problems to work themselves out, what right had she to destroy their faith in something higher than themselves? No bloody right at all! She yanked off her blue jeans and pulled on a pair of gold-coloured silk pants. Then she took off her red checked blouse and slipped on a white silk shirt and the Monkey King's bronze headband. She gazed at the woman in the mirror, dressed in silk pyjamas.

Would her features turn simian when she was as old as Kai-yeh?

She was six when Lord Sun Wukong, through the intercession of Kai-yeh, chose her to be his young messenger. Thrilled and scared that she, and not Rose, was the Chosen One, she had knelt before his altar and drunk a cup of tea mixed with holy joss ash. Lord Sun Wukong was a wise, courageous, shape-changing god in the Taoist pantheon of deities, Kai-yeh told her. Capable of forty-nine changes; he could change himself into a fly, a beautiful woman, a monster or a rock at the blink of an eye. That's what I want to do, she declared. Kai-yeh laughed: That you will, my child. That you will.

Later, in school, she discovered that the English storybooks referred to the deity as the Monkey King. In the temple, however, he was respectfully addressed as Lord Sun Wukong. His altar was covered with a red velvet ceremonial tablecloth embroidered with the Eight Immortals. The cloth reached down to the floor, hiding anyone under the altar from view. This was where she and Rose had slept as teenagers, hugging each other close each night, especially after Kai-ma's death when Rose refused to sleep in the kitchen alone. Kai-yeh sleepwalks and touches me, she complained.

The temple's drum boomed. Her assistant called out in a loud voice: 'Make way for His Excellency, Lord Sun Wukong!'

Cha-li took her rod and glided into the prayer hall.

3

The following week, on Monday evening, Cha-li waited in the parking lot of Tower Block One, Shenton Way. Outside, a thunderstorm was pelting the city hard. After two weeks of blistering sunshine and high humidity that caused her shirts to cling to her back, the weather had finally turned. The storm raged as she sat in her car, watching Lift Lobby Two and the white Mercedes parked near it. Robert Lee should appear at any moment. By seven, the storm petered out. Several men and women walked out of the lift, got into their cars and drove off, leaving large gaps between the remaining cars. Bored, Cha-li continued to keep an eye on movements in the lift lobby as a light drizzle started to fall on the city's grey towers now gleaming wet in the lamplight. Another hour passed, and still no sign of Robert Lee. Lift Lobby Two was brightly lit and empty, most of the executives having left the building by now. For the past two weeks, Robert had left his office between six and seven. Tonight he was late, but he could dash out of the lift any minute. Two evenings ago, she'd had to duck her head and pretend she was reaching for something in the backseat when he'd come out of the lift suddenly with an Indian client in tow. Tonight she was better prepared. She had donned a wig and changed her glasses.

At 8:46 p.m. Robert Lee came out of the lift, alone. He drove out of the parking lot with Cha-li tailing him through heavy traffic to Orchard Road and the Hilton. She did not follow him into the hotel this time. Instead, she drove home to collect Saddam Hussein. Tonight she would try a new strategy.

At ten p.m. she parked her grey Toyota near the playground on Butterfly Avenue and got out. 'Come on, Saddam boy. Okay, okay! Let's go!' Her fox terrier jumped out of the car, pulling at its leash. Laughing, Cha-li jogged after Saddam Hussein—taking the dog out at night was good camouflage. Running down the lanes gave her a chance to observe the corner house on Butterfly Avenue from different vantage points. She could see a pattern beginning to emerge.

As she came around the corner, Robert Lee's white Mercedes stopped in front of the corner house. His passenger, a well-groomed Indian male in a long-sleeved blue shirt and dark trousers, stepped out and pressed the buzzer on the gate. When it opened, Robert Lee drove off.

Back inside her grey Toyota with Saddam Hussein panting in the backseat, Cha-li checked her notes again. For the past several nights, Robert Lee had brought a different Indian male to the house. Sometimes, Robert went in with his guest. But last Tuesday night, he had dropped his Indian guy off and driven away, and Cha-li had tailed him back to his home. Last Monday, Wednesday and Friday nights, Robert had parked his car and followed his

Indian guest into the house. About two hours later, the two men had returned to the car and driven back to the Indian's hotel. Just this week alone, she had followed Robert to several high-end hotels. On Monday night, it was the Fullerton. On Wednesday night, it was Marina Bay Sands. On Friday night, the Ritz-Carlton. On Saturday night, the Shangri-La. But all these details hardly spelled adultery. Robert Lee was simply the chauffeur for his rich Indians. She'd not seen any women coming out of the corner house yet except the one in red who looked like Rose.

She flipped over several more pages in her notebook. Nothing important in there. Her surveillance of Robert's office had yielded little except a list of his dinner appointments with Indian clients, who inevitably ended up going to the corner house for dessert. Which was interesting. Is the house a brothel? Unlikely. Butterfly Avenue was not Geylang Road. Sennett Estate was in one of the city's respectable middle-class areas. It's true that some wealthy Chinese had bought houses here for their mistresses, but this had not dented the estate's respectability. Besides, Cha-li had not seen any young women emerging from the corner house. Was the woman in red the sole magnet that attracted the Indians? But if the woman was Rose, she'd be fifty-five and considered over the hill, no? Unless ... unless she was offering something kinky.

4

On Sunday the matron phoned. Kai-yeh had taken a turn for the worse. When Cha-li arrived at the home, Kai-yeh was hooked up to a ventilator and drip.

'Is he in pain?'

What she really wanted to know was: *Is he going to die?* He was all the family she had.

'He's stable for now. The doctor has given him an injection.'

Cha-li slumped into the chair next to the bed. She stroked the old man's hand. His eyes opened. He raised his forefinger with some effort, and tried to speak. But all he managed to croak was 'Rose.' After that, he had to breathe hard to make up for that expense of energy.

'Kai-yeh, I'll find her.'

Cha-li parked the rental van outside the corner house. Pulling a cap on her head, she got out, pressed the buzzer on the gate and shouted into the intercom, *'Karang guni!* Collect old newspapers!'

The gate opened, and she walked up the driveway. The front door was ajar.

'Come in!' a woman shouted from the kitchen.

Cha-li stepped inside the spacious living room. Its walls were apple white, and the floor was made of white marble. A large white sofa and two armchairs upholstered in white leather sat on a thick beige and grey carpet. The woman who came out of the kitchen didn't seem surprised to see her.

'I knew you'd find me sooner or later.'

'Rose.' That was all Cha-li could manage. Her throat was dry.

Rose, meanwhile, said nothing. She had not moved from her spot near the kitchen. Cha-li peered at her. Wearing a pink housecoat, she looked like the aunties who came to the temple to pray. At fifty-five, Rose was no longer the young dark beauty queen who had held men spellbound as she gyrated onstage with a python in the Great World Cabaret and broke Cha-li's heart. A hard glint appeared in Rose's eyes as she looked at Cha-li, who searched for something to say now that she was face to face with the girl—no, the woman—she had once loved.

Scenes from their past came and went in her head. She saw their two naked bodies, tinted red by sunlight shining through the red tablecloth covering Lord Sun Wukong's altar, as Rose's fingers reached into the deep moist recesses between her thighs, stirring feelings of love, guilt and shame. Ashamed of what she felt, and conscious that she was Kai-yeh's chosen successor, while Rose was just the temple's waif, she fought hard to suppress her feelings. Until one day, Rose was gone. Gone without a word. Frantic with worry, and sobbing her heart out, Cha-li went to the police. A missing person's report was filed but nothing came of it. She wept long and hard every night. For months she haunted the places they used to visit. Kai-yeh was philosophical. Rose is a temple stray. Strays come and go. It's their nature, he said, and encouraged her to study hard.

Five years later, Cha-li became a private investigator. She was on duty in the Malaysian town of Ipoh when she chanced upon a large black-and-white photo of Rose in the Great World Cabaret. It showed a scantily clad sultry beauty with long, dark tresses, and a large python curled around her. Shocked, Cha-li sat through Rose's show before charging into her dressing room backstage. Fuck off, Cha-li! I don't owe you an explanation! The cabaret! Now, that's *my* temple! It's where I dance like a woman. Sexy and beautiful. You! You prance around that temple like a dressed-up monkey! Stung, Cha-li left the cabaret, and hadn't seen Rose again.

'You might as well take off the cap.'

Cha-li pulled off her hat and stuffed it into the pocket of her jeans.

'Why have you come?' Rose asked in a hard voice.

'Kai-yeh is dying.'

'Good! May he rot in hell!'

'He gave you a roof over your head, Rose.'

'Keep your pious shit, Cha-li. You're blind, and a fool. He gave me more than that. Come.'

Cha-li followed her into the kitchen. Rose threw open a door, and Cha-li walked into the kitchen of the house next door. She followed Rose into the dining room where an old woman was trying unsuccessfully to feed a young man strapped to his chair. The young man's large shaved head was lolling on the back of the chair as though his neck was too soft to support it. Spit was dribbling from the corner of his mouth, which was making guttural sounds. The old woman wiped off the spit with a washcloth, and shoved another spoonful of rice into the gaping hole as though to stop the ugly sounds coming from it.

'Ugh! Ugh! Ugh!'

'What your Kai-yeh gave me.'

Cha-li stared at the head and vacant eyes. 'Did he … ? Did he … ?' Helpless, she turned to Rose.

'He raped me. Then I tried to abort him.'

Rose patted the lolling head, which said, 'Ugh! Ugh!' and more spit dribbled.

'Good morning, Madame Mei Kwei! Good morning, Ugh-Ugh!' two girls called out in Mandarin as they came down the stairs, their nipples showing under their skimpy nightdresses. Cha-li remembered seeing them when she was walking Saddam

Hussein. One of the girls approached them and planted a kiss on the lolling head. 'Ugh! Ugh!' The distended mouth dribbled more spit, and the wrists strained at the belt that strapped them to the armrests.

Rose turned away. 'Let's go back. They're getting ready to eat.'

Cha-li followed her back to the first house. The sun had come into the living room, and the light that bounced off the white marble floor hurt Cha-li's eyes. Her head was swimming.

'Is Robert the mastermind?'

'No. Robert has to settle his gambling debts. I ... ah! I need the money and so do these China girls. They have something to sell that the Indians want to buy. Robert brings the Indians. I bring the girls. Everyone is happy. It's not a crime.'

'I don't know about that.'

Rose drew the curtains. 'Report it to the police if you want. I don't care what you do.'

'Why? Why didn't you tell me what he did?'

'Tell you?' Rose's laughter bordered on the hysterical, a wild gleam in her eyes. 'Tell *you?* The bastard's monkey girl? The Great Lord's Chosen One with a paper gold band on your head? And a fake gold chain around your neck? The bastard was holding the bloody chain while you pranced before the devotees, drunk in their adoration. Strike me dead, Cha-li! I couldn't tear open my heart to a prancing monkey in silk robes!'

She wanted to slap Rose, but walked to the front door instead and stopped at the doorway, surprised at the sudden weight in her limbs. Her shoulders sagged. The memory of the gilt headband that she'd worn in those days made her cringe. It was made of cardboard and cheap plastic, painted gold. Later, she had bought the bronze headband to replace it.

The sunlight outside hurt her eyes, which were beginning to tear, the same eyes that had remained shut when footsteps were shuffling in the middle of the night into the kitchen where Rose slept. Rose's mouth was moving, saying something to her, but she couldn't catch the words. She kept thinking of the lolling head and dribbling mouth next door.

'The ... the temple will be demolished. Very soon,' she said without turning around. She couldn't face Rose. She wanted to shut her eyes, shut out the noonday glare, but she forced herself to keep them open, fixed on the green lawn outside sizzling in the midday heat. 'I ... I can get a flat big enough for the three ... three of us ... er ... you and him ...' Her voice trailed off.

AH NAH:

AN INTERPRETATION

'A long time ago in a remote part of China, a man went to live in a forest so far away and so deep that, for years, nobody saw or visited him. The people in his clan village forgot all about him until one day, years later, they were shocked to hear that the man had a son, and his son had passed the imperial examinations and been appointed the judge of their district. When the man's clansmen heard this piece of great news, they were filled with great pride. "At last, heaven has honoured us," they exclaimed and they flocked to the city, hoping to catch a glimpse of the young judge, their fellow clansman. Those who saw him went home and told their families that the young judge had a handsome pointed face with large intelligent eyes.

'Meanwhile the man, now old and bent with age, was overcome with great joy and happiness. His son took him to the city to live in the judge's official residence. Not long after that, the young judge had a strange dream. In his dream a dog had looked at him with such sad and intelligent eyes that he had awakened with tears in his own eyes. He asked his aged father what the dream could mean, but the old man shook his head sadly and said nothing. That same night the judge dreamt about the dog again, and again he woke up with tears in his eyes.

'After the third night the judge could not take it any more. He consulted a monk who listened to his story very carefully. "Set up an altar in the courtyard of your residence," the monk said. "Offer incense and burn joss papers. Kneel and kowtow three times to whatever you see in the fire." Puzzled yet determined, the young judge did what the monk had instructed. He offered incense and ordered his servants to burn large quantities of joss paper. True enough, there it was again! Seated in the heart of the fire was the sad-looking dog! His servants were amazed. The young judge was speechless and his aged father was sobbing. "That is your mother, my son," the old man confessed.

'On hearing this, the young judge knelt down at once, crying out in a loud voice, "Mother!" He knocked his head on the stone floor and kowtowed three times. The sad-looking dog smiled as the fire died out. That night the young judge slept peacefully.

'Strange story, eh? Some stories are like this, right or not? A story is like a pebble. You fling it into the lake and its ripples spread in ever-widening circles as it sinks to the bottom of our unconscious. There it stays forever. That's why stories are dangerous, right or not? They mould our lives.'

A long pause. We sip our tea. I can't take my eyes off this woman in front of me.

'Mummy told me that story when I was three. "Always honour your mother, no matter who she is!" That was what she used to say. For many years I could never see any other meaning in that story. It was always what Mummy said it meant—respect your parents, and that was it. No other interpretation entered my head. It was only after I'd found out that Mummy had betrayed me that I began to see other possibilities.'

'That's how an indoctrinated mind works,' I say.

'Scary, isn't it? Look at the judge's father in the story again. The old man was a nonconformist, right or not? He lived his own life in the forest, took his own suffering like a man and the storyteller rewarded him with a gifted son—a son who passed the imperial examinations, a son who became a judge. What more could a parent want? That was the highest blessing in imperial China! And look at all those villagers. They were the conformists. Living in a community, doing the same things that others did. But, ah, did they get a son who passed the imperial exams? So there you see! That's why this story is never found in your Singapore schoolbooks. D'you think the authorities would let such a story run loose in school? They hate this story. Aha! Not what you're thinking. No, no, they don't hate it for that. Not because it's dirty. Don't think dirty. Dirty minds see dirty things. If you ask me, I can tell you all about dirty men and dirty minds. No, the authorities, they don't like nonconformists. They hate us. And in this story the nonconformist was blessed with a successful and filial son. This story is subversive! Think about it. The nonconformist was rewarded and blessed. Don't you like it when you see it this way? Oh, do say you like it!'

'I like it.' I nod and smile at her.

'You're looking at the name card I gave out at the story seminar. That's right. It just says Ah Nah. Just call me that. Surname? No. No surname. I've no family name. Who's my family? My roots are in the rubbish dump. That's where my own flesh-and-blood mother threw me when I was born. You look shocked. Nothing should shock you by now. That was where Mummy found me. At the dump. She'd heard scuttling noises, she said. She'd spied some rats crowding around something. At first she thought it was just a dead kitten but it turned out to be a newborn baby—me. There! Look. I'm not ashamed. These pink welts above my breasts are where the rats bit me when I was a newborn. What you read in the papers is real. Teenage girls pregnant with fear are fiends. They turn against their own flesh in the womb. Sometimes when I go to the shopping malls, I look at their unlined teenage faces. They cling to their boyfriends' arms and I fear for them. But that lasts only a moment, you know. After all, what's there to be afraid of in life, right or not? Life is a mud pond. You mess around in it. You fall. You pick yourself up and learn to walk again. Then you fall again, and you rise again. That's how we survive, right or not?'

Her mellifluous Cantonese has the polished grace of someone who has studied the language of Hong Kongers for years. When Ah Nah laughs, the whole living room sparkles with her laughter. I never thought a white-haired woman could be so elegant and beautiful. She has left her hair uncoloured—a bold and rare move. Every Chinese woman has black hair these days, even the seventy-year-old grandma. But Ah Nah wears her hair white, looped into a simple chignon, held up by a few hairpins. She looks simple yet so elegant in her loose-fitting silk *qipao* with a single pearl button on her mandarin collar. She sits in the armchair, relaxed and confident with the feline grace of my Persian cat. Her face lights up when she smiles, and the wrinkles curl around her eyes. I make a lightning pencil sketch of her in my notepad. I just have to capture this spirit of intelligent inquisitiveness. We're seated, facing each other in her apartment overlooking Hong Kong Bay. I can't seem to take my eyes off her.

When I was twelve or thirteen, a strange scene took place in our neighbourhood one afternoon. I can still remember that afternoon as clearly as though it were yesterday. I was doing my homework when the phone rang.

Mother answered it. I heard her exclaim, 'Are you sure or not? So? So what happened? Oh, the gods!'

The moment she put down the phone, she rushed into the kitchen, grabbed a broom and dustpan and went out into the blazing sun. I followed her and, to my amazement, the aunties and grannies were out in full force, all pretending to sweep their driveways and water their plants! It was three o'clock in the afternoon and the sun was still blazing! They seemed to be waiting for something. Every now and then one of them would look across the road at our new neighbour's house. But Madam Chan's door was firmly shut.

'Taxi coming!' someone called out.

A yellow-top taxi swung into our lane and stopped right in front of Madam Chan's house. Out jumped an *amah* dressed in a white *samfoo* top and black silk pants. This elegant maidservant opened a black cloth umbrella and used it to shield a teenage girl who was emerging from the taxi. The girl's head was covered with a red cloth. The front door of Madam Chan's house opened, and the *amah* and girl hurried inside. The taxi sped off.

'Did you see that red cloth?'

'Did you see her face?'

'No, lah! How to see? Her *amah* is so smart. Covered her up with a red cloth.'

'She has to. The red will ward off evil and bad luck. It's been barely two days since the old man died on her.'

'It's bad. Very bad! No man will ever want her again.'

Everyone was talking but no one was listening to anyone. Then, seeing us children standing around, listening avidly, the aunties and grannies trooped into Mrs Lam's house. My mother didn't come home till it was time to cook the evening meal. That night when Dad reached home, Mother gave him a blow-by-blow account.

'She's been a *pipa* girl since she was fourteen,' Mother said.

'The papers here say sixteen.'

Dad stabbed at his copy of the Chinese tabloid which featured a black-and-white photo of a girl with a cloth over her head.

'Sixteen sounds better than fourteen. Anyway, don't believe all that the papers say. We should know better, we live next door.'

'So after that, what's been happening?'

'Nothing so far. The door's been shut all day and the curtains are drawn. The poor girl must still be in shock.'

'She should be. An old bugger died on top of her.'

'You watch your words.'

'What's there to watch? It's an ugly world out there. Children should know.'

Encouraged by Dad's comment I asked, 'What's a *pipa* girl?'

There! I told you so, my mother's eyes said as Dad answered my question.

'*Pipa* girl is a pretty term for pretty girls who work in old men's clubs in Chinatown, especially in Keong Saik Street in the old days. My own grandfather was a member of one of those clubs, I remember. Now when I think about this girl next door, I think about Grandpa. But my imagination is very filial. It daren't go any further.'

Mother glared at him. While my parents argued about the merits and demerits of talking about such things in my thirteen-year-old presence, I quickly flipped through the evening tabloid and read about the seventy-three-year-old man who was found dead on top of Ah Nah in Kuala Lumpur. His family had thought that the old man had gone for his morning constitutional when, in fact, he had gone to visit his *pipa* girl. Unfortunately his exertions must have been too excessive, for he collapsed and died on top of her. The teenage girl was so petrified that she went into a state of catatonic shock. She lay under the corpse for more than an hour before Lan Chay, her *amah*, sensing something was wrong, burst into the room and screeched for help. The other residents and clients in the brothel managed to lift the dead weight off Ah Nah. Then someone called the police. Ah Nah was taken to the station to make a statement, and that evening the tabloids hit the town. Since then the scandalmongers and bloodhound press had been pursuing her. Overnight, Kuala Lumpur changed and was no longer a safe and anonymous place to work in. She fled south and came home to her adoptive mother, Madam Chan. But the scandal reached Singapore even before she did, and that was how our neighbour, Mrs Lam, knew of her arrival. As I read the papers that evening, Ah Nah's name was on everyone's lips and our neighbours, including my parents, were placing bets on certain numbers on account of her.

'So you took down the taxi number?' Dad asked, his eyes glinting with greedy dreams of big bucks.

'What do you think? That was the first number I looked at.'

My parents' enthusiasm over the numbers that night was downright disgusting. It was the only time that I was ever ashamed of them. Was that all they could think about? A girl with a red cloth over her head had felt the icy touch of death, and all they could think about was the winning numbers in a lottery.

'It's blood money, I know. If I touch 4D and win, I won't feel good. But everybody's doing it. I'll feel worse if her number comes up and we didn't bet.'

Mother lit three sticks of incense and stuck them into the urn of ash before the Goddess of Mercy. But I was feeling unmerciful. The Goddess of Mercy heard me. Ah Nah's numbers never came up.

'You asked if I think about my mothers? No. This is the first time I'm talking about them. Here! Let's drink to the two of them! To the one who gave birth and the one who gave life! I kowtow three times. Like Na Cha, the Lotus Boy, I shred and return my flesh to the one who gave birth to me. I break and return my bones to the one who gave me life. I am now free! You smile and think this is childish in a sixty-seven-year-old woman. But fairy tales like *Na Cha* are powerful. That's why this version of the boy who shredded his flesh and returned his bones to his father has never entered the textbooks in Singapore. Interpretation shapes meaning. The official interpretation of *Na Cha* is that of a filial son who saved his parents from the wrath of the Dragon King. And the unofficial interpretation? Ah, that's the subversive one. To his stern father, the boy returned his bones. To his pleading mother, he returned his flesh. What was left was his—an untouchable soul to do with as he wished! He took it with him up to the mountains to begin a new life. Free at last from the chains of his father's authority. Look at you! Chained to your seat. Come over here and sit beside me. You're amazed, aren't you? That I, a former prostitute, can talk like this?'

My heart is beating fast. My pulse is racing. I am a grandfather, I tell myself. I am an old man. But darn it! You only live once! I lumber over and sit beside her. Her hair smells sweet. Will she let me hold her hand? The skin on the back of her hand is loose and mottled, but her fingers are long and slender. I can still remember the first time I chanced upon her. I had wandered into our back yard that Lunar New Year. She was standing alone near the wire fence that separated our two houses. She saw me so there was no avoiding her.

'Happy New Year,' I mumbled.

Her eyes lit up.

'Your roses, they are lovely.'

Her voice was soft and shy.

'I planted them,' I managed to croak.

I was fifteen then, and so choked up with pleasure that I could feel an embarrassed heat rising to my face. My ears were burning. I knew that I was turning the colour of beetroot so I bent down quickly and picked a pink rose.

'There! For you.'

I thrust the rose through the wire fence. Startled, Ah Nah stepped back, her eyes wide with fright like those of a young trapped animal.

'No, no, I can't. Mummy won't like it.'

'It's just a rose, just a rose,' I assured her as calmly as I could. I regretted my own boyish boldness. My god, did I do something wrong? My insides were shaking as I pulled back my hand through the wire fence. I flung the rose into the bushes. Ah Nah shook her head and quoted a Cantonese saying:

'Owe a debt of gratitude, repay with a thousand years of remembrance.
Owe a debt of flowers, repay with ten thousand years of fragrance.'

'I didn't know that,' I muttered, crushed by the weight of her Cantonese proverb. The English proverbs I had learnt in school were like 'A stitch in time saves nine' or 'Don't count your chickens before they hatch'. Light little sayings that we had rattled off during English Language lessons.

'I owe others a lot already so I don't want to owe any more.'

Her voice was soft like the whisper of a breeze, so I wasn't sure whether she had said it or I had imagined it that afternoon as we stood under the clear blue sky with just the wire fence between us. I thought she was the most beautiful girl I had ever seen, and that was why I blurted out, 'Run away. You don't have to be a *pipa* girl.' You should have seen Ah Nah's face. She looked at me as though I was mad.

'It's not Mummy who forced me into my line of work. My Mummy loves me very much.'

With that she vanished into the house and we never met or spoke again.

'There must be a God somewhere, you say right or not? But sometimes, when I look around at the world today, I ask God, where are you? I also know I'm a rare old bird. You smile. How many former prostitutes attend seminars? Ha! See! You laugh. But it's sad. Your academic seminars will be enriched if more of my kind attend. Even Jesus Christ seeks our company. He knows that we know what filth and dirt are in our hearts. Do you know how many children my organisation saves each year? In Vietnam alone? How many we lose or fail to save? Now, that I don't know. Many are trafficked into prostitution and sold into slavery by their own dead bitches of mothers. I was lucky. I was not sold. I was pleaded and begged into slavery. I was enslaved by gratitude and filial piety, fed on a diet of stories like the young judge and his bitch mother. My own bitch mother threw me away. My adoptive mother picked me up and fell on her knees, begging me to save her children. "Save your brother and sisters. Help me," she begged. "Their own father is dead. Help me put food on the table. That's all I ask of you, Ah Nah." I was fourteen at the time. What choice did I have? It never occurred to me to say no to the woman who had saved me from the rats. Mummy was kneeling before me with her hair down and her face streaked with tears. And all I could think of was that the Lightning God would strike me dead if I said no to her. Not one cent was I worth. That was how I saw myself. So I gave Mummy all that I earned. I swear before the gods that I did not keep a single dollar for myself. My stupidity lasted an incredible twenty-four years. You say can die or not? That we can be stupid for twenty over years and not know it. I was already thirty-eight when my brother sold my house to pay off his gambling debts. That was when I woke up. That three-storey house was my retirement money and he squandered it in casinos in the Genting Highlands. And he could do it. The house was in his name and Mummy's name. Not mine. How was it that I hadn't known earlier? How could I have known? I couldn't read then. I couldn't read! My sisters, they all went to universities overseas with the money I earned but I, I remained illiterate. I couldn't read.'

Tears roll down her cheeks. She's crying soundlessly. I hold her hand in mine. Down in the bay the water sparkles and dances in the light from the boats. I sit closer to her and close up the space between us. A cool breeze comes in through the window and ruffles her hair. Oh God! God! God! How you work in mysterious ways. Here she is, white-haired and still so beautiful. At sixty-five surely I am free to answer the whisperings of my heart? Or am I just a dirty old man? Ah Nah is right. Interpretation governs meaning. But how did an ex-prostitute learn that?

'Heaven never blocks all our paths. When I came to Hong Kong, KS came into my life quite by chance. I met him at the airport. He was a big and important professor at the university here. He engaged my services. I pleasured him well. In return he got teachers to teach me. I thought it was a fair exchange. I sought learning and he sought a secret pleasure, away from his wife and family. I had to be very discreet, but at least I was using my talent to work for myself. It was much much later that I formed this Save the Children organisation after KS passed away.'

That's all I need to know. My heart is racing. I don't trust myself to speak.

THE MORNING AFTER

There had been a seismic shift the night before. No one noticed it. Singapore the morning after was still the same. The sun rose as usual. Everything looked the same. Except Mother.

'When Cheng Lock brought her home for dinner last night, ha, I thought she was his office friend. So chatty she was. Auntie this! Auntie that! Sweet as sugar she was. She had a motive.'

'Ma,' I protested. 'How can you say that? You've just met Jennifer.'

'If no motive, why didn't she and Cheng Lock come straight out and tell me? Why wait till this morning? Your brother phoned me. From his office. Didn't even dare tell me face to face. Asked me what I thought of his woman. "I've just met her," I told him. That was when he dropped his bomb. They want to marry. Asked how I felt about it. "What's there to feel?" I said. My feelings, not important. So old already. One foot in the grave.'

It was a lie, of course. If her feelings weren't important, my mother wouldn't have taken a taxi immediately after Cheng Lock's phone call and come here.

My feelings were in a state, too, that morning. I didn't know what I was supposed to feel. I was still dizzy from David's news. I wondered if I should tell her about her grandson. Could the old lady cope with two shocks? I was all right. In fact, I was beginning to wonder if I was a normal mum. I ought to feel guilty or sad.

Somewhere inside my head, a judge was sitting expectantly. He expected me to feel guilty. Instead I was listening to my mother complain about my brother's heterosexual love affair.

'There's more. He asked if I wanted grandchildren. "But I've two grandsons already! Your sister's two sons! Are you so in love that you forgot?" I asked him. He laughed. He said he'd meant, what if he didn't want children of his own? That's when he revealed that the woman has two sons from her previous marriage. Asked if I would mind. "What's there to mind? I'm not the one getting married," I said. He asked if I would like the two boys to call me Nai-nai, like Daniel and David. "*Chieh*!" I said. "They can call me whatever. Nai-nai. Por-por. Grandma. All the same! But think carefully," I said. "Make sure you don't regret it. Adopting other people's sons is not like keeping a dog. You say right or not?" That's what I said to him.'

I could hear the anger in my mother's voice, and said so.

'Why do you always accuse me of anger, eh? I'm not angry. Get angry for what? I always tell my prayer group in the temple, let your children be free. My children are free to do what they like. That's my weak point. I'm too soft.'

It was on the tip of my tongue to point out to her that if she hadn't been so stern and possessive a mother, Cheng Lock wouldn't have had to resort to the phone to tell her about his marriage plans. My brother is forty-one. He has lived with our mother all his life. Has never married. Never brought any girl home for dinner. And until last year when he turned forty, our mother was still buying him his underwear. Yes, his underwear. Cheng Lock is the filial son. I'm the recalcitrant daughter. I fought our mother. Kept her at arm's length. Married early and left home.

When I got divorced, I rejected her offer to take care of my sons.

She predicted that my boys would do badly in school because of my neglect. Now a part of me was afraid that she would blame me for David's condition. Condition? What am I thinking? My son is not sick. Why do I have to feel guilty? David has won a state scholarship to study at MIT in the US. Any mother would be proud. But would I be just as proud if he had not done well academically?

My mother did not stop talking even as my attention wandered off. I was waiting to tell her about David. But she was worked up over my brother wanting to marry a woman with two sons. My son is never going to marry a woman. Shouldn't I be the one getting worked up?

'Ma.' I tried to stop her.

But she wanted to parade her virtues. So I had to listen.

'Your brother has a good life and doesn't know it. Which mother is like me? Cook, boil and simmer all day. Then last minute he'd phone to say he couldn't come home for dinner. I would have to eat leftovers for a week. Do I complain? I cook for him, I wash for him, I clean the flat for him. Have I so much as asked for a thank you all these years? Part of my life savings went into that apartment. Now he's getting married. He will expect me to move out of the master bedroom so he can bring home that woman and her two sons. Did you know that they've been living together for a year? He didn't tell me! Only now I know why he's never home. Any other mother would've wailed and complained. But not I. Not a pip out of me.'

'Ma, what are you doing now?' I was getting impatient.

She turned on me.

'Who do I tell if I don't tell you? Who? Your father left me to bring up the two of you. All these years, who knows my tears?'

She started to sob. I made no attempt to comfort her. It was a familiar pattern. My dead father was trotted out each time she wanted some sympathy. I was not surprised that my brother did what he did. It's difficult to handle a mother who cries a widow's tears.

A part of me was proud that I hadn't cried. Last night is engraved forever in my memory. David had stood in the middle of the living room. Still sporting the crew cut from his stint in the army, he was lanky like a robust young tree.

'Mum, I've something to tell you and Dan.'

He did not flinch when he said the word 'gay'. It was the first time that the word had been said among us. Was it Niyi, the African poet, who wrote, '*In the beginning is the Word. In the Word is our beginning*'? Was last night the beginning of my son's new life?

'Mum, I don't want to live a lie. I want to live in the open. In the light. Not hiding in the dark,' he said softly.

Brave words from a nineteen year old. But I was afraid for him. From the outside we're a tolerant, multi-religious, multi-cultural, multi-lingual, multi-everything society. But inside there's a hard kernel. Like an apricot's. We can be most unforgiving. What if the army finds out? He hasn't completed his national service yet. What if the Singapore Public Service Commission finds out and takes away his scholarship? It will break his heart. What if ...? What if ...? I started to pray.

Have I been so blind all these years? No, not blind. Once or twice it did occur to me, what if ...? Fleeting thoughts, never pursued. The mind shies away from such thoughts about one's son. No parent wants to think that it can happen to her son. We're close as a family, the three of us. Dan, David and I. When the boys were growing up, we talked during meals, mostly about what they had done or what was wrong with Singapore. Never, never about sex and sexuality. My fault. My fault. No, no, not my fault. Things aren't so simple. No one knows why such things happen.

When I woke up this morning, I was surprised at my own calm and collected state. My world hadn't fallen apart. David had declared that he was still the same David.

'Nothing has changed, Mum. Only your knowledge. That has changed. Not me. I want you to know about me before I go to the States, so you won't blame the US or the West for corrupting me.'

I was impressed that he had thought about this.

'How can you be so sure?' I asked him, keeping the edge out of my voice.

'I'm sure.'

His answer had the ring of authority that comes from first-hand knowledge.

'When? When did you know? What if you change your mind later?'

I was clutching at straws. Years ago, a student who was a bit of a tomboy had told me that she wanted to undergo a sex change to become a man. But five years later, the girl changed her mind. Last night I'd hoped, no, prayed in my heart that David would make the same happy mistake some day.

'When did you first know?' I asked him again.

David was silent. Then in a voice that quavered with emotion, he said, 'About nine or ten.'

His answer shocked me. Was that why my son was such a neatness freak? Such a good and tidy child? Unlike his elder brother, Dan, I never had to nag David about homework. Was he trying to compensate for his difference at age nine or ten? At that tender age he was already carrying a heavy burden.

'You just knew?' I asked him again.

He looked into the distant past. I saw the tears gathering.

'I prayed, Mum.' He paused, searching for the words. 'I asked God, "Why? Why me?" I asked Him to take it away.' He fell silent again, trying to bring his feelings under control. When he looked up, his eyes were sad. 'I knew God wouldn't take it away when I went to secondary school.'

'But you kept it to yourself.'

I was incredulous. Images of David as a ten-year-old schoolboy in blue shorts and a white shirt, and as a thirteen year old in a white shirt and white trousers, floated past my inner eye. Meanwhile, David stood silent before me as though I had accused him of deceit.

In a quiet voice he said, 'I couldn't tell you earlier. I had to be sure first.'

I hugged him. I wanted to hug away all his years of lonely struggle. I wished I could. 'You're my son. Whatever happens to you, you are still my son.'

I was reeling. Hanging on the wall of our sitting room is a photograph of David at seven. He's leaning against the window. His child's face, serious, his mouth, vulnerable, and the eyes that are looking straight into the camera seem to ask, 'Who am I?' Maybe I'm reading too much into it. My mind trawled the past for signs that I had missed. Could it have been his parents' divorce? No. It couldn't have been. I know of one happily married couple with two gay sons. I turned to Dan. My elder son had been quiet all this while.

'How do you feel, Dan, about David being gay?'

'It's okay, what! What's wrong?'

Dan's answer was gruff. But there was no mistaking his love for his younger brother.

These were some of the things I wanted to tell my mother on the morning after, but she was too upset with my brother's heterosexual love for a woman with two sons.

'Are you listening to me or not?' My mother nudged me back into her presence. 'I said Cheng Lock wants to bring the woman and her two sons home for dinner on Christmas Eve.'

'So?' I looked at her. 'Are you going to say there's no room at the inn?'

My mother was indignant. 'Why do you always think so badly of me, ha? I've already said they can come. He loves her. What can I do? Must accept her, what!'

I laughed. 'Ma,' I sat beside her. 'I've something to tell you about your grandson.'

THE MAN WHO

WORE HIS WIFE'S SARONG

Our family went to his wake and funeral.

'I don't care what others mutter under their breath about him. Kim Hock was a kind man. An honourable man and a loving father. He was the only relative who offered us a room when we first came to Singapore. All the others avoided us. Now that we're well off, it's a different story, lah!'

My mother knew what she was talking about. Like Uncle Kim Hock, my parents were from Penang where we still have many relatives, but my parents have never gone back, not even for a short visit. And I will tell you why.

My mother caused a huge scandal when she got involved with my father. Her family disowned her for living with a married man. It's no longer a scandal these days, but it was a huge scandal during my mother's time, especially among the conservative Nonyas. My parents are Straits-born Chinese, the Baba and Nonya who speak a patois of Malay, Hokkien and English. My sisters and I were in our twenties when my mother coughed out this story on the eve of her silver wedding anniversary. Imagine our shock! I looked at my parents' grey hair and wrinkles, and for the life of me I couldn't imagine that once upon a time they had been passionate young lovers. Anyway, my two sisters and I lapped up their story and teased them about it occasionally. All families should have a few skeletons in their cupboard. They make us more interesting, don't you think so? We Singaporeans are such a staid people.

My mother was Pa's second wife—what Penang people in those days called a minor wife, someone you refer to as *suay-ee* (literally 'small aunt' if you speak the Hokkien dialect). I guess it was to emphasise her lack of importance and status in her husband's family. Such terms are no longer used, and I know young people these days don't care to know about such words. But these dialect words reveal our social and family history. They're part of our cultural lexicon. And there were lots of 'small aunts', minor wives, concubines and mistresses in those days. Of course, we still have them today, known by different names: partner, companion, girlfriend, even goddaughter if the guy is decades older. Human nature has not changed. Today the children and grandchildren of such women could be our doctors and politicians, with reputations to uphold and skeletons to hide.

That your mother or grandmother was a concubine or 'small aunt' was not something you crowed about to your friends in school. When Pa came to work in Singapore, he brought Mother and me with him. Pa's first wife never forgave Mother for 'snatching away her husband'. This was why we'd never gone back to Penang. Then, after Singapore broke off from Malaysia, Pa and Mother also broke off contact with their Penang relatives, including Pa's first wife and her three children. Now, I don't want to judge my pa, but this was what he did. Heartless betrayal at one end, and constant love for my mother at the other. His first marriage was what they called a customary marriage. Just serve tea to your parents-in-law and all the dead ancestors, and you're married. His domineering mother chose his first wife. Pa was her eldest son. He had to do his duty by his mother. And I must say that he did it very well. He had three children with his first wife. Then, in his thirties, he met Mother who was eighteen then. And they had me. His mother, that is my grandmother, refused to accept me as her granddaughter. I remember as a child we had to move house very often. Later I found out that it was to avoid Pa's mother and his first wife who wanted to break up their union. That was why they fled to Singapore.

'Your pa's mother and his first wife cursed me till kingdom come. How I suffered in those days!'

My mother is one those rare gems in her generation who can be utterly honest about her background.

'They always found out where we lived, and then they'd come and make trouble for me. Very domineering, your pa's ma. So was my mother and Uncle Kim Hock's mother. Nonyas are all like that.'

'Looks like it runs in the family, Ma. Are you going to be like that when we marry someone you don't like?' my sister teased her.

'Don't you worry, girl. Why do I want to sit at home to control my children? *Sudah-lah*! Waste my time! I'd rather go travelling with your pa. My dressmaking business, that's enough to keep me busy.'

My mother, in her late sixties, has turned into a regular modern Singaporean grandma. One of those who tog up in leather boots and jeans to do line dancing at the community centre. You'll never catch me doing that! She's come a long way, my mother. From despised second wife in conservative Penang to admired grandma with a dressmaking business in modern Singapore. That's the kind of success you never read about in *The Straits Times*. Who would tell the reporter? Anyway, I was going to tell you another successful love story, but my mother is the better storyteller. Let her tell you about Uncle Kim Hock and his wife.

My Mother's Version

When Kim Hock was born, such a big to-do it was! After six daughters, finally a gem! A son! My god! His parents were so happy. They named him Kim Hock, meaning 'golden prosperity'. But he was a sickly baby, our Kim Hock. Pale skin, dark curly hair, prone to fits and fevers. They nearly lost him when he was three months old. So his mother, my aunt, took him to the temple. They were Taoist, not Buddhist. They gave him to the gods for protection. The medium of the Ninth Prince of the Jade Emperor pierced his baby ears.

'He's got to wear earrings,' the medium said. 'Must also take a girl's name. Call him Noi Noi.'

What to do? Kim Hock had to take a girl's pet name to fool the spirits into thinking that he was a girl and not harm him. Don't you laugh, girl. That's what we believed in those days.

My aunt dressed him in frills and lace till he was six, you know, the poor boy. When he went to primary school, the boys used to call him Ah Girl! In good fun, lah. It's not like the brutal taunting in the schools nowadays. *Nooo*, in those days in Penang and Singapore, when we were growing up, we really believed in names and spirits. Better not laugh at other people's beliefs. Some mothers made their sons wear earrings till they were in their teens.

In those days boys didn't want to wear earrings but their parents forced them to. Nowadays boys want to wear earrings and their parents forbid them to. It's an upside-down world. Seesawing like fashion. Even our religious beliefs have changed.

In those days people really believed that they could pull the wool over the spirits' eyes with a girl's name. Yes, we really believed in those days. Why do you think there are so many Chinese boys with names like Pig, Dog or Horse? They only changed names when they entered secondary school. Then Pig, Dog or Horse became Jimmy, Frankie or Elvis Presley. They changed their names when they changed themselves. Don't laugh. Our names give us our identity. Change your name and you change your identity and destiny. I'm not joking. Kim Hock should have changed his name back to Kim Hock when he was a grown-up. But no, his mother, so scared to lose him, insisted on calling him Noi Noi even after he got married. And so he remained Noi Noi. Mild mannered and adoi! So fair some more, and utterly obedient and filial. At least on the surface, lah! He never went against his mother and she doted on him. Spoilt him rotten. When he had to wear his first pair of shorts to attend school, he threw an almighty tantrum. He stamped his foot and refused. But by then his father, my uncle, had had enough.

'You're a boy! Wear shorts! Wear trousers!'

A big quarrel erupted between my aunt and uncle.

'He's my heart, my life. If anything happens to him, I hold you responsible! Let your ancestors know that! He's their only grandson!'

'Yes! Their grandson! Not their granddaughter! Let him wear trousers!'

Noi Noi was trussed into trousers. He wore them at school like a punishment. The moment he came home from school, he wore his sarong.

He was very smart, I tell you. He did very well at school. He even sat for the Senior Cambridge Examination, and passed with flying colours, as they say. It was a very prestigious exam in those days. Not like your ordinary O level these days. My uncle threw a big feast. He was a court interpreter, a very high post in those days under the British. See. Look at this photo here. Can you see the slim young man in a white suit? That's Kim Hock. See how he's surrounded by his six sisters? This photo marks the height of the family's glory. Before the war. Before the Japanese bombed Singapore. Before the soldiers took my uncle away. They never found his body, you know. People said he was shot because he worked for the British.

The family suffered during the war. Truly suffered. Before the war they'd owned several houses. After the war they were left with that one house in Irvine Road where we rented a room. Before the war they also had a car and a chauffeur. Pak Hassan used to drive Kim Hock to school. My uncle had planned to send him to England for further studies. Then the war destroyed all his plans. Kim Hock's eldest sister died in the last year of the Japanese Occupation. His sister's baby was stillborn. Another sister hanged herself. Raped by unknown assailants, people said. That happened in the second year of the war. The third sister joined a Buddhist nunnery. The other three got married. So Kim Hock was left with his mother, a poor widow by then. Poor by their standards, lah. They still owned the house in Irvine Road. My parents owned nothing.

Since he was the only son, it was his duty to marry. The continuation of the family line rested on him alone. His mother chose a girl from a poor family. Her name was Gek Sim. It means 'heart of jade'. Very appropriate name for her, if you ask me. Jade is a very hard stone. Translucent but not transparent. We never knew what she was thinking about. That Gek Sim was a closed book. Her father was a store clerk, her mother a housewife. Eight daughters and two sons. Ten children. Gek Sim was their eldest daughter.

'So her parents were very grateful to me,' my aunt used to boast. 'They almost went down on their knees to thank me. I could get a girl from a wealthy family for my Noi Noi. But listen, a girl from a poor family is more obedient. And she was born in the year of the Rat. Noi Noi was born in the year of the Ox. Rat and Ox—a good pair. And their horoscopes matched. If I'd known she would turn out like this, I wouldn't have even looked at her.'

My aunt blamed the temple priest for the match. But she herself was to blame. She'd forgotten our ancient stories. The humble rat was a clever little thing. Instead of being the last, it became the first creature to reach heaven on New Year's Day when it jumped onto the ox's nose during the race to heaven. It stood up on the ox's nose and stretched its body forwards. That was how the rat became the first animal in the Chinese zodiac.

Anyway, Noi Noi was nineteen when he married Gek Sim, sixteen. Aye, they married young in those days. My aunt was a terrible mother-in-law. She ruled the house in Irvine Road like those matriarchs you see in Cantonese opera. Poor Gek Sim. She had to learn how to do everything my aunt's way. Nothing pleased my aunt. I tell you, girl, if Gek Sim had been from a rich family, I don't think my aunt would have been so hard on her. Once, she threw a whole pot of chicken curry onto the floor because she didn't like the way Gek Sim had cooked it. The poor girl spent the entire morning on her knees scrubbing out the kitchen. For a week she had to cook and eat curry for breakfast, lunch and dinner till she threw up. When her *buah keluak* chicken stew was too watery, my aunt caned her. Oh ya, she used the cane on her daughter-in-law. Mothers-in-law could do that in those days.

'*Chi-la-kak*!' she cursed. 'You bring no silver and no gold! No manners and no cooking skills! The gold on you, who gave you? All from me! Your father can't even afford a gold chain. Now I ask you for *buah keluak*. What do I get? Didn't your mother teach you to cook? Do you cook like this in your mother's kitchen? Were you cooking to feed pigs? Maybe your family eats such watery stews, but in our family we don't even give it to the servants! No, no! Throw it away! Tomorrow I go to my daughter's house to eat! Lucky I've daughters who can cook!'

Another time it was the laundry.

'*Yao siew*! Accursed one! Look at my *kebaya* blouse! You call this ironed? Look! Look at the creases! Aye! Mother of god! It's torn at the armpit!'

'Ma, it was already torn a bit when I washed it.'

A slap landed on her cheek.

'That will teach you to answer back! No breeding. In *your* parents' house you can be rude. But not in *my* house! My *kebaya* is torn. It's hand-sewn embroidery and lace. Your father's salary for one year won't even be enough to pay for it! Not that I'll ask him for the money. Got so many daughters to feed and marry off.'

Gek Sim did not cry. She did not complain to Kim Hock. She did not run home to tell her mother. Her mother still had seven daughters to marry off. How to tell her? Gek Sim kept things in her heart—that most treacherous chamber in a woman's body! And her heart grew hard. She plotted against my aunt. But she was such a sweet wife to Kim Hock, I tell you. In the end he turned completely against his mother. Didn't even cry when my aunt died. Not a tear. But when Gek Sim died, he threw himself on his wife's coffin and clung to it. Had to be pried away and sedated. He was like a madman. Kept calling her. Calling her name. Of course, people started to talk, lah. Who wouldn't? You don't cry for your own mother but cry for your wife. And they died only one day apart. So many rumours, I tell you. People said his mother's spirit killed his wife because she was jealous. They even said Gek Sim's body turned black in the coffin. That she'd foamed at the mouth. But I don't listen to all this gossip. Kim Hock loved his wife. They were a very loving couple. Strange but very loving to each other. Always talking and giggling together. Do you remember, girl? You don't? Maybe you were too young then. Lucky thing, we'd moved out of their house before all the bad things happened.

My Version

I remember things differently. I was six when we moved into 61 Irvine Road, somewhere near Joo Chiat in Katong. It was a corner house at the end of a row of town houses. One of those colonial Straits Chinese two-storey houses built before the war. Worth one or two million dollars these days. Dark green tiles with pink roses framed its windows. You can't find these ornate tiles any more unless you go to the antique shops in Malacca.

The house was deep. It had three sections. The sitting room in front had the morning sun and the family altar. The middle section was the gloomy part. Gek Sim's bedroom was next to the staircase. The only window in that part of the house was in her bedroom, so the hallway leading to the kitchen was dim and gloomy, even though the door to the kitchen was always left open. We children were told never to close that door. 'And don't you touch the broom hanging on a nail behind it.'

The third section of the house was the kitchen and courtyard. That was where Tommy and Johnny, Uncle Kim Hock's boys, slept at night. His wife, Gek Sim, was called the Landlady. I don't remember Mother ever referring to her as anything else, even though she refers to her as Gek Sim when she tells her story. Gek Sim was always the Landlady. Uncle Kim Hock's mother was White-hair Granny. People said her hair turned white after she found out that her son wore his wife's clothes and sarong. Yes, he wore her clothes. I'll tell you about it later.

I was scared of the Landlady. She had a loud voice. Not softly spoken at all. She could swear profanities as loudly as the men. My mother seems to have forgotten what a shrew Gek Sim was. All our relatives knew that she was a timid little mouse when she first came into the family. Over time, she turned into a termagant who fought with her mother-in-law. No one dared to speak up at the time. You know how relatives are: 'Hands-off, don't interfere, not our business.' Then when the person is dead and gone, they start yakking: 'Should've done this. Should've done that!' I can't stand them.

There were three bedrooms upstairs. We lived in the front

room. Mr and Mrs Tan, both teachers, rented the other room at the back. Mother said that Uncle Kim Hock had to rent out two of their rooms to settle his wife's gambling debts.

Next to the stairs, between the two rooms, was a third room, small, dark, windowless and padlocked. White-hair Granny lived in that room. She locked the door whenever she went out because she didn't trust Gek Sim and Uncle Kim Hock.

I saw her emerge from that room one morning, frail and white-haired. She didn't notice me even though I was standing right outside our room. I stood very still. She shuffled past, silent as a ghost, dressed in a blue batik sarong and a white *kebaya* blouse. In my memory she wasn't the fierce mother-in-law that my mother describes in her story.

I waited till she'd gone downstairs. Then I hung over the banisters and stood on tiptoe to peer through the narrow slits in the wood partition that separated the stairs and the sitting room. I could see the top of her white head. She was saying the Buddhist rosary: '*Nam-mo-nam-mo-nam-mo* ... mercy, mercy, mercy, Lord Buddha.' Over and over again, she chanted 'mercy' while softly hitting a red wooden block.

'I'm fighting the evil one in this house. My life is a war. My prayers are my weapons, arrows to pierce the evil one's heart,' she told my mother.

My memories of our stay in that house are disjointed. I was only five or six. Such a long time ago. I remember I was not allowed to go downstairs to play. So I played on the landing and the stairs. One day I discovered that if I lay down flat on one of the steps, I could peer through the banisters into the kitchen at the end of the dim hallway. And that was how I spied on Uncle Kim

Hock and the Landlady late one night.

He was wearing his wife's sarong while doing the ironing. I swear it was bright pink and lime green with a pattern of flowers and leaves. And the blouse that he was wearing was also pink! Not a pink shirt, mind you. A pink blouse with a bit of lace. And red clogs on his feet. No, lah! It's not my imagination. Nothing wrong with my memory and imagination. I can remember the scene to this day. He had a cigarette dangling from his mouth and his wife was laughing. Seated on a chair, she was puffing a cigarette, just like him, and laughing at something he'd just said. It was very strange. They were behaving normally yet Uncle Kim Hock was wearing his wife's clothes. She was wearing a black sarong knotted above her breasts. Her bare shoulders gleamed like a hard slab of brown lard under the naked bulb which hung above them from an electric cord in the ceiling. She was a big, fleshy woman. Next to her, Uncle Kim Hock looked slim and slender. I couldn't hear what they were saying. They seemed to be sharing a joke. Then they stopped. White-hair Granny had walked in. She looked at them.

'Noi Noi!' she cried out.

Then she turned and started to climb the stairs. I was so startled that I fled into our room and hid under the bed.

'Girl, what's going on?' Mother asked.

Just then, White-hair Granny came into our room.

'That witch! She's turned my son into a woman. My Noi Noi is wearing her clothes and doing the ironing,' she sobbed. 'A manager of the biggest pharmacy in town and he cycles to work. To save money for her. I've no face any more. How can I face my relatives? My son! My son cooks and washes at home like he's the wife and she's the husband. That witch doesn't lift a finger. And I'll tell you another shameful thing—she gives Noi Noi fifty cents as pocket money every day.'

'No, Auntie!' I heard the shock in Mother's voice. 'You're imagining. That's just enough to buy a bowl of noodles.'

'You don't believe me? Just look at the table in the sitting room tomorrow morning. Look before Noi Noi leaves for work. You'll see two coins: twenty cents and fifty cents. The twenty-cent coin is for Johnny. He goes to school. Tommy stays home. A bit slow, that boy. My poor, poor grandson! I swear she's sold the boy's brain to the devil to spite me.'

I was a curious child. The next morning I looked at the table. Sure enough, there were two coins. Then I sat down near the doorway to wait for my school bus. Uncle Kim Hock came out of his bedroom. Dressed in his white shirt and white trousers, he looked like one of those clerks who worked in the Colonial Civil Service. I could smell perfume on him. His face was smooth and clean-shaven. He took a coin. I glanced at his feet. He was wearing dark velvet slippers instead of a man's black leather shoes. Now, I know that we wear all sorts of things to the office nowadays but black leather shoes were the standard footwear for men working in an office in those days. Johnny came in. He took the twenty-cent coin.

'Dad, I've to buy a writing exercise book today.'

Uncle Kim Hock dug into his trouser pocket. He took out three ten-cent coins and handed one to Johnny.

'Thanks, Dad.'

Then Uncle Kim Hock saw me. He smiled and patted my head, but my eyes were fixed on his dark purple velvet slippers.

'A strange way for a manager to dress, if you ask me,' Mother said.

'Don't interfere. None of our business,' Pa said.

'But his mother is my aunt. She says he swallowed his wife's spittle. He's under his wife's thumb. She wears the pants now and he wears her sarong and embroidered *kebaya* blouses. Adoi! My aunt doesn't know what to do! She suspects he's been charmed. Said he must've drunk her breast milk and spittle. That's why he listens to her and acts so ... so strange. He used to be such an obedient son, you know. My aunt would say do this, he'd do it. Do that, he'd do that. Now he doesn't care what my aunt says. Doesn't even talk to her. He's truly drunk his wife's spittle. Listens to everything she says.'

'Maybe yes, maybe no. I listen to everything you say. I left Penang because of you. People think I've drunk your spittle too,' Pa laughed.

Mother flung a pillow at him. They had a pillow fight and I joined in.

'We should move out,' Mother said on another day.

'But we've just moved in. Not easy to find a good room in Singapore for this kind of rent,' Pa said, and so we stayed on.

We stayed put until my baby brother died. And my young heart blamed Uncle Kim Hock's wife. And why not? She'd bewitched Uncle Kim Hock so she must've killed my brother. I was sure of it because of something that I'd seen as a child. It made me stay away from the house after we moved out. My parents too stayed away from Irvine Road, but that was because of the pain of losing their only son in that house. They didn't go near that house for more than thirty years. I had my own reason for staying away: I truly believed that Uncle Kim Hock's wife was a witch because of what I'd glimpsed.

One evening I was playing on the stairs as usual, peering through the banisters into the kitchen. An aroma of sizzling beef and onions wafted up the stairs. Uncle Kim Hock, dressed normally in a sleeveless vest and trousers, was holding a frying pan over the stove, frying beefsteak and potatoes for Tommy and Johnny. I could see Tommy. He was carrying his one-year-old sister astride his hips with one hand, and laying the table with the other. Johnny was setting out the glasses. They were all talking excitedly. They loved beefsteak. My mother, being Buddhist, never cooked beef. White-hair Granny was Buddhist. She would never touch the meat. Yet Uncle Kim Hock and Gek Sim often cooked beef for their dinner. I think that was their way of making sure that White-hair Granny would keep away from them.

Anyway, that evening I saw Gek Sim come out of the bathroom with her hair dripping wet. She was wearing her black sarong, knotted below her armpits. She walked over to the stove. Steam rose from the black pot when she lifted the lid. I gasped when she plunged her hand into the steaming pot. She raced into the dark hallway towards the stairs and me, holding a ball of steaming white rice in her hand! She shot me a piercing look. I bolted up the stairs and locked our bedroom door. 'What's going on?' Mother asked. I didn't want to tell her. But that same night I had nightmares and my baby brother cried all night. He was running a high fever.

The next morning Mother rushed him to the doctor's. My baby brother was warded in the hospital that same day. He died the next day. One month later we moved out of 61 Irvine Road.

In my childish heart I knew I should have been the one to die. Gek Sim's evil look had shot past me and hit my baby brother. He was killed because of me. This was the guilt I carried as a child, and suppressed as an adult. So now you see why I had to visit the house in Irvine Road when I was studying psychology and counselling. I had to exorcise my guilt. Part of our training.

'Anyway we stopped going to the house when the witch was alive,' Uncle Kim Hock's sister said. 'Bad luck to meet her and get a tongue lashing for nothing. Our mother died of heartbreak, I tell you. I swear it. Not only did her hair turn white but her heart broke. That witch kept a spirit child that ate away our mother's heart. People said she hid it behind the door—the door in the hallway.'

My heart jumped when I heard that.

'Tell me more,' I pressed her.

'That spirit child helped Gek Sim to win back the money she'd lost in the gaming houses. Oh yes, that Gek Sim was a gambler. Very addicted, I tell you. Had to gamble every day. Lost money like water through the fingers. That's why my brother never grew rich. She kept a spirit child behind that door to help her win back her money. But she got to feed it. Timing was very important. It had to be fed before sunset, the twilight hour just before dark. And she must be the one to feed the spirit. No one else could do it. But that evening, before she died, she came home late. She'd won a big sum of money. Several thousands, people said. Her biggest win. She was so happy. She took the whole family out to celebrate. That very night she collapsed and died. The spirit child was so hungry that it ate her instead.'

No, no, no, I don't believe the story. That was what Uncle Kim

Hock's sister told me. But I didn't know what to think, frankly. Of course, I didn't want to believe a word about this spirit child thing. To change the subject, I asked her about Uncle Kim Hock.

'Kim Hock? He's one of a kind! After his wife's death we urged him to sell off the house. Two deaths in two days so close together, it's not good. Bad luck. Sell the house. Bad *feng shui*. Bad air. We tried to advise him but my brother did nothing. Very difficult talking to him. He just sat there. No spirit left after the witch's death. We expected him to be ... I don't know what we expected him to do. But he was empty. Like he'd lost his soul. We stopped visiting him after some time. No point. He just sat there. Wouldn't say a word. Later we found out that he'd sent Johnny to a boarding school overseas. The one run by the Christian Brothers. Tommy was sent to Boys' Town. He works as a carpenter now. They're all married and working, his children. But Kim Hock, he continued to cycle to work until he retired. Paying off the witch's debts, no doubt.'

'I'd like to visit him.'

'What for? He's senile now. Lives alone in that house. Refused to go into the old folks' home. Refused to live with his children. Anyway, they can't have him. He's so weird. You'll know when you see him. His wife put a charm on him years ago. Turned him into a queer. Before that my brother was normal, I tell you. Our brother was normal. And a very obedient and filial son. He used to listen to everything our mother said.'

But I had to visit 61 Irvine Road for reasons of my own.

'Hello! Hello! Anyone home?'

The front door was not locked. I walked in. The house smelt of dust and mould. It looked the same, just very old with paint peeling off the walls. The hallway was dark even though it was daytime. I heard music in the kitchen. Entering the kitchen was like entering a time warp. Everything was as I remembered it thirty years before.

Uncle Kim Hock was stooped over the ironing board. Thin and gaunt, his hair was completely white. He must have been seventy-eight or more. Even though it was daytime, he had switched on the light: a naked bulb attached to the end of an old electric cord which hung down from the ceiling. He was ironing a pink blouse under the light. On the table was a pile of clothes.

'Ah, so you've finally come, *Sayang*. Sit down. Sit down.'

He gave me a vacant smile, revealing teeth yellow from years of nicotine.

I sat on a chair. Come to think of it, I must have sat on the same chair that Gek Sim sat on each night when she watched him do the ironing. That would explain why he thought I was his wife. He'd called me *sayang* which means 'darling' or 'beloved'. He pushed a box of cigarettes towards me.

'As I was saying, Mama was fuming mad this morning. "Mama," I said, "you let me be. You didn't mind the frills and lace when it suited you. What's wrong with a bit of pink lace?" Ha-ha! You should've seen her face. Poor Mama!'

He put down his iron, took a cigarette out of the box and put it in his mouth.

'Want a smoke?'

I shook my head.

'*Sayang*, you tried, didn't you? Tried every trick of Eve. Still nothing happened. Your belly still flat as a pancake. Man and wife. More than two years and still so flat. I know, I know. You suffered. Yes, yes, my old lady was terrible, horrible, insufferable. A Nonya shrew. Ha!'

A sly smile crept up his face and the wrinkles creased around his sunken lips as he looked expectantly at me. I think he was expecting me to applaud.

'Termagant, deity of violent tempers. Did you pray to her? Mama's eyes followed us like a hawk. Like your belly would swell if she looked hard enough. Ha-ha! Poor Mama. She dragged me to temples, consulted a Malay *bomoh*, a Chinese *tangki*. My god! Those mediums even got her praying to a parrot in a cage. They told her, "Your son's bewitched." My foot! Bewitched!' He chuckled.

He flicked the ash from his cigarette, stuck it back between his lips and pulled a bright pink blouse out of the pile on the table. He flattened and smoothed its creases on the ironing board.

'Always a careful ironer, I am. Fussy about my clothes, you can say. "Wear red. Rub him down there with a hard-boiled egg. Give him black chicken herbal soups with lots of ginseng. Good for the manhood, you know. Take a rose water bath." Mama and her silly friends were teaching you to seduce me, weren't they? Poor thing. No wonder you became ill. I became ill. And Mama wailed. I know, I know. She blamed you. Called you names. Wailed that she pawned her jewellery to pay for our wedding but got back nothing. But she was the one who wanted the wedding. Not me. Lucky we gave her grandsons in the end, didn't we?'

He held up the pink blouse and turned to me.

'And lucky you like pink too,' he chuckled. 'Oops-a-daisy! Strong wind today. Monsoon season. Storm coming tonight. That's what the radio man said this morning. Storm tonight.'

Carefully he pressed the hot iron onto the pink blouse.

'D'you remember, Gek? Same strong wind like this. It started to rain that day when I returned from the hospital. You rushed into our bedroom, dumped the clothes on our bed—clothes you'd torn off the washing line. Then you rushed out again. I was in bed. I sat up. Hey, don't laugh. It's true. I actually sat up to help you fold the clothes. Then I saw your pink silk blouse. Oh my! So soft and fragrant. And oh, so pink. I *lurve* pink! Oh, how I *lurve* the smell of pink. I buried my face in your blouse. I put it on and we did it that night, didn't we? That's the night we gave Mama her first grandson.'

He laughed long and loud, and started to put on the pink blouse. A gust blew into the kitchen. The sleeves of his pink blouse flapped about him.

'Help me with it, Gek.'

I helped him put it on just as the storm broke. The window shutters rattled, and the light bulb swung wildly at the end of its electric cord.

'Thank you, *Sayang*. When you gave birth to Tommy, you said his little willie gagged Mama's mouth. Ha-ha! Twice you gagged her. Tommy and Johnny. Born two years apart. Who said I wasn't fertile? Aye, *Sayang*, I've missed you.'

'Uncle Kim Hock!'

'Huh?'

'Uncle Kim Hock. It's me, Molly. I used to live here as a girl.'

He shook his head. When he spoke again, his voice was stern.

'My sisters sent you. They think I'm a senile faggot. Leave me alone. Go! An old man is entitled to his memories.'

'Uncle Kim Hock ...'

'Go, go! Please go.'

I walked out of the house. I didn't know what to think. Then, and only then, I remembered. Die, lah! I'd forgotten to say goodbye to my brother's spirit. And that was why I'd gone to the house in the first place. So the next morning I returned to 61 Irvine Road.

'Uncle Kim Hock! Hellooo! Can I come in?'

Like the day before, I walked straight into the kitchen. I thought I should just let him know that I was back before going upstairs to see our old room and say a prayer for my little brother. And that was where I found him—upstairs in the bedroom that used to be ours. He looked like he was asleep on his bed, still wearing his wife's pink *kebaya* blouse that was embroidered with a pattern of white flowers and green leaves, and his wife's pink and green batik sarong.

I called the police on my mobile phone and then I phoned his sister.

This is another reason why our whole family went to Uncle Kim Hock's wake and funeral—I was the one who found his body. There was great unhappiness and friction between Uncle Kim Hock's sons and his three sisters over how he should be dressed for burial. The sisters wanted their brother to be buried dressed in a Western suit. But their two nephews, especially Johnny, were adamant that their father should be buried in the manner in which he'd dressed himself to meet death.

'A shame,' the aunts cried. 'What will people say?'

'What shame? Our father's been a good father,' Johnny yelled at them. 'He took care of us, educated us. He brought us up after our mother died. He couldn't choose the soul he brought into this life but he sure could choose the life he lived. It's nobody's bloody business how he's dressed and buried!'

There weren't many people at the wake, just the family: his three sisters and their families, his two sons and their wives, his four grandchildren and us. We gathered in the front room of 61 Irvine Road. I didn't know Johnny and Tommy well—we'd not kept in touch—but I liked the way they'd stood up for their father. And that was filial love for a parent who was different from other parents. The two guys didn't care a hoot about face the way so many of us do. They saw a loving father who did his best for them. I say, judge a man by how his children treat him after his death. Tommy and Johnny loved their father.

Ya, ya, I know. People said their mother was a witch. And I did see what she did with that ball of rice. But I was an impressionable child of six, filled with tales of witches and black magic. Can you really trust the memory of a six year old? Or what others say, especially those who didn't like Kim Hock's wife? And if you think about it, Uncle Kim Hock loved his wife and she him. Not in the way the world expected. Not in the way Uncle Kim Hock's mother and sisters had expected. But it was love nevertheless. The love that accepted him for who he was. I can't claim to know him well. I can't claim to know his wife. She was the dreaded landlady in my childhood, the witch. But she was the mother of Tommy and Johnny, and the grandma of their four children. Witch or no witch, she must have taught them something about love. They didn't judge their father, why should we?

And was there a spirit child behind the door of the hallway? If there was, it's gone. And the world has changed. Singapore has changed.

'Adoi, girl! Of course, Singapore has changed. Young men wear their hair long these days. In the 1980s the law was so strict. Men weren't allowed to keep long hair. These days I've even seen some middle-aged Chinese guys sporting ponytails. They wear colours of the rainbow: earrings, nose rings, *macham-macham* rings on their fingers and toes, silver studs in their tongues. I've seen them in our shopping malls. Nobody says such dressing is abnormal. If you live long enough, you'll see all kinds of things. And that's progress, lah,' Mother said.

I guess someone has to take the first step to cross an imaginary border. My line-dancing mother did just that when she became my father's minor wife. Now I'm not the least bit ashamed of Pa, God rest his soul. He loved Mother but betrayed another for her. Yet we accept that as part of love. And certainly it is love, but only if you're on the receiving end. Somehow I think that the love between Uncle Kim Hock and Gek Sim was, by far, a greater love than that of my parents. But that's just my view. Call me unfilial if you like.

MY TWO MOTHERS

Kwai Chee ...'

'What?'

'Will you come back for dinner? I'm going to ...'

I shut the door. Cut her off in mid-sentence. Didn't bother me that I was rude. I was a teenage pimple on the face of the earth. I wished Yee Ku and Loke Ku hadn't adopted me. I wished somebody else had. Somebody like Miss Lee or Miss Nazareth.

My two mothers were old enough to be my grandmas. They were already in their sixties when I was fourteen. I can't remember when I started feeling shame. It probably began when I was six on my first day at school in 1958. The other children had a father and a mother. And I? I had Yee Ku and Loke Ku. Both wore black silk pants and white *samfoo* tops with a mandarin collar. Both carried black cloth umbrellas. They shaded me from the sun as we stood in the school field with the other children and their parents. The teachers thought they were maidservants sent by my parents who could not come.

That day I discovered that my two mothers were *amah jieh*, traditional Chinese domestic servants. They belonged to a sisterhood called the Seven Sisters. They left their village in southern China in the 1930s to work as *amah*s in Singapore. I have a black and white photograph of them. It shows seven women in matching white *samfoo* tops and black silk pants, standing in a row. It was taken on the day my two mothers prayed to the Seven Sisters in heaven, plaited their queues and vowed never to marry.

The Cantonese word *ku* means paternal aunt. But it means more than that in my case. I was their adopted daughter, but I couldn't call either of them Mother because they were unmarried. Two unmarried women living together were my mothers but I had to call them Aunt or *Ku*. Now you understand why I was confused and angry as a child.

They named me Kwai Chee or Precious Pearl. When I went to secondary school, I dropped my Chinese name. I called myself Pearl. It sounded more sophisticated in English. I told my classmates that my parents had died. I lied that Yee Ku was my grandmother. She had given up work to bring me up. Loke Ku was our breadwinner. She worked as a live-in maid for a family. She came home once a week to check on us, and once a month she stayed the night and slept in the same bed with Yee Ku. If I needed to buy anything that cost more than ten dollars, I had to ask Loke Ku. If I failed a test, I had to answer to Loke Ku. But if I were punished or if I hurt myself, Yee Ku comforted me.

'There, there, don't cry. Big girls don't cry.'

'Ah Yee, don't spoil her. She's got to learn.'

Loke Ku was the disciplinarian. But I wasn't spoilt. And I did learn. Not love, but shame. A part of me hung my head. I invited no one home. Not because home was a small rented room above a car workshop in Jalan Besar. More because I felt my family was not normal. I had two mothers instead of one. Mothers I had to each call Aunt. Mothers who were unmarried domestics living together. And in the secret chamber of my secretive heart,

I suspected them of being something more. I couldn't say what it was as a child. It had the faint smell of wrongdoing. Of something that people frowned upon. How did such an idea enter my head when no one had actually said anything to me? Had I picked up things as a child from the whispers among the neighbours downstairs? From the way they looked at me? Or was it from things that one of my secondary school teachers said, like girls should not hold hands or worse?

I don't know. I don't know.

I was a confused and angry girl in those days. I was sullen. I studied hard. I buried myself in my books. Not because I enjoyed studying but because I wanted to succeed and leave home. I wanted to get away from the two of them. And I was ashamed of myself for feeling that way.

In 1965, when I was in the Girl Guides, I met Joyce Lee and Julie Nazareth. They were the adopted daughters of Miss Lee and Miss Nazareth, teachers in Upper Paya Lebar Girls' School. Miss Lee, tall and slim, with straight black hair knotted in a bun at the nape of her neck, taught Maths. Miss Nazareth, plump and maternal with a short frizzy brown perm, taught English.

'And you live together as a family in the same house?' I asked.

Julie heard the surprise in my voice.

'Ya, we're a family.'

Her dark eyes challenged me. I said nothing more. Miss Lee was Chinese. So was Joyce, her adopted daughter, although Joyce looked Eurasian to me. Julie was Indian like Miss Nazareth. Two single women and their adopted daughters. And they were a family. They lived in the same house, drove to school in one car and went home together after school.

'Anything wrong, Pearl? Why so quiet?'

'Nothing wrong,' I lied.

I was always lying in those days, you know. I couldn't say what it was that was bugging me. Not straightaway anyway. The next Saturday, after our Girl Guides' meeting, Julie and Joyce took me home for tea.

'Mummy, this is Pearl.'

'Good afternoon, Miss Lee.'

'Hello, Pearl.'

'And this is my mum,' Julie said.

'Hello, Miss Nazareth,' I said.

Over tea, scones and jam and *bubor cha-cha*, the conversation somehow got round to family and what a government minister had said in the newspapers.

'That Mr Chan Soo Beng in the Prime Minister's Office. He defines a family as one man, one woman and their children,' Miss Lee told us.

'Oh yeah, absolutely. People whose parents have died are orphans, not family, don't you know?'

Miss Nazareth buttered a scone and handed it to me. I couldn't tell if she was serious or joking.

'What about widows, Mum? By his definition, widows and their children are not families either,' Julie said.

'Or ... or,' Joyce jumped in, 'what about one grandma, one unmarried uncle and the children of his dead sister? Is that a family?'

'Of course not, silly!' Julie scoffed. 'According to Mr Chan a family is one man, his wife and their children!'

'Jeepers, such a broad definition! That should include

everybody in Singapore! What about us, Mum?'

There was a pause. Then Miss Nazareth said, 'Some families are born; some families are made.'

'But ours,' Miss Lee looked at Joyce and Julie, 'is especially cooked. We selected our ingredients.'

We laughed. I caught myself wishing that Miss Lee or Miss Nazareth had adopted me instead of two illiterate *amah*s. Class and education clouded my young mind.

In 1975 I graduated with a BA Honours degree. The night before the graduation ceremony I put on my gown and hat for Yee Ku and Loke Ku. They were not attending the event.

'You're sure you don't want to come?'

'No need, no need. Just seeing you in your gown and square hat is good enough for us,' Loke Ku said.

On my part I didn't try to persuade them to attend. They would be out of place in the university auditorium.

'Here, Kwai Chee. Let me iron your gown.'

'No, no, Yee Ku, don't fuss. I'll do it myself.'

'Take a taxi tomorrow,' Loke Ku said. 'I'll call for a taxi. Don't rush. Go early.'

'I know. I know. Please. I know what to do.'

They got up early the next morning to offer thanksgiving prayers to the gods. Loke Ku walked me to the taxi stand. Yee Ku, too old and weak by then, stayed at home.

'Yee Ku is cooking your favourite dishes tonight. Abalone soup and stewed mushroom with chicken.'

'Can both of you just stop fussing over me? I don't know what time I can come home. My friends and I are going out to celebrate. After all these years of studying, we need a break!'

I jumped into a taxi and drove off.

In 2000, years after my two mothers had passed away, I was the writer-in-residence at the University of Iowa.

Laura Jackson, the editor of the university's press, took me home to meet her family. Her partner, Kathleen, was a nurse. Over dinner they told me how they had felt something for each other since they were teenagers. In their late twenties, after years of muddled thought and struggle, they committed themselves to each other with their families' blessings. I thought of my two mothers then and, suddenly, tears came to my eyes.

'A bit of dust,' I said. I caught myself denying them once again like St Peter before the cock's crow. That evening things came full circle. I was introduced to Laura and Kathleen's two daughters: Kelly, four, and Sally, three.

'The girls are half-sisters. They share the same biological father.'

I looked from one to the other.

'A very good friend of ours,' Laura said, 'donated his sperm to us.'

'You're pulling my leg.'

'No, we're not,' Laura smiled. 'He even signed an agreement to give up his rights to the girls. I wanted to be a mum real bad. Kathy and I, we wanted a family. We asked Carl. He's our best friend. Oh, he's married. Got his own kids. He agreed to help us. One afternoon in the bedroom downstairs here, he did what he had to do. I was upstairs, lying in bed, waiting. He handed Kathy the bottle. She syringed his sperm, rushed up the stairs and squirted it into me.'

'It was a success. Laura gave birth to Kelly,' Kathy said.

'Watching her breast-feed Kelly, I realised that I wanted the experience of giving birth—to be a mother.'

'One year later we asked Carl again. My god! We owe that man big!' Laura laughed.

'This time it was Laura who rushed to take the syringe upstairs to me.'

'Nine months later Kathy gave birth to Sally,' Laura added. 'Giving birth to the girls bound us as a family. Kathy stopped work to look after our two daughters.'

'So your daughters have two mothers.'

'She's my Mummy Laura!'

'Mumsy Kathy!'

The two girls shrieked and leapt into their mothers' laps.

'Isn't that wonderful, darling? You've got two mummies to love you.' Laura hugged the girls.

A lump rose in my throat.

'Hm, well, I ... er ... I've two mothers too.'

That evening I did what I couldn't do all those years in Singapore. I told Laura and Kathy about Yee Ku and Loke Ku. As I talked, my body grew light. My heart expanded and I saw what I'd failed to see before. Yee Ku and Loke Ku lived together for more than fifty years. If that isn't love, commitment and fidelity, I don't know what is. Theirs was a more lasting relationship than many marriages today. That night, for the first time, I was proud of them—and grateful.

Two strangers, unrelated to you by blood, take you into their midst because your parents have died or don't want you or are too young or too poor to take care of you. So two strangers take you into their midst and give you a new life. How do you ever say thank you?

That night I remembered them. When Loke Ku came home once a month to stay the night, she would sit in her cane chair on our tiny balcony that overlooked the back lane. Yee Ku would sit in her canvas chair. After dinner they sat, fanning themselves with a palm leaf fan while I cleared the table. They did not look at each other. They did not speak. But they were connected. An invisible cord bound them as it bound me to them, two old *amah jieh*, sitting on the balcony above the back lane, insignificant and irrelevant in modern Singapore. Yet this image of them, rising like a pale moon above the rooftops of the shophouses in Jalan Besar, had held me all these years.

I had dinner with Kathleen and Laura several times. They choose to live in Iowa City because the university town recognises their relationship as legal. The church also welcomes them as a family. Iowa City, the city of writers, is an oasis in a hostile desert. The rest of Iowa isn't like this. In Des Moines, the capital, the pastor of a church and his followers burnt the US flag in front of the statehouse when I was there. They wanted to demonstrate their condemnation of gays and lesbians. Last Christmas Laura and Kathleen sent me a photo of their family. Kelly and Sally, now aged nine and eight, are in school. And I, the daughter of two mothers, wish them well.

THE CLEANER'S SON

In memory of
Sister Susan Chia, R.G.S. (Religious of the Good Shepherd)

1

1 April 1986. Ah Gek rips the page off her Chinese calendar.

Another day gone.

'*Hoi*! Get up! Drink this,' she holds out the bowl of hot soup, but the heap on the bed makes no sign that he has heard her. '*Hoi Kow Kia*! Sit up!'

Not a muscle moves. She feels like pouring the soup on his head. A grown man lying on her bed day after day. This is the bed she had shared with his father since the day they lived together as man and wife. They had paid a bomb for it. Had to get a loan from the *Bai-yi*. Wouldn't have been able to set up home without the Indian moneylender's help. When they moved in here, she had just been sacked by the Chias. Mercy, Mother Mary! What made her think of such painful things this evening? Ack! The past is past!

'*Hoi*! Get up!' She shouts at her son again.

His face, half covered by the blanket, is turned to the wall. An unwashed smell of decay and vomit hangs over him. The air in the tiny two-room flat is foul; the window is shut again.

He must've gotten out of bed to close it when she was out. There's been no fresh air in the flat since he came crawling home sick as a dog.

'*Hoi*! Kow Kia! Get up! I made you ginseng soup with chicken. Get up and drink it! Won't kill you! It's been cooked over a slow fire for three hours. So don't waste my gas. Get up! Get up!'

'I didn't ask you to do it, Ma.'

The weariness in his voice makes her blood boil. He can't even muster enough strength to contradict her. She would rather that he fights her than lie down like a sick dog. 'Sit up, will you!'

'Leave me alone.'

'How can I leave you alone? How can any mother stand here and watch you like this? Look at you. No strength. No work. No money. Day after day, you sleep. You're wasting away. You'll die if you don't take care!'

'If I die then I die, *lor*.'

'You think it's so easy to die? If it were so easy, I would've died long ago! When you and your sisters left me, did you think I didn't want to die then? You think I want to live and see my son like this day after day? If you want to die, don't die here. Go and die somewhere else. Not here. Not in my home. I don't want to wake up one morning and find you dead. Don't you dare give me this pain! You've given me enough heartaches already.' Her eyes are welling again, but her voice is sharp and hard. 'I've had it up to here. If you want to die, go and die elsewhere. What I don't see, I don't care. But as long as you're under my roof, you will get well. Get up! You hear me? Up! Up! Sit up!'

She yanks off his blanket. His hand flies up. She drops the bowl. Soup splatters all over the floor. She swears at him. Vows she will never cook him another nourishing soup again. He struggles to sit up. Watching him, she is both furious and relieved. Relieved that he still has some life in him. His arms stick out of his singlet like two matchsticks. He has lost so much weight. Today he looks even thinner than a week ago. His rapid weight loss scares her.

She goes into the kitchen. Returns with a pail and rag and starts to mop up the dark liquid with quick, angry moves.

'Twenty dollars, twenty dollars worth of ginseng! My sweat and blood only to mop it all up!' She twists the rag over the pail, twisting the cloth to squeeze out the thick brown soup while he watches her from his bed. 'I'm wringing out my heart. That's what I'm doing! Mop and clean! Mop and clean! All my life! From the time I was eight I've had to mop up other people's mess. My Pa's drunken vomit! My Ma's gambling debts. Your uncle's shit! Your father's spit! And now you! My own son...!'

'Quiet!' A violent coughing shakes him. His hoarse raspy voice cuts her like a glass shard. 'Please, Ma. I ...I need ... rest.'

The dripping rag in her hand she looks away, his plea booming in her ears. Her irritation ebbs and subsides. Guilt washes over her. She has wanted him to get well quickly so he would leave her apartment. She, his mother, wants him to leave. Flushed with shame, she gathers up the fragments of shattered bowl, wipes the floor, and goes into the kitchen. She throws away the porcelain shards and rag. Fills a pail with water and returns to mop his room and the tiny hall where she sleeps on the floor these days now that he has taken over her bed in the room. A mother is always a mother. She can't bear to let him sleep on the floor like before although he had said he didn't mind sleeping on the floor. Before he and his three sisters left her, all four of them had slept on the floor in this room, just big enough for their foam mattresses which they rolled up and pushed under her bed each morning.

Agh! Why is she going back to the past again? That was when they were children. Things have changed. She mops and cleans the kitchen before she goes to bed, and takes out the aluminium pot and steamer for tomorrow's cooking.

2

4.30 a.m.

She is up before the alarm goes off. She switches on the light in the tiny bathroom and glances at the cracked mirror hanging from its rusty nail on the wall. Her face framed by a mess of grey hair is crisscrossed by a latticework of lines. Two deep channels run from her nostrils to each corner of her mouth. Lines, and more lines cross her cheeks and forehead. Aye, this is what a husband and four children can do to a woman. They leave lines across your face and belly like a farmer's plough. Ach! Enough! Leave such thoughts alone. She runs a comb through her hair and ties the strands with a rubber band. She has no money to waste on hairdressers and foot massages. Not like her neighbour, Mee Sua Soh. But thank God, at her age, she can still squat over the toilet bowl. Thank you, Mother Mary for blessing me with good knees, she mutters and washes her hands at the sink before she takes out the dough and turnip filling from the fridge to make *soon kueh* dumplings.

Fresh steamed *soon kueh* is her specialty and the people in the office love them. She pushes open the kitchen window to let in more air. Then she lights the gas stove to boil water for the steamer and starts kneading the dough, picking up speed as she kneads. When the dough is ready, she takes a small lump, flattens it between her palms, cups it to form a shallow shell and fills it with a spoonful of the pork and turnip she has cooked the night before. Then she folds the shell into a half moon pressing and folding the edges together to seal it before slipping the dumpling onto the steamer's tray and take another small lump of dough to make the next dumpling. On and on she works like an automaton as the clock ticks. She keeps an eye on the steamer, ready to take out each tray of dumplings as soon as it is cooked.

The kitchen is hot and cramped, barely big enough for a stove, a small fridge, a sink and some shelves that Kow Kia's father had nailed to the wall when they first moved in. They were lucky to be able to rent this one-room flat in this Bukit Ho Swee estate from the Public Housing Board. Back then thousands had to wait for years for a home of their own. She was only seventeen, and already pregnant with Nancy, their first child when they married. The day they moved in, Kow Kia's father, oh dear, he was so very eager and he ... and her eyes light up as they gaze into the distance. It's so embarrassing to think about it after all these years but she still remembers how he...ah... how he had lifted her up and carried her into the flat. Just like the *ang moh* newly weds in the American movies. Laughing uproariously he threw her on to the bed and ... and they did it. Again and again that first night of their married life. They were so happy then. Not a care in the world.

The wok hisses. A cloud of steam rises from the steamer when she lifts off the cover. She takes out the tray of *suon kueh*, sprinkles fried onions on the steaming dumplings and packs them into the styrofoam boxes. Six *suon kueh* per box. Twenty boxes. One hundred and twenty pieces of *suon kueh* each morning. At forty cents a piece, that will be forty-eight dollars. Minus thirty or so for turnip, pork, chilli sauce, sesame oil, soy sauce, fried onions, gas and bus fare, that leaves her with eighteen dollars. Let's say fifteen dollars a day. Ten days. One hundred and fifty dollars. Not bad. Not bad at all. Blessed Mother Mary, look kindly on me. Let me sell off all the *suon kueh* today. Have mercy on me, she prays in the Teochew dialect in the way that old Granny Chia and Father Edmond Tay had taught her during catechism classes.

Can Jesus understand Chinese, Granny? She had asked.

Don't worry, *lah,* girl. Granny Chia had laughed. Jesus and Mother Mary, they can understand everything. Whatever language – Teochew, Hokkien, Malay not just the English tongue of the *ang moh*.

She had followed the Chia family to the Catholic Church in Au Kang where most of the Catholic Teochew families used to live. At first, she did it just to get out of the house. Then she was amazed to see so many Chinese people praying in a way that was so different from her parents' praying. All the women wore a veil on their heads in church. Granny Chia and Mrs Chia wore black lace veils, and the four Chia girls had white veils. They each carried a little black book called a missal and a rosary with a silver cross. They looked so pretty and elegant on Sundays that she longed to be like them. Granny Chia bought her a white veil and taught her to say the rosary. Mrs Chia even took her to the Church of Our Lady of Perpetual Succour in Thomson Road for the novena service every Saturday and prayed for her conversion. Aye, those were the wonderful days of her youth. Her employers were generous and kind. She ate what the family ate, worked hard and never gave them any trouble. Granny Chia and Mrs Chia had their hands full looking after six children. The four girls were five, seven, nine and ten. And the twin boys, Peter and Paul, were newborns.

At sixteen, she was put in charge of the kitchen and the ordering of provisions for the family. She could order anything as long as she told Mrs Chia or Granny. They trusted her. And she never cheated them. She did all the cooking under Granny Chia's supervision. The family was pleased with her, and Mrs Chia bought her two new dresses for church and increased her pay to fifty dollars a month the year she met Kow Kia's father.

She packs the last box of *suon kueh* into her bag and pulls back the curtain that separates the sleeping area from the kitchen. Kow Kia is still asleep, his head hidden under the heap of bedclothes. She crouches beside his bed and pulls out the handbag she has hidden behind the boxes under the bed, careful not to make a sound. She feels bad about hiding her handbag. Still, she has to be careful. His presence cramps her. She feels pressed against the wall at times. She stands up and draws the curtain that she had hung up to give her and Kow Kia's father some privacy when the children were growing up. It was very difficult when the four of them were teenagers. The flat was so small. How could she blame them for roaming the streets till late at night?

When Kow Kia and his sisters left home, the flat became very quiet and empty; the space felt large even though all the things were still around. She lived in a daze, staring at the tv not knowing what the talking heads were saying. The hours crept past. There was nothing to do. She felt wasted like rubbish washed up on the beach. No one wanted this old body of a mother. Then Mee Sua

Soh, her neighbour in the next block, found her a cleaning job.

Ah Gek, don't sit at home all day. You'll think about this and that till you go mad. Now that you can work, go and work. Having money is better than having children. These days we can't depend on children any more. When you ask them for money, they think you're asking for their blood. Right or not?

She had never been inside an office before. Everything looked so officious and orderly. And all the young men and women looked so smart and important. She could not look them in the eye. Mee Sua Soh laughed at her.

Let me tell you, Ah Gek. They look good on the outside only. I clean the loos, I know. They're filthy inside. Such dirt the women leave behind in the toilets. Tampons, *lah*! Blood *lah!* Foul smelling pads stuck behind the water pipe. I used to spit when they leave my toilets! *Ji-la-gak*! I cursed them. Their mothers never taught them how to use toilets properly. Even cats cover their poo. Right or not? But not these educated young people! Still, washing the loos in an office is much better than washing the loos in the malls. Don't worry. This office, the people are very nice.

She was happy to work. Even managed to save a little. Until Kow Kia turned up on her doorstep one night. The green pallor on his face shocked her. But Kow Kia being Kow Kia insisted there was nothing wrong. Just the flu, Ma. Just tired. I come back to rest a few days. Can or not?

How could a mother say no? She was happy he had come home. She cooked and boiled and steamed for him but his health grew worse. These last two months, he hadn't left the flat at all. She had offered to pay the doctor's fee if only he would go and see the doctor. But no, he was stubborn. And proud.

Cannot get ill, is it? Ill only you must fuss and nag. Nag me all day. I know you want me to leave your house. Don't worry. I will leave.

It's true; she wants him to leave. She has gotten used to living alone these past few years. Yet in every mother's heart, her son is always her son. Dear Mother Mary Blessed Ever Virgin, have mercy on me. She looks up at the plastic statue on top of the cupboard, makes the sign of the cross and promises to say several rounds of the rosary in the evening if she sells off all the *suon kueh* today. Then she opens the front door and lets herself out.

The lighting in the common corridor is dimmer than usual. One of the overhead lights has blown. Dim even in the daytime, the corridor runs down the centre of this block of rental flats. The corridor is no man's land; its walls are smeared with dried spit, bicycle tire marks and shoe marks. Cardboard boxes, cartons, shoe cases, an old pram, a ladder, two stools, two rusty bicycles chained to the pipes, and piles of old newspapers line the walls. If this block were in the Prime Minister's constituency, such clutter would have been cleared away. A faulty light? No problem. It would be replaced the next day. As Mee Sua Soh said the bigger your Minister, the faster things get fixed.

A child wails.

'Shut her up! *Buat suay*! Early, early in the morning she howls like *Limpek* is dying! Ah Ba is not dead yet! Stop crying! My luck is bad enough already!' The man yells. His wife yells back. Something is flung against the door. The child cries louder. Ah Gek hastens past her neighbour's door with her plastic bags of *suon kueh* and presses for the lift.

3

Kow Kia turns slowly onto his back, careful not to make any sudden move that could press against his sores and aggravate the pain. The skin on his back feels raw and damp; he wonders if they had bled while he was asleep. He tries to sit up but it demands too much energy and effort. He lies still, willing himself to stay calm as the clatter and chatter of the neighbours grow louder as the light outside the window grows brighter. He closes his eyes, and tries not to think of Honeybear. Just breathe. Just keep breathing. Don't think. Don't feel. Breathe. Just breathe. In. Out. In. Out. He can hear the band playing, and Honeybear is singing: *Enjoy, enjoy yourselves tonight! Oh celebration! What jubilation!* The spotlight is on the two of them gyrating their hips on that beautiful stage in Manila. Bright pink ostrich feathers waving and dancing on their heads, their four-inch stilettos glittering silver and gold as they kick their heels and thrust their hips sashaying down the aisle through the cheering throng of men, blowing kisses as drunks and loved crazed fans and American tourists stuffed wads of US dollars down their bras and sequinned panties. Bangkok, Pattaya Beach, Phuket, Manila and even Jarkarta, those were the days when the two of them went everywhere together, seldom a day apart.

Honeybear. Honey Darling, please get well. You *have* to get well, Honey.

Shh! Don't cry. Don't cry, da. Honeybear's voice hardly rose above a whisper the night the ambulance came for him. We will be together always. Always, I cross my heart. Why think so much ahead? Don't think of the future, *lah*. Don't despair. Don't worry about me. *Allah memberi rahmat kapada ku*. God All Merciful will have mercy on me.

4

'Hello, people! Breakfast is here! Come and get your *suon kueh*! And pay up! Pay up!' Peter Chia called out to his colleagues.

'Hey, Peter, are you getting a cut from Auntie?'

Ah Gek suppressed a snort. That Ting woman is flirting with Mr Chia again. See, see her wagging her finger and tapping her little red painted finger on his shoulder. Shameless! Baiting young Mr Chia like this. But it's none of her business. These young things who speak English *fah-li-fah-lah* like the *ang mohs*. But Peter Chia is different. He's always polite to her. And so helpful too. Helping her to hand out the boxes of *suon kueh* to the young women crowding around his desk. Such a sweet young man, and the only one, who stands up whenever she enters his cubicle to empty the wastebasket and clean his table, and he always has a few words for her.

Have you had your coffee yet, Auntie? He would ask her.

Not yet, Mr Chia, she would reply. She never calls him Peter, not even after the two of them found out by chance that she, Ah Gek, was his family's maid years ago when he and his twin brother were born.

Just call me Peter, Auntie Ah Gek.

Cannot. This is the office. How can I do that? You're so high up now. *Aiyoh*, I better clean your office quick. Then go and drink my *kopi*.

Her English is rotten; she knows that. But kind Mr Chia, he never embarrasses her. Never corrects her. Never complains about the way she speaks. Not like this Ting woman. Ah no, that busybody told the boss to send cleaners like her for English language classes during the Speak Good English campaign.

Complained that workers like Ah Gek give their publishing house a poor image.

How can we allow Singlish here? We're this country's foremost publishing house. This is our headquarters for crying out loud! We're the flag bearer. We publish English books for schools. Singlish should be banned from this office. It's ungrammatical. It grates on the ear. I can't stand all this *lah* and *lor*, and *leh* and *meh*! They drive me nuts!

That Ting woman was referring to me, she told Mee Sua Soh one day. That snooty talked like her skin is white. Ya, *lor*! Mee Sua Soh agreed, and there and then the two of them dubbed Miss Ting as *ang-moh-sai,* a piece of English turd. *Ang-moh-sai*, she says it in her head. It makes her feel better. Calling them names is the only way that people like her can get back at people like Miss Ting.

'Mr Chia, this box is for you. Special. Eight *suon kueh* inside.'

'That's not fair! How come Peter gets more than us? How much is each box?' Miss Ting holds up a box.

'Two *dollah,* forty cents, *lor*.'

'Actually your *suon kueh* are more expensive than those in the market!'

May be it's Miss Ting's high-pitched whine or the accusative tone, or her own impatience, but whatever it was, she retorts in a mix of Hokkien and English, 'My *suon kueh* all made by hand, *hor*! The skin, you see or not? Very thin. Got more filling inside, *hor*! More meat. More veg-gee-table. The rice dough. I ownself make. The chilli sauce I make. Not from bottle, *leh*! I no buy bottle chilli sauce. My dried prawn and turnip, all good quality! My pork got no fat. Very lean, one. Prices go up. I no increase my price. You don't believe me? You go home. Ask your mother. Ask her. How much the pork, the dried prawn, how much the turnip sell in maar-ket!'

'Oh dear me, there's no need to shout and tell a long story, Auntie.'

Silenced, she counts out the change and hands it to Miss Ting.

'No, keep the change.'

'No thank you, Miss Ting. Take your change, *leh*. I don't want ten *dollah*. I poor but not greedy.'

Without a word Miss Ting takes back her change and walks off followed by Peter Chia who whispers 'thank you.' Later, during their coffee break sitting on the backstairs of the office, Mee Sua Soh tells her she was stupid.

'You made Miss Ting lose face in front of so many people. She's the deputy director. It'll bring you trouble. You watch it. She's not the sort to forget. The whole office is talking about you now.'

'Let them talk, *lor*! What to do? It's done already. She was waving her ten dollars in my face. Like her ten dollars is so big.'

'Shh! Not so loud. Miss Ting doesn't understand Teochew. But other people understand. They will report to her. Why are you so worked up? Miss Ting can make life very difficult for you, you know! She's this close to the boss.'

Mee Sua Soh presses two fingers together.

'You think I don't know? But she could've ruined my business just now. The gods in heaven know I need the money. Kow Kia must eat well to get well. So who has to cough out this extra money for medicine and food? Your old cow here. If people in the office like my *suon kueh*, I can sell. But I cannot sell cheap. The price of pork has gone up. Even pork bones cost more these days.'

She tears the red bean bun into two and gives one half to Mee Sua Soh. They wash down the bread with sweet black coffee. She's glad that she has a friend like Mee Sua Soh.

'My *ang moh* talk always gets me into trouble.'

'You know that your English is half past six, why you bother?'

'Not me. It's that sow!'

'Who are you calling sow?'

'Don't be thick! That Ting woman said she couldn't understand Teochew. Asked me to talk English in her office! And I do know a bit. I've worked for years in an English-speaking family when I was a maid!'

'Eat up! Eat up. Here. Try this.'

Mee Sua Soh hands her another bun, warm and glistening with sesame oil. Hungrily, she bites into it, savouring the taste of sweet minced pork and fried lard.

'Aaah, this is so good.'

'Costs me ninety cents. Everything's gone up. Water and electricity. All gone up. Bus fares went up last month. But the gar'ment still says we're doing well.'

'Of course, the government is doing well! It's people like us who are not doing well. Look at Kow Kia. Is he doing well? All that money I spent on herbs and soup! It's like pouring money down the drain.'

'Talking of money, Ah Long Chek,' Mee Sua Soh lowers her voice. She glances up the stairs to make sure that no one is coming down. 'Sick or not, he expects you to pay him back this week. You missed again last month.'

'But I paid him last month. I gave two hundred and fifty to

Si Tua Pui.'

'That deadbeat fatty said your payment last month was for the month before. You missed the month before? Tua Pui said you missed twelve weeks, that is, three months. Ah Loong Chek, he's not pleased. He is very strict about prompt payment.'

Mee Sua Soh's words dampen her mood. She tries to recall all the payments she'd made to Ah Long Chek alias Tua Buck Long alias Big Eye Dragon. The names alone are enough to make her heart pound faster. But she had had to go to the Dragon and his assistant, Si Tua Pui. Who else in this world will lend you money without any collateral? And no questions asked. She has no collateral But Big Eye Dragon is known to keep an open hand, and will lend you whatever sum you ask. Only thing is his *kaki* - his men can break your bones or your livelihood if you can't pay up. They can smash your food stall, splash paint and faeces on your front door, break your leg and make it look like an accident. And no one dares call the police.

'I've lost count how much I owe.'

'Si Tua Pui said you owe two thousand and...'

'What? Two thousand? But I only borrowed five hundred!'

'Keep your voice down. Si Tua Pui warned you not to fall behind, didn't he?'

'But how can five hundred become two thousand?'

'Interest, *lor*. It piles up. You owe them two thousand and six or seven hundred. I can't remember the exact figure.'

Ah Gek groans.

'And don't forget your twenty-five percent interest. At the end of six weeks, you have to pay back the loan plus twenty-five percent. That's why I advised you last time. Pay back quickly. But you didn't pay back the whole sum. So you owe more and more. Interest upon interest. It all adds up very fast. Compounded.'

Ah Gek stands up, brushes off the breadcrumbs on the front of her blouse, collects her plastic cup and climbs the stairs back to the office, too angry and despondent to say another word.

5

The corner coffeeshop was in Bedok Northwest. And just as Mee Sua Soh had told her, there were several men seated at the tables, drinking beer and iced tea, looking like your regular neighbourhood uncles in shorts and loafers. One or two of the men sported a thick gold chain round their necks. She waved to the woman taking orders for drinks. When the woman came to her table, she placed her order as instructed: One *kopi* with three spoons of sugar, and two spoons of condensed milk.

One of the men at the next table glanced up. The woman took her order and returned moments later with the cup of coffee. She placed it on the table and muttered: Wait a while. Si Tua Pui. He's in the toilet.

She remembered smiling at the name. *Si Tua Pui*. Dead Big Fatty. A common nickname for loafers in Housing Board neighbourhoods. But for a moneylender to be called Dead Big Fatty that was unusual. She didn't think she would have anything to fear from Fatty. She took a sip of her coffee and made a face.

The *kopi* is too sweet, is it?

The man who sat down heavily in front of her was not fat and flabby as his name suggested. He was a stout thickset man. He did not smile. His eyes were small for his large face. Two deep lines ran down either side of his nostrils. His large nose looked like he had broken it in a fight. He took out a pack, extracted a cigarette and offered it to her. Smoke?

No, thank you, she heard herself squeak.

Judging by his sun-browned face, he could have been a fisherman or a construction worker in his younger days. She put his age at about fifty to fifty-five.

This *kopi* is twenty-five per cent sweeter than the normal cup. Just add twenty-five percent more sugar. Every six weeks. You understand?

His voice was gruff, his Hokkien unpolished. He spoke like he was telling her how to make a good cup of coffee. He flicked his lighter, lit up and inhaled deeply. He held the cigarette smoke in his mouth for a few seconds before letting it seep out through his lips and nostrils. Like a dragon breathing smoke, she thought. Then she noticed the large jade ring on his finger. The kind of grey-green jade known as 'dead man's jade'. Encased in a thick gold band, the jade stone had gleamed like a threat. A warning. How much *kopi* do you want to order? He asked her.

Five hundred, please.

Mee Sua Soh had warned her not to mention money. Instead, she was to state the amount of coffee, milk or sugar she wanted.

Tell me where you live. I will send someone to deliver the coffee powder to your home.

He took out a cheap ballpoint pen and scribbled her address into a dirty notebook stuffed with pink and yellow slips of paper.

Tomorrow night. Ten o'clock. You be at home.

Mee Sua Soh had warned her she'd better pay up in full. She had pleaded for time. She couldn't rustle up so much. Later, Si Tua Pui sent word through Mee Sua Soh again. Big Eye Dragon was not pleased. And that was the first time, she was aware of the chain of command. Like a ladder. The top man sent word down to the lowest rung. And it crossed her mind then that Mee Sua Soh was on the lowest rung of this ladder.

6

Her big mouth was to blame. She was fired. And there is still no word from Mee Sua Soh about another job. It has been more than a month now. Her savings will vanish if she doesn't get work soon. She goes into the bathroom. She comes out of the bathroom. She paces up and down, mops the stove for the umpteenth time and re-arranges her shelves. Then she stands at the kitchen window squinting at the splinters of sunlight from the glass panes and the sun-scorched walls wondering if she should go downstairs to the coffee shop to collect discarded empty drink cans. She can sell them to the *karung guni* man when he comes around to collect old newspapers. Might earn her a dollar or two. But has she sunk so low that she has to rummage in the rubbish bins of coffee shops? Her neighbours will have something to say. And if her three vixens find out, they too will have something to say about their mother's lack of shame these days. Not that they will find out. They haven't visited her for some time now. Not since their brother came home.

She fans herself furiously with a piece of cardboard. No breeze today. No sign of rain. No sign of the hot spell ending. The grass along the road has browned. Singapore is seething in this heat and humidity. In the car park below, heat waves rise from the sun-beaten tarmac. Her headache is threatening to return. Four-thirty, and the sun is still a fiery ball. If only there's a bit of breeze the air won't be so oppressive. Her clothes are soaked. But no, she won't switch on the fan. Must save electricity. Earlier, Kow Kia had complained of feeling cold despite the hot weather. He's lying in bed as usual with his face turned to the wall. She has stopped trying to coax him to eat. What's a mother to do? He's a grown man. Can't force him to eat like she used to when the children were small. Besides, she has no appetite herself. And it isn't because of the heat. It's been two months since she lost that job. Eight weeks since she shouted at Mr Rajah, the cleaning supervisor. He said people had complained to the boss about her. Said he had no choice. Had to ask her to leave. She'd broken the rules.

What rule? What rule?

Hey! Don't shout at me *lah*, Ah Gek. Not me complain, you know. You're not allowed to sell things in the office.

But no one told me!

Read your contract.

Read your head! Did that fart of a man expect her to read the English words?

Your head, my head, it doesn't matter now, Ah Gek. You sold *suon kueh* in the office. Lady Boss said this is a publishing house not a market.

Ah so! It's Miss Ting, that *kaypoh*! That busybody!

It wasn't the wisest thing to say. She knew that and Mee Sua Soh also said that. But she had said it and now her bridge is burnt. The company will never give her another job again. A daily rated worker. The company owes her nothing.

'*Si kia*!'

The screech jerks her awake. She must've dozed off.

'*Si kia*! Dead child!'

Her next door neighbours are at it again. She too used to

yell at her children like this. All the women in the block did it. They yelled at their kids all the time. Her own brats made her so furious sometimes that not only did she screech and yell at them, she also caned them and wanted to strangle them. They were a pack of yapping, fighting animals when they were young. Couldn't understand words at the normal volume; she had to screech at them or hit them on the head. Never a moment's peace with them yapping at her heels, getting in her way and knocking into her every which way they turned. It was a tight squeeze, this one-room flat with four kids. The children had to eat their meals in the corridor outside. Kow Kia's father, who wasn't so stoned and drunk then, had placed two large wooden crates along the wall outside their flat, and he brought home soapboxes for the children to use as stools. Nancy, the eldest, took charge, yelling at Lily and Molly. Nancy used to smack them but Lily fought back. Only four years old, the little mite fought her sister tooth and nail while Molly the second girl squealed, Ma-aaa!! Lily and Nan are fighting again!

The girls wore her out. Such screeching little vixens they were. But not her Kow Kia. He was different. A quiet child, a sweet baby boy. How he'd clung to her breast even when he was asleep, and wailed in angry protest whenever his sisters tried to carry him, his baby arms flailing out at them. She loved the feel of his plump little body against hers when he was born, the way he wound his baby arms around her neck, nuzzling against her breast, his baby mouth sucking at her nipple. He was always hungry, always needing to suckle and afterwards peeing all over her so that she had to change her clothes several times a day some days. But she never minded it. The truth was she was suffused with love for her son. She loved his clinginess, his baby greed, his sourish milk-curdled smell and his fresh-from-sleep sweet infant smell. At two, he was such a healthy brown and chubby toddler that his sisters promptly named him, Kow Kia or Little Pup, and the name had stuck.

Her little pup brought his father good luck too. She remembered the foolish grin on Ah Seng's face when she told him that their fourth child was a boy. He couldn't believe his luck. A son? I have a son? He was beaming when she placed the boy in his arms. Your son, she'd said to him. Speechless with joy, Ah Seng gazed down at the bundle, unable to say a word. Not a word. How proud and happy she felt that morning. Her son's birth changed Ah Seng's status in her eyes. From then on, she saw him not as her husband but as the father of her son and took to addressing him as 'Kow Kia's father.' Later, even their neighbours addressed him as such. He was earning a decent wage working at a construction site then. Life was good even though there was not much left after paying for rent, utilities and food. But they had enough to eat.

Aye, those were good days, the good old days before the crane crashed down on him. Before he broke his leg. Before he started to drink. Before he turned moody and crazy. Before he started to beat her and the children. Before he took a chopper to her neck. Before she ran away with the boy. Before he jumped down the block. Aye, before all that happened, that year, that happy year after Kow Kia was born, Ah Seng took her and the girls to the Great World Amusement Park. It was the first day of Chinese New Year. A hot glorious day. Entrance to the Park was free on Chinese New Year's Day, and Kow Kia's father had money to spend. He had won a small prize betting on the birth date of his son. They feasted on plates of chicken rice and roast pork, and he bought the girls huge bowls of ice *kachang* for dessert, and tickets for rides on the Ferris wheel and merry-go-round. The girls were so happy! And she was so happy just looking at her brood and their beaming father. Ah Seng made them delirious with fright on the Ferris wheel. What if we fall, girls? Eh? What if we fall? Don't look down! We're going higher and higher and higher! Hold us! Hold us, Papa! The girls had squealed as they clung to their father. But little Kow Kia slept through it all. He was asleep in his father's arms. Kow Kia's father, who had never carried his daughters, was carrying his baby son that Chinese New Year. It was the happiest day of her married life.

How come we humans realised we're happy only after the happiness was gone? Sorrow strikes like a hammer's blow but happiness, fickle and light as a butterfly, brushes our shoulders and darts off. Why is her life so full of hammer blows? If it isn't one thing, it's another. Money is always not enough. Never enough. Each month had been a struggle to make the dollars last till the end of the month. The children were always in trouble. School trouble when they were in school. Men trouble or money trouble when they grew up. The girls hitched up with one bloke after another. How many? She'd lost count. Only when the four of them left her did she enjoy some peace. But then Kow Kia came back. What had she done to deserve such children? And she's a baptised Catholic some more.

She gazes at the implacable blueness of the sky outside her window. A blue unchanging cloudless sky. Vast, silent and oppressive. The heavenly Father is a distant figure, absent from her life in a one-room rental flat among neighbours who burn paper offerings to the same deities that her parents had worshipped. Her Catholic God and His saints are keeping away from her neighbours' *Ti Kong* in Heaven, the pantheon of Chinese saints like the Kitchen God, the Earth God, Prosperity God and Longevity God. A Catholic since age fourteen, she hadn't been near a church for years. Not since Father Patrick Lee humiliated her in front of the women in the Legion of Mary. Stop living in sin, Ah Gek. Go and marry the father of your children. And have them baptised. Later, he scolded her again during confession for going to the government clinic for abortion and ligation. That was the last straw. She lashed out at him in the confessional. Father, will you pay for my fifth child then?

Since then, she'd never gone back to church. So now God must be punishing her. Something was sapping Kow Kia's blood and energy. Like a rat in the gutter, guilt gnawed at her. But surely, surely, Heavenly Father, you remember how at fourteen I rejected my parents' false gods.

Her parents, drunk on a future that never came, were forever shaking a milk tin filled with pieces of rolled-up paper, written with the numbers zero to nine.

Bless us! Bless us with a lucky number! Her mother had even knelt under the banyan tree while her father cried out to a large python in the wire cage.

Lord Python. Do what you will with her but please give us a winning number.

She was disgusted. How could her father offer his own wife to the reptile god? Gamblers were willing to do anything. Scurrying from one shrine to the next, from a hole-in-the-wall to a hole-in-the-banyan tree, from temple to cemetery, her crazed parents had prayed under trees, knelt beside drains or knelt on the beach in the dead of night calling up the spirit of a drowned man to tell them what numbers to buy for the next big lottery draw. By the time she was thirteen, her mother had lost all her jewellery. She could remember times when there was no food in their attap hut in Sembawang. Her brothers and sisters were crying but there was no sign of their father. One night, her distraught mother had lined up all six of them to kowtow to the God of Wealth. Fighting hunger pangs, each child had to pick a number out of the milk tin. That night, instead of buying food, their mother betted her last ten dollars on the numbers they had picked. A month later they lost their attap hut and had to move into a rented room. Eight of them, parents and six children, crammed into one small room. From then on, she stopped going to school and left home the night her parents prayed to the python god.

'Forgive me for judging them. My fault, my fault, my most grievous fault!'

Her fingers tap her heart three times in a ritual prayer that was drilled into her by her former employer, Mrs Mary Chia. *Mea culpa, Mea culpa.*

'*Hoi! Si kia*! You dead bastard!'

A bottle shatters the still afternoon air. The drunk next door is at it again. His wife screams at him, and the children wail. The block's daily afternoon opera has begun. What shit! These men! They drink their way to hell and damnation. Just like Kow Kia's father. She's mad whenever she thinks of him. His death was so pointless. A wall! Climb over it, *lor*! But no! He bangs his head against it. Chose drink and death. *Ack*! Why waste her time thinking of him? It's past five already. Time to pray. She reaches for the box of matches and lights a candle. Places it in front of the Blessed Virgin Mary. Time she returns to saying the rosary. Beads of the desperate. That was what Mrs Mary Chia had called it. A fitting name for the string of beads. She makes the sign of the cross, holds the string of blue glass beads in her hands and begins: Hail Mary, full of grace, the Lord is with thee... A prayer so achingly beautiful to her ears when she first heard it as a lonely fourteen-year-old maid in the Chia household. Each night she had watched the family praying together, yearning to be part of their circle of father, mother, grandmother and children, each one on their knees, counting their rosary beads, murmuring in unison,

Hail Mary, full of grace...

She had knelt at the fringe, praying with them, happy to be connected to them by a string of beads. The family that prays together stays together; Mrs Mary Chia taught her. But Kow Kia's father, he refused to pray. And her children followed their father's bad example although, in her heart of heart, she must admit that this was not entirely his doing. She herself was erratic in her praying after she'd left the Chia's employment. They had sacked her when they found out that she was pregnant at seventeen.

'Our Father Who art in heaven, holy be thy name...'

She ends the first decade of beads and gets up to sit on a chair. At sixty-six, her joints are not as strong as they used to be. But to do penance properly, she has to be on her knees. So she kneels again.

'Please make Kow Kia well O Blessed Mother Mary! I promise to recite the rosary every day for the rest of my life if you ask your son, Jesus, to make him well.'

She prays to the Virgin, mother to mother. She was not above bargaining. Prayers are offerings to a divine deity in return for favours granted or sins forgiven. You pray for what you did or what you desire. The bigger the favour, the bigger the sin, the longer you pray. A fair system. Hammer on God's door. That's praying, Father Patrick said. Knock and the door shall be opened unto you.

'Hail Mary, full of grace...'

Her prayer in Teochew rises and fall in a lilt that sound quaint to modern ears accustomed to Teochew spoken in the market place. The words of the prayer are formal and tonal unlike the Teochew of daily speech. She clutches the string of beads in both her hands, pushing down a bead after each Hail Mary. When she reaches the tenth bead, she recites, 'Our Father...' and starts again bead by bead, one bead for one prayer until she'd said the 'Hail Mary' prayer fifty times and the 'Our Father' and 'Glory Be' ten times each.

She has been praying like this every evening for the past fortnight. Her plan is to say this number of prayers each night for a month. By the end of thirty days, she reckons she will have said 'Hail Mary' one thousand and five hundred times, 'Our Father' and 'Glory Be' three hundred times. She imagines each prayer as a knock on God's door. Knock, knock, knock! Out in the great beyond, He's bound to hear her and answer. A soft groan comes from behind the red checked curtain. She remains kneeling and continues to pray with her back to the curtain while her ears pick up every move and sigh behind it. 'Hail Mary, full of grace, the Lord is with Thee. Blessed art thou amongst women and blessed is the fruit of thy womb ...'

7

Just what the hell is she doing? When is she going to stop this mumbo-jumbo? Her words dropping like marbles on the hard floor and bouncing off the walls. Praying for him, she'd said. More like hitting him with a hammer on his head with each 'Hail Mary'. He's broken out in a cold sweat again. His soaked tee shirt clings to his back. He feels drained. Last night, she'd badgered him to see a doctor again. What can the doctor do? Bound to give him bad news and a prescription for the expensive drugs he can't afford. How else can these medical blokes buy their BMWs and Mercedes? That's how the business works. If I die, I die. I'm prepared, he told her, and she'd cried. Said he was killing her with his intransigence. Big Teochew word – intransigence! Where did she learn that kind of Teochew? Like from the opera.

Silence on the other side of the curtain. The praying has stopped. At last he can breathe. He sits up, feels for his slippers and drags himself to the bathroom, and leans against the wall to catch his breath. Then the praying starts again. He swears under his breath. Why can't his mother be silent? Sit quietly like other old ladies. But no, she can't sit still and do nothing. If she sits down, her hands must reach for a cloth to wipe the table or wash a cup. Her eyes dart from one corner of the flat to the other, checking for dust, for dirt, for this, for that, all the while her hands would be wiping, sweeping, grabbing, her mind clicking, counting, adding, and her mouth yelling at her children. Sit up. Drink up. Wake up. Own up. Don't lie. Don't die. She can't help herself. Has been like this ever since he was a boy. If her mouth wasn't yapping, her hands were kneading dough and anger. Face taut with fury, her hands pounded the pastry, flattened and moulded the rice dough into *soun kueh, chooi kueh, ang ku kueh*, any *kueh* or cakes that would bring in a little extra to supplement his miserable old man's miserable wage. Hard anger was buried in those hands. He couldn't eat her cakes. Couldn't stomach them. Used to throw up when she forced him to eat the unsold *kueh*.

'Hail Mary, full of grace...'

Damn! His throat hurts. His tongue feels bloated and thick. He looks into the mirror on the wall, opens his mouth and sticks out his tongue. A cream-coloured fuzz covers it. There's an ulcer at the corner of his mouth. Yesterday, she had looked at it and pronounced him, 'heaty.' He'd almost laughed. *Heaty*? What a joke! He wishes it were just the heat that's bugging him.

When they were children, his sisters had borne the brunt of their Ma's temper. She was a firecracker with a short fuse. Bang! Bang! Bang! Little things set her off. When the old man was alive, their flat was a boiling cauldron of quarrels and fistfights. She hurled things at him. Pots and pans were flung at the wall in the middle of the night. He banged his fists on the table, and thumped her and them, the children if they got in the way. The pots and pans in her kitchen were dented, the bowls and plates chipped. Nothing was whole. She hammered her children's heads with anything she could grab. A bowl. A plate. A mug. A pot. Once she hurled a stool out of the window. It landed on the path downstairs. Luckily no one was hurt, but it'd scared the shit out of him. She could have been jailed for 'killer litter' if someone had reported her to the police. Oh, she was reckless in those days. But she was the only one who stood up for him when the old man whipped him at the slightest excuse. He loved her then. When she hurled that stool out of the window, he was prepared to lie to the teeth to the police to protect her.

'Ugh!' At the sound of his cough, she stops praying.

'Kow Kia! You want water? Toilet?'

He waves her off and is glad she doesn't try to help him. He closes the bathroom door, but he can't shut out her droning, which is not as loud as before, but that's only because she's listening to his laboured grunts in case he falls or faints. He chaffs at the lack of privacy. Untied the strings of his pants and gingerly lowers his bag of bones over the squat bowl, relieved that he hasn't soiled his pants. His bowels are loose and watery again. If not for this damn diarrhoea, he needn't have come back. There's nothing here for him, just lousy memories of his old man. He knows he broke her heart when he left home at fifteen. But god! The flat had reeked of his sisters' female things and smells. Their tits and bums had rubbished his face. The four of them had had to share the half of the room not occupied by their parents' bed. The half that the old man had grandly called the sitting room. Sitting room, ha! More like a pigsty. His sisters' clothes were everywhere.

One day, thinking all of them wouldn't be home, he'd tried on one of Nan's fancy bras. A flaming red bit of lace. Very beautiful. He gazed at himself in the mirror in the bathroom. The mirror wasn't cracked then. It was Ma's broom that cracked it when she found him wearing Nancy's red bra. That night she told his Pa. The old man undid his leather belt and thrashed the living daylight out of him. His body was lacerated by the time his yelling brought their neighbours to their doorway. They yelled at the old man to stop, but not a single one lifted a hand to stop the thrashing. That was how he ended up sleeping in the corridor outside. The old man wouldn't let him sleep in the flat after that.

Listen! He's your son!

YOU listen! He's not my son! Your womb was diseased! What have you given me? You call this worm a son?

Two years later, the old man threw him out, and wouldn't even let him sleep out in the corridor. He groans as he rises from his squat on the toilet bowl.

'Kow Kia! Are you all right in there?'

His grunt reassures her. She returns to her rosary, listening as she recites the words for his grunts and exhalations. She lives in fear of a thud on the wet cement floor. If he were to slip, God help her! She won't be able to lift him. She'll have to call the neighbours. But they may not want to come inside. And she won't blame them. Kow Kia's body is covered with sores.

'Kow Kia! Kow Kia!'

She bangs on his door. When there's no answer, she yells, 'Call an ambulance, somebodiiii! Kow Kia! Don't leave me!

8

'Ma, how did he get pneumonia?'

'Molly, why you ask Ma? How would she know? You blaming her or what?' Nancy pounced on her sister.

'I wasn't blaming her!'

'Didn't you hear what the Indian doctor said? Kow Kia's immune system is a gone case!'

'Please stop. I've a headache,' she tells her daughters.

A hostile silence settles on the table as they drink their coffee in the coffee shop. Her three daughters eye each other like boxers in the ring. She turns to Lily who can speak English better than the other two.

'What's ICU?'

'Intensive care unit,' Nancy answers, showing off that she knows about hospitals too, not just Lily. 'Kow Kia will have to be warded there.'

'No, Nan. The doctor didn't say Kow Kia has to go to ICU now. Only if he gets worse. He said Kow Kia must have more blood tests. The doctor ... he said we must wait for the test results first. He's in the Communicable Diseases Centre.'

'But there's something else, isn't it?' She looks at Lily who is digging into her handbag for a tissue. She's certain she heard something else. Something very serious, judging by the Indian doctor's face. Something about a disease that had hit America, Africa and Asia. She presses Lily for an answer.

'Yes, Ma. A deadly disease that has infected thousands in *Mei Guo*, *Fei Zhou*, and *Ah Zhou*.'

As the Chinese names of the three continents roll off Lily's tongue, she sees faceless young men falling like dominoes and her son is among these skeletal hordes. She's suddenly tired, very tired as her daughters' rapid exchange of words fly like arrows around her. No cure? Even cancer can be cured these days. How come no cure? They can make guns to kill people they can't make medicine to kill a disease?

'It's called the gay disease in America,' Molly says, 'the scourge of the twentieth century.'

'That's rubbish! It's not a gay disease.' Lily's tone is authoritative. 'I saw a tv documentary, married people can get it too. The tv didn't show the woman's face. Her husband gave her the disease and she passed it to her baby. It's contagious.'

Ah Gek groans, holding her head, two fingers rubbing her

temples. Her daughters' words are like knives in her skull. She regrets phoning them. Talk, talk, talk. That's all they do. Years ago, the three of them used to sit facing her like this across the table at home, the table with the blue Formica top cracked by Kow Kia's father when he flew into a rage one night and hurled the table at Kow Kia. It cracked the poor boy's head. And the girls were not spared either when they tried to protect their brother. Now, they've grown hard. She looks at Nancy, her eldest. Hair dyed a copper red. Face thick with make-up and a lipstick that's much too red. She and Nan had fought each other bad. Fought over everything, mostly over the men Nan went out with. But she has stopped fretting about her daughter's life. Stopped caring. Some day, men will tire of Nan. Will find her old, compared with the young chicks from China, Vietnam, Myanmar. What then? What will Nan do when she reaches fifty, sixty? Clean toilets? Molly is no better. Wearing a tee shirt so tight that her boobs stick out more than they ought. Lily is the only one who gives her some money each month. Fifty dollars isn't much but at least, it helps to pay for her bus fares and the rare taxi ride.

'Ma, you shouldn't bring Kow Kia home,' Nancy tells her.

'What do you expect me to do then? Leave him in hospital to die? He's my son, my only ...' She chokes up.

'Drink your tea, Ma. Drink.' Lily makes her drink her tea. 'Just listen to us first. You don't have to do what we say. But you listen first. Kow Kia's illness is long term. Not just one or two weeks. He's not going to die tomorrow. With proper care and medicine, he can live a long time more. The doctor said that.'

Like a drowning woman she grasps at the hope. Even a faint glimmer on the horizon is good. She'll grasp at anything that might save her boy. O Mary, Holy Mother of God, please let him live. Let my son live. 'Is there no medicine?'

'It's very expensive. Like more than a thousand a month. And that's excluding hospital check-ups, X-rays, blood tests, doctor's fees, etcetera. A lot of money, Ma. How to find more than a thousand a month?' Lily sighs.

'More than a thousand a month,' she repeats.

'There's no government subsidy for these medicines.'

'No subsidy? But we're poor peo...'

'I know, Ma. But the government doesn't pay for such medicine. If you have Medisave, you can withdraw up to five hundred a month to pay for Kow Kia's medicine.'

'I don't know if I have this...this Medi...' her voice trails off.

'People with not enough savings, die, *lor*. No subsidy. The poor pay like the rich! That's equality. Not enough Medisave, too bad! Nobody asked you to go and get this kind of disease.'

Nancy's cynical laugh jars her nerves. Ah Gek gulps down the rest of her tea and stands up. 'I will look after Kow Kia myself at home.'

'Ma. Listen, go and see the MP. May be the MP will help.'

'No use, one, *lah*! At most they will just write a letter.'

9

'Two coffee! One coke!'

'Coming!' Ah Gek hurries over to the tables with her tray of canned drinks and tall glasses of *kopi ping*.

Saturday night. The coffee shop is a hubbub of noise and activity with kids screaming and the television blaring overhead in the corner. She cleans a table, stacks the used plates and bowls into her red pail, sweeps the detritus of bones and used tissues into the blue pail and wipes the table with a grey dishcloth. A young couple sit down.

'Thank you, Ah Po.'

She gives the girl a grateful smile. This is her second month working in the coffee shop, and this is the first time a customer has greeted her so politely. Usually, people take no notice of her, and she would rather that they don't. Her only wish is for them not to dunk their used tissues into the bowls of leftover noodle soup. Customers, especially the young women, crunch up their used tissues into a ball and leave them in the bowls of soup. She loathes handling these soggy tissues. Families with young children are worse. They leave a huge mess on the tables. She doesn't mind if the old folks do it. Old folks she can excuse. But young people with education and money should have better manners. Her mood is bitter tonight as she trundles back and forth between the tables with her cloth and pail, and trays of drinks. Her head feels heavy, and her back aches. She's been on her feet since ten this morning. This being the weekend, she has to work longer hours, the boss said. By the time she lugs the last pail into the kitchen, it's past eleven thirty. The China woman who does the washing up gives her a nod.

'Aah! My back hurts!'

'Arthritis,' the China woman grunts.

Arthritis or not, she can't afford to lose this job. It doesn't pay much, but work is work. If she doesn't want it, someone else from China or Myanmar will take it. That's what Mee Sua Soh said. Take it or leave it. It's better than foraging in the dustbins for empty drink cans to sell. Better than stretching out a hand to her wretched daughters. Where's their help? In the end, it's all talk. She sloshes the contents of the pail into a large oil drum, and rinses the dishcloth furiously under the tap. Splashes water on her face and soaps her hands. Her knuckles are red and swollen. Her fingers are bent like claws and can't straighten. The veins on the back of her hands are like green worms beneath her brown skin.

'You finished?' the China woman asks.

'Ya, going home.'

She has clocked eleven hours, and is paid thirty-eight fifty. A good sum. She can save a few dollars. And that's a consolation. She can buy pork bones, some herbs like cordyceps, ginseng and wolfberries to make a soup for Kow Kia. She's counting every cent. His hospital bills have not yet been paid. Neither are her rent and utilities. The Housing Board has sent her another reminder to pay her rent. She's several months in arrears. There're just too many bills to settle.

'Not taking the bus, Ah Gek?'

'Nah! Why waste good money?'

She cuts across the empty car park. Her only indulgence these days is a smoke. Even then, she tries not to do it every day. Just one stick every two days. But she needs a cigarette now and fishes one out of her bag. She holds it to her nose, inhaling its woody fragrance and sits on a stone bench in the playground.

Aah, a rest and a smoke before walking to the public phone. She lights up and sighs. Sometimes when she walks past the brightly lit 7-Eleven convenience store, she longs to buy one of those packs inside, but they're beyond her means. Such exorbitant prices! The cigarette makers and suppliers are thieves. She can't afford to buy a whole pack, and shops no longer sell cigarettes by the stick, not like in the old days. Only the coffee shop boss is kind enough to sell her one cigarette at a time. As a favour, he said. But she reckons that she's paying him forty percent more this way. But what to do? She needs a smoke now and then. It takes her mind off worrying. To make up for paying him more, she had nicked a cigarette from his tin on the counter this afternoon. He won't miss it, and she won't do it often. She needs a smoke real bad tonight. Si Tua Pui is after her. He had sent word through Mee Sua Soh pressing her to pay up. Big Eye Dragon is upset her loan has not been repaid.

I've no money to pay him yet.

Didn't your daughters give you some money?

Lily gave me some last month. But I had to settle my water bill.

If Si Tua Pui finds out, he'll wring your neck.

Wring my neck also no use.

Your interest is piling up.

I know, I know, but Kow Kia is very ill. I'm caught in a bind.

You're caught in a bind? What about me? I was the one who introduced you to Si Tua Pui. He comes after me if you don't pay him. And Big Eye Dragon goes after him. You better ask your daughters for more money. Swallow your damn pride for goodness sake!

But it wasn't her pride. Molly has disappeared. Nancy wouldn't take her calls. And Lily is always at work when she phones. Lily who works in a factory is the only one with a decent job and family, and some feelings, but Lily too won't come up to the flat to see her brother.

He's not a leper.

I've got my boys to think about, Ma.

He is your brother. You, Nan and Moll are heartless!

Can you not think only of your son? In their line of work, Nan and Moll have to be careful. If people know that their brother has this ... this disease, the two of them might as well sit around and swat flies all day! Which man will want them?

She draws a last smoke from the cigarette, stubs it out and saves the unsmoked portion in the matchbox for after she has phoned her daughters.

'Alllo! Allo! That you Ah Tee? Ah Mah here! Tell Mama to come to the phone!'

'Granny, don't shout. I can hear you. Mama is working night shift.'

'Are you telling the truth?'

Maybe she has been too hard on Lily. She shouldn't have said, 'leper.' How could Lily be doing night shift for so many weeks?

'Ah Tee, after I put down the phone, you call Mama for me. Tell her Uncle Kow Kia has to go to the hospital again!'

'Can't. We're not allowed to call her while she's working!'

Gunshots and screeching cars in the background almost drowned out her grandson's words. 'What're you two boys doing at home?'

'Watching tv.'

'Where's your Pa? Is he home?'

'No! Granny, I've to pee!'

Ah Gek puts down the receiver. That loudmouth guzzler is out again when he should be home with his sons while Lily is at work. When he's not driving his truck into Malaysia, he's always lounging in the coffee shops ogling at the China girls and they fleece him blind. Poor Lily. She clings to him for the sake of the children.

She dials Molly's number next, and has to shout because the music in the background is too loud and the man at the other end seems deaf.

'Molly who? We have Molly Wong. Molly Ang. Molly Soh.'

'Molly Tan.'

'No such person!'

She puts down the phone. Is there any point phoning Nancy? Someone had told her that Nancy is working in Geylang Lorong A. She didn't know which house in Lorong A but she did walk down the lane one evening after work, hoping she would bump into Nancy. She didn't like what she saw when she walked down those backlanes. Women lolling on plastic chairs, standing in doorways, along the road and street corners. Middle-aged and mini-skirted, they crowded these shadowy lanes and covered walkways. Younger women with less need to hide their wrinkles paraded under the streetlamps. Men with hungry eyes prowled among them. She searched for her daughter's face in the crowds until, suddenly ashamed, she turned and left. What would she do if she met her daughter? Did she really want to see her Nan plying her trade?

You slut! She had screeched when she found out what Nancy was doing. Have you no shame?

What's so shameful? You want me to be like you? A cleaner of loos? Cleaning up other people's shit? It's an honest living. I'm not stealing!

You're prostituting.

Jesus did not condemn prostitutes, Ma. Lots of people are

prostitutes. Some people prostitute their brains to earn fat pay! I use only my body!

O blessed Mary ever Virgin, forgive my daughter!

Once she dreamt of Mary, a silent figure in blue, trailing after her son. In her dream, she'd stood with her head bowed before the Holy Mother who towered above her. She saw herself shrinking smaller and smaller until small as a bug she'd scuttled away from the Virgin Mother. She had failed as a wife and mother. Fought her husband. Fought her children. Fought them throughout their childhood to adulthood. Yet not one of them would bend to her will. Not even Kow Kia. She'd loved him the most. Did he live with a Malay man? She was blind when she should be mute like the Holy Mother. Maybe that's what children want from their mother. An inscrutable maternal silence.

10

She reaches her block and takes the lift up. At the tenth floor, some of her neighbours are still awake but their doors are shut. She can hear their television as she walks past. The stench in the corridor is awful. She wonders if Kow Kia is awake.

O God! She pulls up sharply outside her flat, knocking into her neighbour's bicycle. Her door is smeared with red paint and faeces.

'Kow Kia! Kow Kia! Are you all right in there?'

Hands trembling, she fumbles for her house key.

'Vandals! Swine! No wonder people shut their doors! Did you hear anything, Kow Kia? Are you asleep?'

She rushes into the bathroom.

Kow Kia sits up. His mother is hauling a pail of water to the front door. Moments later, he hears her sniffling in the kitchen. There's the sound of papers being crushed and stuffed down the rubbish chute. He wants to tell her that he had heard the men. They had knocked and banged on the door. Bold as daylight they were. They knew no one in this block would dare call the police. Every family in this block needs to borrow money some time or other. Smearing red paint and faeces on the door is mild. Loan sharks have done worst things. He struggles to stand up. He wants to go outside and help his mother clean the door. He stops when he hears Mak Som's voice in the corridor.

'What happened, Ah Gek?'

'This, *lah*! Look! Look! All this shit on my front door!'

'*Adoi*! This is very bad. But my Chinese friends, they tell me, faeces mean good luck. Faeces bring good luck! Don't worry, *lah*. I help you wash.'

Chattering in a mix of Hokkien and Malay, he hears Mak Som clucking away like a mother hen, comforting his mother, and he's grateful.

'The red paint. *Tak boleh chuchi!* Can't clean off easily. Never mind, *lah*! But this brown gob is very easy to wash off. *Sabun sikit-sikit, air sikit-sikit boleh!* Can wash off with soap and water. Brush hard. Then spray insecticide. After that, *mana ada* smell? No more bad smell.'

'Very sorry, Mak Som.'

'*Ack*! Sorry, for what? No need to be sorry, *lah*! We're neighbours. Everybody here borrow money. We're not rich people. What to do?'

Mak Som is the only one who comes out to help his mother. Other neighbours stay inside their flats. No one wants to get in the way of the loan sharks. Or a filthy diseased man. He decides not to go out to the corridor. Best not to let Mak Som see him.

'*Kam sia*, Mak Som.'

'Thank me for what? I didn't do anything. I only talk. You wash.'

'Can I offer you a drink?'

'No, thank you. *Alamak!*. It's one thirty already! You better go in. Better rest.'

He knows it's not the lateness of the hour that has stopped Mak Som from coming inside for a drink. No one has come into the flat ever since he returned from the hospital. Not his sisters. Not the neighbours. Not that the neighbours had said anything bad about him to his mother. But even if they had, she wouldn't tell him. The neighbours still greet his mother. He has heard them talking to her in the corridor. Yet the few times he struggled out to the common corridor, just for a change of air after lying for hours in bed, the neighbours' doors slammed shut. The children, who used to come into the flat for his mother's *suon kueh*, have stopped coming. He's not surprised. It's inevitable.

Ya-lah! What to do? Singaporeans are like this, *Sayang*! All want to avoid trouble. That's what Honeybear would have said if he were alive. He can hear the bugger laughing. They don't want to come into your flat, never mind, *lah*! Tell them. You keep your germs. I keep my germs! Share your sperm but not your germ! Good, eh? It rhymes some more!

Honeybear had a corny sense of humour. Sometimes in the witching hours between two and four in the morning when his body is shivering in a cold sweat, he has been comforted by his lover's voice, not so much by the words said but by the timbre of his voice like the bass of his old guitar. There it is again. His cackling laugh. And his face. His unforgettable face. The skin stretched tight like thin parchment over the face. No flesh under the skin. Dark dried scabs of old sores clustered around his lips and nostrils. Honeybear's eyes, once bright with mischief and laughter, once beautifully lined with kohl and mascara, were dull opaque disks. His beloved, his sweet babe, his darling, his whatever, he stuffs a fist into his mouth to stop himself from sobbing out loud.

It has been two years. After the first rush of anger, after the initial shock, after the news from Honeybear about the deadly virus had sunk in, after the accusations and counter-accusations, after the bouts of fear and drunken stupor, after their tears had dried and their eyes could cry no more, what was left between them? What else? What else? Death, when it came, was swift and sudden. The funeral was rushed. He didn't know that the law in Singapore then had ruled out embalming, had required that the dead be thrust into a black body bag and buried within twenty-four hours. There was no time for goodbye. No time for closure. He didn't even know that his Honeybear was gone until he was gone. His real name was Malek bin Abdul Samad, he was told. He didn't know that. He didn't know at the time.

So much then for living together. How many secrets did they keep locked inside their hearts? How little they knew about each other. How little. He didn't even know where his Honeybear was buried. Did the authorities or his family bury his body? Or was it burned? Was his body flung into the fire like a diseased log, the flames scorching the vermin in his flesh? The body he had once held against his own healthy body. But no, no, Muslims do not cremate the dead. Did Honeybear ask for him? Did his beloved want to see him one last time? One last time. But even if he had wanted to, Honeybear had no way of getting to him. Damn, damn, damn. He's imagining things again, imagining his beloved's last moments when he should have been by his side, holding his hand, easing his passing. He buries his face in his pillow. God, where were you when Honeybear was dying? Where? Bloody hell, where were you, Kow Kia? You shouldn't have left for Manila. He hit himself. He heaves his skeletal frame out of bed and shuffles to the kitchen.

His mother is at the sink, washing her hands and face. From where he's standing, she looks grey and thin. Her blouse is hanging loosely from her shoulders. She seems to have shrivelled in the last six months. Had it been six months since his return from hospital? He bites his lower lip. He's dripping sweat again exhausted by the effort to get up and walk. When she sees him standing in the doorway of the kitchen, she moves to one side thinking that he wants to go to the bathroom.

He shakes his head, unable to speak. His throat is sore. He points to the kettle on the table. She pours out a glass and gives it to him. His hand shakes when he takes the glass from her hand. It shakes again as he holds it to his mouth, his teeth chattering as he drinks, water dribbling out of the corner of his mouth and down his neck. He's aware that she is watching him, watching the water dribble from his mouth to his neck. Gingerly he puts the glass down and wipes his mouth with the back of his hand. Her watchfulness irritates him. He wishes she would relax. Let go of her worry. He won't die if she were to relax a little. But tonight, looking at her tired face, he softens. He wants to tell her that he knows why she had borrowed the money and why he said nothing. What can he possibly say? What's there to say? Where else could she get the money for his medicine if she didn't borrow? He had thought of ending his life many times to end her burden. But each time he had thought of her, and his courage failed him. Pray, she always urged him. But where's God? Heaven is void.

'Ma.'

She looks up, waiting, but the words are lodged like fishbones in his throat. He coughs. No other word comes out. He turns away.

Kow Kia! Kow Kia! He hears her calling from a great distance. Kow Kia! She's waving to him. He's in the playground, climbing the monkey bar. He must be four or five years old. Look at me, Ma! Look! Look! He's balancing on one foot on the top rung of the monkey bar. Maaaa! Headlong into the sandpit he falls, wailing like a banshee for his mother. She picks him up. Young, warm and smelling of sweet lavender talc she wraps her arms around him and he buries his face between her breasts, breathing in the sweet sour milky fragrance of her nipples. The hot ginger tea burns his throat. He coughs and spits out a gob of green phlegm.

'Thank God! Thank God! You're all right. Don't die on me, Kow Kia. You hear me? Let me die first. You must live. Can you stand up now? Try. I'll help you. Lean on my shoulder. Yes, yes, lean on me. Don't worry. Just lean on me. I'll get you back to bed. You fainted. Such a scare you gave me.'

11

The thin reedy voices of three women and one man fail to comfort Ah Gek, kneeling with head bowed at the back of the church. She has slipped in when the church doors opened at six. Never having attended early morning mass before, she is glad that the church is empty except for a sprinkling of old folks. At communion time, she joins the queue inching its way to the priest. She clasps her hands and opens her mouth. When the priest places the consecrated host on her tongue, the feeling of reverence that sweeps through her is so strong that she dares not chew on the wafer and waits for it to melt in her mouth.

'Lord, have mercy on me.' She prays for strength and courage. She has to do it. If she doesn't, she will never be able to help Kow Kia and clear the huge debt she owes Big Eye Dragon. 'So help me, God.'

'Arise, the mass has ended. Go and serve the Lord,' the priest intones.

12

Ah Gek crosses herself, relieved. She has cleared Custom & Immigration. Standing on the road divider in Johore Bahru town centre, she watches the never-ending stream of cars and joins the others as they dash across the road. Si Tua Pui has told her the job is easy.

Very simple, one! You take some *suon kueh* to JB and bring some *suon kueh* back from JB. What's so difficult?

She had asked him why she had to take a bag of *suon kueh* into Johore Bahru, and bring back another bag of *suon kueh*. It didn't make sense.

Must everything make sense to you, *meh*? Can you not be such a busybody? What for you ask so many questions? The big boss said to do it this way. You do it this way. When you're done, he'll cancel your debt and will give you more money some more. Good, right or not? You're getting a good deal, Ah Gek. So! Just do what you're told. Now this is what you do. Take a taxi into JB. When you come back, take the bus. Easy, right? Once you reach JB, go to the central market. Go to the Chinese section. Not the Malay section. Got it? At the Chinese section, look for the *suon kueh* stall. You can't miss it. There's only one stall selling *suon kueh*. Husband and wife. You go up to the husband. Give him your bag of *suon kueh* all packed in styrofoam boxes. Tell him, they're from me. He'll know. His wife will give you a bag of her own homemade *suon kueh*. Very delicious, hahaha! You bring those back to Singapore and give them to me. Simple, isn't it?

She pushes her way through the crowds in the packed open-air market. Pushing and shoving, elbowing and nudging, people yell at her to get out of the way. Wooden clogs nick her heels. Baskets knock against her. A flood of humanity weaves in and out of the narrow spaces between the makeshift stalls. The air reeks of beef and mutton. She hurries past huge shanks of beef and carcasses of goat and sheep. A few goat's heads hang from steel hooks, their goat eyes like opaque glass marbles. She has heard that the Malays in Johore love to suck goat's eyes cooked in a curry. She has nothing against eating eyes. She herself loves fish eyes especially the eyes of a grouper or red snapper steamed with garlic, red chilli and fermented black beans. But a goat's eye? No, thank you.

She elbows her way out of the crush, spies a pig's head hanging by its snout on an iron hook. Ah, the Chinese section of the market. She can breathe freely now, walking between the stalls hawking slabs of pork, chunks of ribs, and strings of pale intestines hanging from metal hooks. Her nostrils no longer feel assaulted. Kow Kia's father used to tell her that umbrellas have different handles; people have different tastes. That was what he used to say whenever she nagged him about not going to church with her. Ack! If I go to church, who will pray to my ancestors? These days religion no longer bothers her. She will pray to any god who can make her Kow Kia well again. Ah! There it is! The *suon kueh* stall.

'Si Tua Pui asked me to give you this'

She gives the man the plastic bag of styrofoam boxes filled with *suon kueh*. His wife hands her another plastic bag.

'These are our *suon kueh* for Si Tua Pui.'

'Thank you,' she says and leaves. They didn't even exchange greetings or names. Later, she would regret that she didn't look at their faces properly.

At the bus station she boards the bus for Singapore. Just follow other people, Si Tua Pui had instructed her. When the bus reaches the Malaysian Immigration checkpoint, she alights with the other passengers who rush forward towards the queues in front of the immigration booths. She joins one of the queues. When her passport was stamped, the bored-looking officer, a Malay woman wearing a headscarf, didn't even look up.

She hurries back to the bus. The Singapore Immigration building at the other end of the causeway is the next stop. She is tense. Her bladder is full. She had avoided using the washroom in the Malaysian Immigration building because of its wet floor and dirty toilets. She would rather wait till she has crossed the border back into Singapore; wait till she has crossed the line that separated order from mess. She hurries out as soon as the bus pulls into the bus bay. Several other buses are also spilling out passengers who rush toward the immigration booths with their bags and children in tow. She has no luggage. Just her handbag and the bag of *suon kueh*. She quickens her steps. Everyone will rush for the toilets soon. She wants to go through immigration quickly and reach the washroom before this tourist horde.

A young woman in front of her in the queue is having a hard time with her year old toddler. The child is screaming and kicking, refusing to sit in his pram. His poor mother has to take him out of his pram, carry him astride her hip with one arm and push the pram with the other. As the child continues to scream and kick, the mother and child are holding up the queue.

'Here. Let me help you.'

'No need, Auntie, I can manage,' the young woman says.

But her wailing child is flailing his arms, kicking his legs and twisting his body. It doesn't look like the young mother can carry him, and handle the pram as well.

'Here I push. I push the pram for you.'

Ah Gek places her hand on the pram but the child's kick lands on her knuckles. The sudden pain causes her to let go of her plastic bag. *Suon kueh* tumbles out of their styrofoam boxes into the pram.

'*Aiyah*! See, *lah*! See, *lah*! I told you no need! I don't need your help! I've enough trouble already, Auntie! You're giving me more trouble!!!!'

'It's all right. It's all right. I'll clean your pram!

Ah Gek tries to retrieve her boxes of *suon kueh*.

'I told you already! I don't need your help! Go! Go! Leave me alone!'

The woman pushes her away. People crowd round. An immigration guard strides towards them. The raised voices, the child's crying and screaming, and the young mother's angry shouting disorientates her. She is faint with fear when two immigration officers gather up her boxes of *suon kueh*, and lead her into their office.

13

Kow Kia sits up in bed. Holding the small mirror to his face he stares at the dark purple lesions where the skin is broken around his jaw. His cheekbones and nose stick out like craggy outcrops. The mirror shows an old man with sunken eyes and cheeks. The disease is slowly but relentlessly remoulding his features. His face has become the face of the disease, the face of his withered soul. He has no words to describe the turbulence in his heart. His head aches. He regrets he did not kill himself long ago. He should have. Now it's too late. Too late. His death will negate what his mother has done. He has to live. For her sake. A dry, hard sobbing shakes him. He pushes the mirror under his pillow and lies down to wait. This is his new routine now. Waiting. Every day, he waits for news of his mother, waits for the food that Mak Som brings on days when Lily can't come. His life these past months has revolved around waiting for what little news his sisters could give him, waiting to find out what his sisters and the authorities are planning for him. He has very little control over his life, except his breath, and thankfully his bowels. He can still choose to inhale and exhale, and make his way to the bathroom without soiling his pants. Sometimes lying for hours in the silent flat, unable to sleep at night, he misses his mother's snores, and is forced to listen to his own breathing. Count one, two, three, four, up to twelve before he releases his breath, and inhale again. He does this sometimes to remind himself that he still has some control over life, some will power to control the breath in his wasted body. In. Out. In. Stop. Out. Stop. He can slit his wrist. If he wants to.

He had stayed up, waiting for her, trying not to fret when she failed to return home that fateful night. She hadn't said a word about not coming back. It was not like her to go off and not tell him. She talked to him even when his back was turned to her. He heard footsteps in the corridor, but they were not his mother's. Her walk was a soft rubber-soled shuffle, not a hard stride. He was surprised that he remembered such things about her, surprised that the months of lying in bed had made his hearing acute to the sound and rhythm of his mother's footfalls, and the movements of neighbours down the corridor. He remembered he had glanced at the clock, heard the ticking of the minute hand. Then he must have fallen asleep until Lily's shouts roused him.

Kow Kia! Kow Kia! It's me! Wake up!

Ah, ah! Coming. He'd answered, but he couldn't make his voice any louder. The lymph nodes around his throat were swollen.

When he opened the front door, Lily had stepped back involuntarily. A reflex action that had stung him to the quick. She stood some distance away from him, her face pale when she said, 'The police have arrested Ma.'

14

'I've brought you pork bone soup, fried rice and chicken porridge. One container each. Should last you two days.'

Lily puts the large plastic bag on the doorstep. He knows she won't come into the flat even if invited. Not that it matters. He understands his sister's fear and he is grateful that she still finds the time to bring him food and news of their mother.

'Ma will be in court tomorrow. Her picture was in the papers again yesterday.'

Lily hands him a copy of yesterday's Straits Times.

'How...how is she?'

'She's lost a lot of weight. Gone very thin. Can't sleep, can't eat, she said. She thinks too much. I told her to take it one day at a time. Not to worry about you. I haven't been sleeping well myself too. Sometimes I ask myself, why, eh? Why did she have to go and do something stupid like this? Something so stupid! Don't look at me like that. I didn't say it to Ma. But each time I visit her; each time I see Changi Prison, I start fuming. Why? Why? Why did she do it?'

He bends down to pick up the bag of food. He can't bear to look at Lily's anguished face. Carefully, he folds the newspaper and puts it on the shoe rack next to the door. He will read it later.

'Don't blame Ma. Blame me.'

'Don't say that!' Lily's voice is sharp. 'Don't you say that! You didn't make her go to JB! She should've gone to the MP for help, to the hospital, or the family service centre. We told her so! All their lives! She and Pa! Always borrowing from loan sharks! For this! For that! Remember Pa? After he broke his leg?'

It's on the tip of his tongue to tell Lily that one of his sisters should have gone with Ma to get help. Instead, in a voice dulled by resignation, he mutters, 'Ma owed the Housing Board many months rent. They wanted to evict us.'

'All the more she should go to the MP. They won't evict her. Just think of the bad publicity! Housing Board throws old woman with sick son out of their flat! So heartless. You think the bosses in the Housing Board want such publicity, *meh*? She should've talked to me! But she kept things to herself! Kept it in her heart! Aaah! I just have to get this off my chest. I can't say it to Ma. I can't say it to Nan. I don't want to start a quarrel with her and Molly.'

'Lily, listen. Ma did it for me.'

'Now don't you start me off. Ma doesn't want you mixed up in this.'

He shakes his head. He's the only reason his mother went to the loan sharks, and Lily knows it. 'Has she got a lawyer?'

'The court has given her a lawyer. No need to pay. They've a special word for it. Pro something ... *pro bono*. For poor people. Ma's poor. And we're not earning much. I told the police I've a family to support. Look, I've got to go. Ah Lau is always so irritable when he drives me over. He's waiting downstairs. Can't park his lorry here. I've got to go. And you,' she looks at him from across the distance that separates the diseased from the healthy. 'I don't know what's going to happen to you after tomorrow. I can't bring you food every day. I've got to work. Got to visit Ma, got to run here, run there and take care of my boys, take care of so many things. I can't take leave too often. Now it's still okay. Ma's picture is in the papers. Everyone at work is very sympathetic. And the busybodies fawn all over me. But if I take too many days off, people will complain. I might get the sack. You understand or not?'

'I'll manage. Don't worry.'

'Ma asked about you. She's very worried. I see it in her eyes. She misses you. You take care, Kow Kia. Take care of yourself. Okay? If ... if anything, anything,' Lily's eyes are reddening, 'you phone me. Call me. You understand? Call me no matter how late, you call.'

Numbed and pained, he nods.

'Ma knows you can't manage by yourself. A nun, Sister... *aiyah*! I forgot her name. This sister from the Good Shepherd Convent visited Ma in prison. And Ma told her about you. This sister told Ma she will help you. Take you to a home where ... where they will take care of you. So, tomorrow or next week, if that sister or some other persons come...'

Lily looks as though she's going to cry.

'If the sister comes or if other people come, you open the door and let them in. Okay? Don't say no. Just...just go with them. Ma...she wants them to take care of you. Give her that comfort, okay?'

He nods again, unable to speak. Lily too is silent as they stand facing each other across the corridor.

'You better go, Sis.'

'Do you need anything else? I'll bring it on my next visit. And if you...if you're in the home, they'll let me know. I'll visit you there. Do you need anything?'

'A phone card.'

His voice is hoarse. He pulls out a small hand towel and coughs into it, careful not to befoul the air with his coughing.

'Get me a card for my phone. The line was cut. I...I didn't pay the bill. If I've a phone, you can call me. No...no need to visit.'

A deep racking cough rises from the cold hollow in his chest.

'Pass me your phone. I'll buy a card for it.'

He goes into his room and returns with his mobile phone. Lily does not take it immediately. She digs for some tissues in her handbag and wraps her hand in tissue paper before taking his phone. She puts it in a plastic bag and knots the bag tightly.

15

A thick hedge and green leafy trees mute the traffic on Marymount Road. The home is clean, airy and quiet. Two fans on the ceiling stir the torpid afternoon air. Grey-faced listless men wait for the hours to pass. The men show no sign of curiosity about one another, preferring to keep to themselves. And if they do talk, it's about the present, the here and now, never about the past, and never about their families. Most of the time, they lie on their beds, eyes closed, shutting out the world. And the two or three, who open their eyes, turn their gaze inward.

He remembers the same inward gaze on his old man's face in the weeks before he jumped. The same inward, self-absorbed gaze. He had come home from school that fateful afternoon to find his old man, sitting in the cane chair, his good leg stretched out on the floor. The other leg, amputated at the knee, was sticking out of the seat like a sawn-off tree stump. His father's eyes were red, glazed, and unseeing. The room was littered with broken beer bottles and glass shards. Without a word, he took a broom and started to sweep the shards into a dustpan. A move that his old man took as criticism. His crutch hit him hard on the head. The sudden force caused his nose to bleed but he didn't move away. He didn't cry out. He didn't retaliate. Looking back, he realised why he had stood still and let the old man hit him. He didn't have the heart to fight the cuckolded cripple. 'One-legged Tortoise.' That was what the neighbours had called his Pa, and why his father drank himself silly. *Lau Or Kui* was Hokkien slang for a cuckold. He was fourteen then, and convinced that his Ma, known in the neighbourhood as the 'Toilet Auntie', must have done things inside the toilet cubicles besides cleaning them. And yet, he could not hold it against her. She was a good mother and a long-suffering wife. The old man was impossible after he lost his leg and job at the construction site.

'John, your sister is here.' Sister Susan wheels him into the visitors' room.

The afternoon sun is blazing outside. Pinpricks of light glitter among the trees. Lily brings him the latest news. In between reading out the newspaper report to him, she gives her version of what the prosecution said on the last few days of the trial.

'The *suon kueh* sellers in JB vanished. The Malaysian police can't find them. No one saw them or knew them. So Ma is gone case. Listen to this. The law in Singapore is very clear. Drug trafficking is a capital offence. The mandatory punishment is death. The evil that drug trafficking inflicts on thousands of people demands that we punish drug traffickers severely. The problem has to be tackled at the source. And the newspaper also said. The accused had four hundred grams of heroin hidden among the pieces of *suon kueh* she was carrying in several styrofoam boxes packed inside a plastic bag. The main prosecution witness, the mother of the toddler, said that the accused had tried twice to put the bag into her child's pram. Ingrate! Ma was just trying to help her push the pram!'

Lily sounds loud and harsh in the quiet of the visitors' room.

From where he's seated, facing the doorway, he can see the dazzling red and purple of the ixoras and bougainvilleas blooming in the brilliant sunshine. Sunlight bounces off their dark glossy leaves, and the sun's glare makes him close his eyes. The anger in Lily's voice tears through his frame. His gastric pains return.

'And do you know what else is said by all those *kaypoh*s and busybodies in the coffee shops? They talk like they know the law in this country. Just because they went to court for a few days to listen and gawk. Ya, they gawked at Ma and Nancy and Molly and me. Like they're at a show, pointing their fingers at us! And the reporters! I wanted to slap them. They kept taking photos. I didn't care. They want to take my photo! Take, *lah*! But Nan and Molly hid their faces behind newspapers. I told them no need to hide. Why hide? Those uncles in the coffee shops know who you are already! And you know what one uncle said to me? He said a murderer kills one person, affects only one family. Drug traffickers kill hundreds of thousands. Destroy whole of society. *Oi*, uncle, I said. I didn't care. I asked him. What about the fat cats? What about those who sell tobacco and alcohol? Run casinos and make millions? Own prostitute houses? They also ruin hundreds of families and thousand of lives, what! Do you want to hang them too? He kept quiet. I was so furious. You see now what Ma is up against? She's got no chance. The law is the law.'

The anguish in Lily's voice, the unshed tears and dark rings around her eyes stab him. He feels useless. Utterly useless. He stares at the flowers in the brilliant sunshine. Lily is the only one who visits him. The other two blame him, and rightly so. His head feels heavy and feverish. He longs for his mother's hand, for the rough palm that stroked his forehead sometimes. He'd dreamed of her hand last night. It had brushed against his face, and he'd caught a whiff of the pine-scented detergent that seemed to cling to her skin.

'Kow Kia, you okay?' Lily is staring at him. 'Are you all right?'

'Just very tired.'

'I'll come again. Maybe next month.'

'I want to see Ma. Ask the lawyer to plead with them. I've...I've got to see her. I want to see Ma one last time. Before... before...'

He bangs his head against the back of his wheechair.

'Kow Kia! Stop it! The government is the one killing her! Not you! *Not you*! Get that into your thick head! Our Ma is going to die! But she wants you to live! Understand or not?'

16

The grounds of Marymount Convent and its chapel is a sea of flickering candlelights. The Good Shepherd sisters and parishioners are holding a vigil for his mother. The mood of the gathering that numbers more than five hundred is quiet and sombre as night falls and Sister Susan leads them in prayer.

Sitting in his wheelchair, his hands trembling uncontrollably, his heart is a tumult of feelings. He has received news that the family will be allowed to see their mother one last time. Lily kneeling on the grass beside him is sobbing quietly in her husband's arms. Nan and Molly are kneeling beside the nuns.

Sister Susan places a rosary into his trembling hands. 'John, meet Peter and Marc, the organisers of this prayer vigil. They've something to tell you.'

Two men, a Chinese and an *ang moh* shake his hand. His voice quavering, he thanks the two of them.

'It's the least we can do,' Peter Chia smiles. 'Your mother is a good woman. She used to work in my office and I bought *suon kueh* from her. I wish I'd known about you earlier, John. You see I am like you … HIV positive. Marc here is my partner. We have spoken with your sisters and doctor. We would like to take care of your medication. With the right medication you can live a normal life. We travel to Bangkok periodically to buy the pills. Much cheaper there.'

He doesn't know what to say. His sisters are standing around him. Lily's hand reaches out and her fingers intertwine with his. The touch of his sister's hand sends a sharp joy through his heart. He holds on to Lily's hand as they listen to Peter Chia speak to the sea of flickering tea lights and candle-lit faces.

'My grandmother and my mother, Mrs Mary Chia, remember Madam Ah Gek very well. She was our family's maid when my brother Paul and I were born. She learnt to say the rosary and followed my grandma to church every Sunday. My mother said that Madam Ah Gek was very hardworking. Very honest. She was only fourteen when she came to work for my grandma. Her family was very poor and Madam Ah Gek and her brothers and sisters often had no food to eat. My mother wept when she heard about Madam Ah Gek's death sentence. Thank you all for coming to this vigil and rosary service to pray for her and her family. My grandma is eighty-nine and she's bedridden. She can't be here but she is praying with us at home. Let us pray for mercy and compassion to prevail. A petition is going round over the Internet. We're pleading for Madam Ah Gek's life to be spared. Let's pray that justice in our society will be tempered with mercy.'

A soft murmuring rises from the sea of flickering lights as a lone flute plays, and Marc sings,

'God of mercy and compassion,
Look with pity upon me....'

* * *

ADDENDUM

To His Excellency
The President of Singapore

Dear Sir,

I wrote the above story with the kind help of a writer who visited the Good Shepherd Convent. It has been 10 years since my mother was sentenced to Death's Row. My sisters and I beg you to review our mother's case.

Yours very respectfully,
John Tan (Kow Kia)

GLORIA

She wraps her brown brawny arms around him, holding him between her knees, hugging him close against her breasts. He leans back, sinking into the fold of her arms, his eyes fixed on the tv screen in the living room. But her eyes are not on the tv. They're gazing through the black iron grille of the balcony, gazing at the distant lights of the ships anchored out at sea, gazing towards where the brightly lit buildings shine like altars to their Chinese gods, and beyond that to the dark sky, the same dark sky that arcs over Manila City, the same dark sky with the same bright moon shining on the garbage of the Pasig River. Oblivious of the glances of her ma'am, seated in the armchair in the living room, her hand is stroking the child's back. The family is watching tv after dinner, and she has slipped out of the kitchen to join them. But she does not sit with them. Although her ma'am has not said anything, she knows that it will be regarded as presumptuous if she sits with them in the living room. So she sits on the cane chair in the balcony, and the boy, Timmy, the youngest of the two boys and a girl under her charge, has come out to sit with her. She wraps her arms around his warm tubby belly, inhaling the lavender fragrance of the talcum powder she has rubbed on him after his bath. When she has saved enough, she will buy a small tin of the same Johnson & Johnson talc powder to take home to Migoy and Amy, her two youngest. She kisses the boy's head.

"Timmy! Come in here!"

With a start, her arms drop to her side. The boy runs to his mother.

"What're you doing in the balcony, darling? Full of mosquitoes out there. Sit here with Mummy. Gloria!"

"Yes, Ma'am."

"Have you finished washing the dishes?"

"Yes, Ma'am."

"What about the kitchen towels? Did you wash them and hang them up to dry?"

"Yes, Ma'am."

"Bring out the chocolate cake in the fridge. And don't forget the plates and forks this time."

"Yes, Ma'am."

She goes into the kitchen and returns with the cake, the plates and forks on a tray. She sets it on the coffee table.

"How am I going to cut the cake without a knife? And you forgot napkins."

"Yes, Ma'am."

She goes into the kitchen again, returns with the cake knife and some napkins.

"No, you don't cut it. I'll cut it. You still have laundry to do tonight, don't you?"

"Yes, Ma'am."

"Well, what're you waiting for then? I don't need you here."

She retreats into the kitchen, and sits on the floor of the narrow alcove where the laundry is hung and where she sleeps at night. She sits beside her suitcase, the green and brown canvas suitcase that Tita Flora had lent her when the village knew that she was coming to Singapore to work. She sits beside it, her brown brawny arms wrapped around her shoulders, rocking her upper body back and forth, back and forth, as though she was rocking her baby. Her little Migoy.

* * *

"Good morning, ah, Mrs Ling."

"Good morning, Alice. This is my new maid."

"Oh, your new maid, ah?" The receptionist at the clinic looks at her. "What happened to the old one?"

"I had to change her," her ma'am replies.

"To change maids, you got to pay extra or not?"

"This maid agency is very good. The employer is allowed to make two changes. No need to pay. You pay a transfer fee only at the third change."

Her ma'am hands over a sheath of official papers across the counter.

"Glori-ah An-ton-nia Bern-na-dette San-tos," the receptionist reads out her name in the singsong lilt of the Chinese in this clean and green city where even the trees look neat and tidy, very different from the unruly trees back home. But the sunlight is the same, the same. The sun that shines in this rich city is the same sun that shines on her *barangay*.

'Glor-ri-a!' the receptionist turns to her.

"Yes, ma'am."

Her voice squeaks like one of those tiny white mice in the pet shop. The clinic is full of watchful eyes. The eyes of these strangers are scrutinising her, eyes that say she's the stranger, not them. She keeps her head down, suddenly ashamed of her shabby blouse and faded black pants. The receptionist continues to address her in a loud voice as if that will help her to understand better.

"You, ah! You take this cup and go to the toilet. You pass urine into the cup, okay? Make sure enough urine is inside the cup, not outside; otherwise cannot do the pregnancy test. You got pee or not? If cannot pee now, you drink some water."

The woman turns to her ma'am.

"Must always tell them to drink water. Some of them, no pee, also go inside the toilet and stay there a long time. And their employer is out here waiting and waiting, and the maid is still inside the toilet. Many people complain to me. Other patients also want to use the toilet. So now I tell all the maids. Go drink some water first."

Her ma'am smiles and shakes her head. "I know. You've got to spell out every single step before they do it right."

"Ya, lor! Glor-ri-a, you go pee now."

Head down, she walks towards the closed door.

"Oi! Not that door! The other door! That other one!" the receptionist shouts across the crowded waiting room.

A young man rises from his seat and points her to another door. He gives her an embarrassed smile. She nods, goes in and locks the door. The words, 'thank you', are stuck like a fishbone in her throat. She leans over the sink, turns on the tap and cups her two hands to drink some water. It's only when she unzips her pants and squats over the plastic cup that she lets her tears fall.

A mother since age sixteen, she's thirty-six but looks fifty-six. This is the medical examination to decide her fate. Make sure that she's not pregnant before they will confirm her employment.

What they don't know is that she doesn't want to get pregnant any more. She'd pushed Alex away. After the first four, she didn't want it any more. Didn't want more babies. But how could she keep saying no to her Alex? He wanted her even when they already had ten mouths to feed. And the wife should submit to the husband and not push him into sin, Father Paolo Biviendo had preached. These priests. They know only God's will. She cleans herself, zips up her pants, and washes her hands at the sink. She's through with these priests. It's up to Suzie and her now. Suzie will take care of the others. They will have to depend on their eldest sister. It'll be five long years before Alex is out of prison. In the meantime, she'll work and make money. Make lots of money. Pay back the agent; pay back the lawyer; pay back Tita Flora; pay back Ma Lulu and the others. She opens the washroom door, carefully holding with both hands the white plastic cup half filled with yellow urine.

* * *

"Speak up, Gloria. I can't hear you.

"Yes, ma'am," she repeats a little louder.

"Now the maid agency says you can cook. Is that right?"

"Yes, ma'am."

"Good. I want you to cook simple nutritious meals for the children. One meat, one vegetable, a soup and rice. I myself don't know how to cook so you take charge of the menu. If you don't know anything, ask. See this stack of cookbooks? You can look at them. I bought them for the last maid. You can read, can't you?"

A slight movement of her head. Neither a 'yes' or a 'no'. She's unsure of the consequences if she should admit that she'd only been to school up to grade four.

"I'm very particular about cleanliness. When I come back from the office, I don't want to see oily stains all over the stove or walk on an oily floor. This kitchen must be clean and spotless. You understand?"

"Yes, ma'am."

"If you run out of detergents, cleansers or anything, tell me. Don't keep quiet like the other maids Don't tell me at the last minute or when I ask or when I find out we've run out of food and things. I'm busy working every day. I go to the supermarket once a week so you must let me know in advance. Here. This notebook and pen are for you. Write down all the things I've got to buy for the week. You understand?"

"Yes ma'am."

"See this box? I've put fifty dollars inside. It's for little emergencies. You run out of condiments or the children need to buy something in school, then you take the money from this box. Always ask the shopkeepers downstairs for a receipt. Put the receipts inside. I'll check the box once a week and replenish it. You understand?"

"Yes, ma'am."

Her head is reeling. Fifty Singapore dollars. How much is that in peso? That is …that is…that is two thousand pesos. She's amazed but she's careful not to smile. Two thousand pesos for her to buy things each week. She has never had so much money before.

"Let me see. What else do I have to tell you? Oh yes. Do you know how to use the washing machine? I've pinned up the instructions here. Just read and follow the instructions. If you don't know how operate it, ask John. He's the oldest. John! John!"

"What?" The boy is surly at being called into the kitchen.

"Show Gloria how to operate the washing machine, and the other electrical things if she doesn't know."

"Very simple to use, what! Just read the instructions."

"I will teach Gloria, Mummy!"

"Timmy! You teach Gloria?" Sarah runs into the kitchen, wagging her finger at the little one. "Hahaha! He'll teach her all the wrong things, Mummy!"

"But I know! I know!"

"Quiet. You children, out. Go on. Out of the kitchen. I want to talk to Gloria."

"Yes, ma'am."

"The agent has explained things to you. But I will go through it again. You get three hundred dollars a month. The agency will deduct two hundred and seventy every month for ten months until you finish paying back what you owe them. So I will give the agency two hundred and seventy dollars, and give you the remainder, thirty dollars, each month. Do you understand? You get thirty dollars every month. The rest goes to your agent. So you must spend within your means. I'm sick and tired of maids borrowing money from me. No borrowing. My last two maids always borrowed. Father ill. Brother sick in hospital. Mother dying. Sister getting married. Brother going to college. Or uncle lost his harvest in floods and typhoons. All sorts of stories I've heard. I lost six hundred dollars just listening to the stories of the last two maids. Sir said, no borrowing. No advance payment. Do you understand?"

"Yes, ma'am."

"Are you clear about the meals and kitchen? And the schedules of the children?"

"Yes, ma'am."

"Don't just say yes ma'am, yes ma'am when you don't understand. Do you understand?"

"Yes, ma'am."

* * *

"Eeee! The pork tastes funny!"

The girl spits out the meat on to her plate. Timmy follows suit.

"You don't like pork, Sarah?"

"This pork tastes funny. What is it?"

"Pork adobo."

"Yuks! I don't like it. I want fish fingers."

"Me too! Me too!" Timmy claps his hands. The doorbell rings. She runs out to open the door for the eldest boy back from school.

"What's for lunch, Gloria?"

"Yukky pork!" the girl giggles. "We're having fish fingers instead."

"Yeah, I want fish fingers too, Gloria."

Without a word, she goes to the freezer. "How many you want?" she asks.

"Ten," the eldest boy says.

"Me too," the girl follows.

"Me too, me too," Timmy clamours.

But there are only fifteen fish fingers in the box. She heats some oil in the frying pan, and empties the whole box into it. When the fish fingers are a golden brown, she gives the eldest boy seven pieces, and the two younger ones four fish fingers each.

"It's not fair! You gave John more!"

"Cos I'm the eldest!"

"You're not!" the girl shouts.

"I am!"

"You're not!"

"I'm the oldest!"

"I was the oldest before you came to live with us!"

"You think I want to live here with you? You lizard face!"

"I'll tell my Mummy you called me lizard face!"

"Tell-*lah*! Tell-*lah*! Cry baby! This is my Dad's apartment!"

"It's also my Mummy's apartment!"

"Children! Children!" She tries to calm them.

"Mummy!" The girl is already calling her mother on the phone.

She is summoned to the phone.

"Yes, ma'm. No, ma'm. Yes, ma'am." The children watch as her eyes brim over. "I understand, ma'am." She puts down the phone and goes to the moneybox.

She takes out the fifty-dollar note. She likes the crisp, clean feel of the white and blue note. It's not limp, dirty and crumpled like the red *Limampung Piso*, the fifty peso note that she's used to handling. Fifty dollars. She can buy so many sacks of rice, so many kilos of fish, especially the bangus and tilapia that her children dream of eating, and so many yards of cloth to sew shirts for Bet and Vern, may be a blouse and skirt for Mol and Suzie, and buy shoes for Ninoy and Beng. Ahhh, a great many things she will buy with two thousand pesos!

"Gloria! Where're you going?" the girl asks.

"The shop downstairs. Your mummy says to buy more fish fingers."

"I want to go too," Timmy insists.

With the two children leading the way, she has no trouble taking the elevator from the 21st floor to the ground floor. She doesn't tell them that the speed makes her dizzy. But she will tell her children when she sends a letter home. Timmy and Sarah lead her across the empty car park, which in the evening will be filled with shiny clean cars parked in neat straight rows. Everything is clean, neat and orderly in her ma'am's condo. No one says sub-division here. Not like in Manila. She will write and tell her children. They walk past the rows of palm trees, the swimming pool and the tennis courts. What Sarah calls 'our neighbourhood shop' is in fact a small air-conditioned supermarket like the ones back home where the rich people in Quezon City shop, and where she has gone with Tita Flora to deliver the laundry. She's working in a rich neighbourhood for a rich family. Her ma'am scolded her just now because she didn't spend the fifty dollars.

What's the matter with you, Gloria? You know there's only one box of fish fingers. You know it's not enough. Why didn't you go downstairs to buy another box? What's the money in the box for? I don't want the children to quarrel just because there's not enough food. For goodness sake! Use your brain. Go to the shop and buy another box of fish fingers! What's so difficult about that? I'm in the middle of a meeting. I don't want the children to call me about these little things. Do you understand?

She walks down rows of bottled soft drinks, cans of beer, bottles of soy sauces, fish sauces, tomato ketchup, spices, condiments, and boxes of cereals she'd never seen or eaten before; and milk powder packed in tins, pasteurised milk in packets and bottles, and jars of jams, tins of meat, chicken and fish crowded the shelves. The tins of Spam, and sardines in tomato sauce make her mouth water even though she's still full from her lunch of rice and pork adobo. Ahhh, she feels blessed. She's walking through this wonderland, armed with the knowledge that she has money power. She has fifty dollars. But the shopkeeper doesn't understand her when she speaks. He behaves as though she's not speaking English.

"What, ah? You new, ah?"

"Uncle, she's our new maid. Her name is Gloria," Sarah, the little busybody, explains.

The shopkeeper looks at her. "Oh, Glori-ah. What you want to buy, ha?"

She opens one of the glass doors of the refrigerators and takes out a big box of Bird's Eye Fish Fingers. Then for good measure, to show that she's in charge, she walks over to the other side of the shop, and picks out two pink kitchen towels, a mop and a red plastic pail. When the children ask for ice cream, she lets them choose what they want. Two years, may be three years, from now if her ma'am extends her contract, she will let Migoy and Amy choose what they want in the supermarket in Fairview. One day. Some day. She hands over the fifty dollars to the Chinaman shopkeeper.

That night, her ma'am tells her not to cook pork adobo any more.

"The children don't like it. You have it for lunch tomorrow."

"Yes, ma'am."

Her brood would've rushed for the adobo. When there was enough pesos, she would buy the leftover fatty pork from Jong Boy's meat stall on the corner of the narrow lane between the tricycle and motor repair shops and Nana Ahchut's *sari-sari* store. Nana Ahchut had refused to let her buy on credit, not even the stale bread loaves and egg-sized *pan-de-sal* for the children's breakfast. *If I do that, Gloria, I will have to close down. Touch wood! I've many mouths to feed like you!* Nana Ahchut shouted through the iron grille, her fat face framed in the small window through which all the store's transactions were made. No one was allowed to enter the tiny store. *Been robbed too many times.* Nana Ahchut glared at her as if what Alex did was all her fault. The kids learnt to go without breakfast. They learnt to make a bit of rice and salted fish last until dinnertime when she returned from the laundry where she waited with other women to do the washing. If she were lucky, she had more kilos of clothes to wash, and earned more pesos. But that was not enough. Never enough to feed ten mouths. Her children were always hungry and scrawny like the chickens in Tita Flora's backyard scratching the dirt for scraps.

She scrapes into the bin the chunks of half eaten pork, rice and vegetables that the three children and their parents have left on their plates.

"We don't eat leftovers. Throw them away unless you want to eat them for lunch tomorrow," the ma'am said.

Why should she eat leftovers in this island of plenty? For once in her life, she will not eat leftovers. She'll even have an egg for breakfast.

* * *

Her new radio alarm rings. She gets out of bed and starts to dress. At six-thirty, just as the sky brightens, the ma'am comes out of her bedroom. They leave the apartment together, and take the elevator down, she carrying the basket and the ma'am carrying her purse and car keys. It's Saturday, the day when the children have tuition classes instead of school. It's also the day she goes to the fresh food market with the ma'am. She looks forward to this weekly trip although the ma'am dislikes the wet market, and would rather shop in Cold Storage, but Sir does not like the meat from the supermarket.

She sits in the front passenger seat with the basket on her lap. The ma'am starts the car; they rarely talk in the car. When they reach the market, the ma'am parks the car and strides ahead in her tee shirt, denim shorts and high-heeled slippers. She follows with her piece of paper and the blue plastic basket. Their routine has not changed this past one year. But today, she intends to vary things a little.

"Two chickens." She points to two large freshly slaughtered chickens. By now, the chicken man is used to her. Then she points to a bag of chicken bones and adds it to her usual order. "To make soup, ma'am," she says. "Timmy likes chicken soup."

"Ok. Is this enough?"

"Enough, ma'am." She keeps the pleasure out of her voice.

They move on to the Malay butcher's stall to buy beef, and then walk to the other side of the market to buy pork from the Chinese butcher. By now, she's used to this funny way of selling meat in the markets in Singapore. Only the Chinese sell pork, and only the Malays sell beef. Back home at Jong Boy's stall, things are easier. No one makes a fuss if a leg of mutton or beef is hanging next to the head of a pig. When she mentioned this to the other maids at the church she goes to on Sundays, they laughed. Last year, when she was still a new arrival, they had told her that all Chinese in Singapore are Buddhist, and all Indians are Hindu, and they don't eat beef.

Of course, we eat beef, Gloria. Cook beefsteak for us if you know how to do it. As long as the children eat what you cook, and Sir does not complain, that's fine with me. I just don't want to come home and hear a host of complaints from the children. You understand?

Her ma'am does not care how much food she buys and cooks these days.

"Pork one and a half kilo," she points to the rump, which has a bit more fat. "And lean pork one kilo. The bones four dollars."

At the fish stall, she adds two kilos of fish and half a kilo of shrimps, and tells herself to stop; don't over do it. The ma'am might ask questions even though the ma'am's mind is always busy at the bank, and she works late like Sir. Both earn a big fat salary. They won't mind paying extra. They won't even miss it. She knows because the ma'am and Sir talk at the dinner table. Last Christmas, the ma'am's bank gave her six extra months' salary as a bonus. The family bought a new car, and went to America for a holiday. During the two weeks they were away, she worked for the ma'am's mother, and the old lady gave her fifty dollars. When the ma'am returned, she also gave her fifty dollars on Christmas Day. It was the first time that she'd received so much money. The money is in the bank now. She can't touch it. The ma'am had made her deposit her money in the neighbourhood Post Office bank.

Don't be stupid, Gloria. You maids always sent your money home. You shouldn't. How do you know that your family is not wasting your hard earned money? You must save for yourself. Put the money in the bank here. Earn interest. I'll use my name to open a joint account with you. Don't worry. I won't run off with your money. And you keep the book. At the end of your contract, you can withdraw all the money and go home with a lump sum. Do you understand?

"Gloria! What're you thinking? Are we through?"

"Sorry, ma'am. I forgot to buy sweet *tauhu*."

"You're still saying *tauhu*. People here will think you want bean curd for frying. It's *tau-huay* for sweet bean curd."

"Sorry, ma'am. Timmy wants."

"Here's ten dollars. Go quickly. The market is getting crowded. I'm tired."

The ma'am will let her buy anything if it's for the children. Her ma'am walks ahead carrying her purse and car keys. She follows with the blue basket loaded with food and two large pink plastic bags filled with enough meat and veg to feed eight adults for a week. And the ma'am hasn't questioned her. Is this a sign? Is God being fair at last? Maybe God knows her troubles and gives her this chance. She can't be choosy. If she's given the chance, wouldn't she be a fool not to take it? Suzie is gone.

I know this will break your heart, Gloria. Suzie has left home. She didn't tell anyone. Not me. Not her brothers. Not her sisters. Not a soul. Oh, Gloria, she left them in the dark. Such a shock to me when Migoy came running to say their sister is gone. Tita

Flora wrote.

She remembers holding that letter in her hand as the tears gathered and the news sank in. Bent over the kitchen sink, she had clutched her breasts. Her heart was broken again. How long could a heart remain a heart? Her heart had been hacked too many times. First, by Alex, then Ninoy and her drunken *Tatay*, the father she wished she'd never had. All day she was poorly. The ma'am, thinking she had caught the flu, had taken her to the clinic where the nurse had made her take a blood and urine test. *Just to be sure*, the ma'am said to the nurse in Chinese. *Just to be sure*, the nurse's silent nod agreed. Did they think she was stupid and diseased? That she would infect them with her broken heart? That she was too stupid to understand their *Chink-chong* code? Did the ma'am think that she'd caught something and would pass it to the children? Just to be sure. Always, it's just to be sure. The ma'am who has everything wants to be sure of everything. She who has nothing is never sure of anything. She cannot even be sure of the child who dropped out of her womb. Suzie's gone. Her flesh and blood has left her.

No letter. No phone call. Not even a note. *Did Gabriel Jose leave the village too? Did she elope with him? Did you check with Gab's family? Did you ask them?* She had cried and screamed into the public phone at the post office till her phone card ran out of money. How did this happen? Who could tell her? Would Suzie have run away if she were there? If her Papa were there? Alex. Alex. He was a fool to think he could leave the warehouse without the guards knowing. A fool to get himself arrested. A fool that no lawyer would defend because there was no money! Fool! Fool! Fool! Susie. Her child! Her baby. The first in the family to graduate from high school. Her pride.

She had to ask herself: What do you do when your only hope runs off because she's afraid of the burden you placed on her thin shoulders? She runs away because she doesn't want to end up like you and her aunts fucking, eating and shitting in the hovels under the bridges of Pasig and Quezon City. Cardboard palaces that the typhoons blow away and the floods wash away. Can you blame Suzie for taking off? Can you blame your daughter if she doesn't want to be like you? What do you do? Where can you find her? O God! Where can I find her? Is this why you have given me this opportunity? This skill? These men?

Carefully, she wraps the extra pieces of fried fish and pork sausages in sheets of tin foil and pushes them to the back of the freezer behind the Tupperware boxes of frozen pork, prawns and fish. No one will bother to look into the freezer. On Sunday, her day off, she will take the bus to Lucky Plaza in Orchard Road and pass the package to Ramos and Roddy, and they will pay her.

* * *

Sarah runs into the kitchen waving an envelope.

"Glori-ah! Letter for you! From Japan. Can I have the stamps?"

"Later, later. Go and play."

The girl runs out. Hands trembling, she tears open the envelope. She sits on the floor in the alcove of the kitchen beside Tita Flora's suitcase, and stares at the two photographs. She brings the letter to her nose and inhales its sweet fragrance. The letter is written on pink perfumed paper with a border of tiny flowers in pale blue. *Dearest Mama*. Her eyes start to brim. Nine months and eleven days after she's run away, Suzie writes, *Dearest Mama, how are you? I am well. I am working in a hotel in Tokyo... Dearest Mama. Dearest Mama.*

"Gloria! Sarah says you've a letter from Japan. Do you have anyone working there?" the ma'am asks her after dinner.

"Yes, ma'am. My eldest daughter."

"Oh. Is she working as a maid too?"

"No, ma'am. She's a secretary in a big hotel in Tokyo."

She takes out the photographs as proud proof of her daughter's new status.

"My daughter graduated from high school."

"Oh. Very pretty girl. Did you say she's a secretary in a hotel?"

"Yes, ma'am."

"And she's dressed like this?"

Something in the ma'am's question has poisoned her eyes. Her sight is maimed. She stares at the photos. She can no longer see her daughter. Instead she sees a young teenage girl in a bright red negligee reclining on the large bed. A bright red sunny smile plastered on her face. The other photo shows her in a black mini skirt and high-heeled black leather boots outside a grand-looking building with bright lights and Japanese men in the background.

"It's her bedroom, ma'am," she insists, barely able to control the tremor in her voice as she thrusts the photos back into the envelope. No. She will not tear out the stamps for Sarah.

* * *

One year, eleven months and twenty-nine days later.

"Mummy, where's Gloria?" Sarah asks licking her fingers clean.

Linda has ordered in home delivery of two large pizzas, three orders of garlic bread and salad for the children.

"Gloria has gone shopping, dumbo," John reaches for the largest slice of pizza. "She's flying home tomorrow."

"I will miss Gloria, Mummy."

"Don't be daft, Timmy. Miss her? For what? We'll get a new maid soon." Pause. Then, "Right, Mum?" John turns to her.

"Yes." Linda gives him a bright smile. It's so seldom that he calls her 'Mum' that she's willing to overlook his comment about not missing the maid. But it's not right. She'll have to correct him later.

"It's okay, Timmy. You can miss Gloria a little."

"I'll miss her a lot, Mummy."

"Then you're stupid!"

"Mummy!"

"It's okay, Timmy. *Kor-kor* John is just teasing you."

"But it's stupid to miss the maid. They always leave. I don't miss any of them!"

"John, that's enough," George says.

The boy stuffs his mouth with garlic bread and ignores his father and the rest of the family.

"It's okay, John, if you don't want to miss anyone. Here. Have another slice of pizza."

She pushes the pizza box towards him. The boy makes no move. She rises and hands him a slice of pizza on a plate.

"Thanks," a pause, then, "Mum."

Sarah giggles. George smiles. Ack! She's worrying too much as usual. John's just a bitter boy ever since his mother left him. And there are all sorts of stories about wicked stepmothers. George said that she shouldn't force the pace; let things happen naturally. But she likes to nudge things forward a little. She glances at the clock.

"Da, it's nine o'clock. Gloria's not back yet."

"Don't worry. It's her last night in Singapore. May be she wants to paint the town red. Didn't you go with her to close the joint account, and she withdrew all her money?"

"Ya. That woman has saved quite a bit. Nine hundred and ninety something. Times that by thirty pesos. How much is that?"

"Hey, you're the one who works in the bank," George laughs and turns on the tv to watch the news.

"Thirty-one thousand six hundred and forty-five peso," John announces.

"Not much for two years' work," George turns around.

"Not much here but a lot in the Philippines. Luckily I asked her to open the account. She sent quite a bit of money home. So many children. Ten. She's packed two large suitcases. She muttered something about opening a stall. What they call *sari-sari*."

"Did you check her bags?"

"What? You think she might've squirreled away some of our things to take home to sell? I gave her all the children's old clothes and some of yours and mine too. But I'll check her bags tomorrow before we leave for the airport. If I check tonight, she can still re-pack while we're asleep. If a maid wants to steal, she'll find ways to do it. What can you do? She lives with us, and we're not home all the time. Hey. You three! Go to bed! This is adult talk. Go to bed! Brush your teeth! If she's not back by eleven, I'm going to lock the door and go to bed."

"What time did she leave the house?"

"After lunch. I gave her the day off. She said she wanted to buy gifts for her family."

"If she's not back by midnight, we'll call the police and report her missing."

"You think she doesn't want to go back to the Philippines?"

"How do I know what she wants? I just don't want to lose our deposit at the Manpower Ministry if she goes missing."

"I hope she doesn't get into an accident or something. The next maid we get must be younger and unmarried."

"Aha! Not scared she might seduce the Sir?"

"George, be serious. You don't joke about such things, okay?"

"Hey, read the papers. The media is always biased against us. They always highlight the man doing the seducing. What about the woman, eh? A young maid."

"Okay, enough. You go and quarrel with the media about it. I'll get a fat and ugly one for us. But young and single. Not another mother.'

"You're the one who insisted on an older woman and a mother."

"I know; I know. My mistake. Have you seen Gloria with Timmy before I put a stop to her hugging and kissing? She likes to cuddle my darling."

"Our son likes her."

"It's not healthy. All this hugging and pawing! That's why I stopped her from bathing Timmy."

"Ahhh! A case of maternal jealousy."

"Shut up, George. I don't like maids to hug and kiss my kids.

I can do that myself. I told her before. Chinese people. We don't like strangers to kiss and hug our children. She said Filipinos do it all the time. I told her I don't care what she or other Filipinos do back home. But in my home, I set the rules. I don't want the maid to hug my kids."

"Aye, women and mothers!"

"Sexist!" She throws a cushion at him. George ducks. He clicks the remote and switches on the tv. She switches it off.

"I want to talk. Did you hear John call me, Mum, just now?"

A tired "Yes, I told you he'd come round if you give him time."

"Ya, claim credit for it. You think it's so easy to be your son's stepmum? I noticed a change when I stopped Gloria from hugging the two younger ones. I mean just see it from John's angle. He's the oldest. Already he sees himself as the outsider. The other two are my own, and what does the maid do? She's always hugging Timmy, and Sarah when Sarah allows it. I know she misses her own kids. I've heard her telling Timmy about her ten children."

"Okay, what? What's your point?"

"The point is that John felt better after I stopped Gloria from hugging Timmy and Sarah. He's eleven. Too old for Gloria to hug him. But he's still a child and feels deprived. Seeing the maid hug the other two and not him makes him feel even worse about being my stepson. Got it? So, no hugging except by me. I'm the mum who hugs all three of them. I hug John whether he wants it or not. Just to show that I treat him as my own. And you think I'm acting like a jealous ..."

"Come here."

Her husband wraps his arms around her and plants a wet kiss

on her lips. The phone rings. George picks up the receiver.

"Yes. Yes. That's right. Please wait a sec. I'll check with my wife. Is her name Gloria Antonia Bernadette Santos?"

"Yes. What's wrong?"

"Shhh! Yes, she's our maid. Okay. Okay. We'll be there in half an hour."

* * *

It's almost two in the morning by the time they are home again. They were silent throughout the ride home from the Tanglin Police Station. Linda clasps and unclasps her hands. George had told her expressly not to say anything or ask any question until they got home. He didn't want a scene. He handled everything at the station. But the moment he shuts their front door, he sits down beside her, and they confront the bovine face of their maid.

"Sit down, Gloria. Take the chair opposite us. Now take out your handbag. Show us how much you have in there," she begins.

The woman empties the contents of her purse on to the dining table.

"Count your money."

They wait till she has finished.

"How much do you have? Come on. Tell us. How much do you have inside your purse? You've just counted the money. How much?"

The brown sullen face wears a sheen of sweat and oil; the dark eyes are averted; they would not meet her eyes.

"I'm not budging until you tell us, Gloria."

The woman looks at her, stupefied.

"I mean it, Gloria."

"Three hundred and twenty-eight dollars and seventy-five cents, ma'am."

"You have three hundred and twenty-eight dollars in your purse, Gloria. More than three hundred Singapore dollars! Why the hell did you have to steal? Why did you do such a stupid thing on the eve of your departure? Tomorrow you will be charged. Do you know that? Tomorrow, you will go to jail and miss your flight! Sir will forfeit his deposit with the Ministry of Manpower and I don't know what else will happen to you! You're a fool!"

She feels the pressure of George's restraining hand as she stares into the stupid woman's eyes till shame makes the woman look down.

"Put your money back into your purse, Gloria," George says. "Where were you when you were caught?"

A long silence. Then she mutters, "Scotts Shopping Centre, Sir."

"The police told us that the security guards searched your bags and person. They found two bras unpaid for, two packets of AA batteries, a transistor radio and three shirts for men. All not paid."

"I was going to pay, Sir."

"Don't lie to us, Gloria!" she yells. How good it is to yell at the cow! She's been bottling up her anger all the way from Tanglin and up the East Coast Expressway till they reached home. "The guards stopped you at the exit! If you were going to pay, you should've been at the cash counter! What were you doing at the exit with all the unpaid goods? Ha? Tell me!"

Again she feels the press of George's hand, retraining her.

"The police have impounded your passport. Tomorrow we have to take you to the subordinate court where you will be charged," George tells the brazen liar. "You know that in Singapore, shoplifters are jailed. Depending on how seriously the judge views your case, Gloria, you could be jailed for one or two weeks. Do you understand? We will not bail you out. You will miss your flight home tomorrow. We have already paid for this flight. If you want to go home after serving your jail sentence, you will have to pay for your own air ticket. Do you understand?"

The woman nods; her eyes are dumb as a cow's waiting for the butcher's knife.

RETIRED REBEL

I worked for twelve years with the British army, but I didn't look up to the British even then. In fact, I looked down on them. I was a rebel, I tell you. "Don't talk pidgin to me," I told the Brits. "You want to speak to me, speak proper English," I said. In those days they thought we locals couldn't speak English. I gave it to them proper. When I was a fresh recruit, every time my corporal wrote on the board I had to get up and correct his spelling. I would erase his words and write them again with the proper spelling. After a while he got really embarrassed, you know. "Jimmy," he said to me, "I speak. You write on the board what I say." Those English soldiers! They only know how to spell their own names, nothing else. Can't write. Can't spell.'

She could see how his eyes still shone with the fire of his youth as a young Asian in the British army. He reminded her of her father back home after he had had a drink or two. Cheap beer bought from the *sari-sari* store loosened her *tatay*'s tongue, and he would entertain friends and family with his exploits as an odd-jobman for a company that worked for the Americans in Subic Bay.

'I had my schooling at St Joseph's, you know, where the Christian brothers really taught us how to read and write. So we could hold our heads high. Once, I got a sergeant real hot. I was a corporal by then. The other corporals had been complaining to me about him for a long time. "Wait, wait," I said to them. "Don't do anything yet. Give him rope enough to hang himself first." Then one day my chance came. We were in the mess, playing scrabble. The English corporal was teaching us how to play. Then the sergeant came in. He went up to the English corporal. "You're wasting your time teaching these locals," he said to the corporal. I got up at once. I told the other corporals to leave me with the sergeant. Then I gave it to the bugger. I said: "I've lived with you chaps for years. Slept in the same room with you, eaten with you. But I've yet to see an English soldier get up in the morning, brush his teeth, wash and have breakfast. You chaps just go for breakfast the moment you get up and eat without brushing your teeth. You English taught us the word hygiene, but I don't know whether you can spell it. It's h-y-g-i-e-n-e." I spelt it for him. I tell you, his face went all red. "If you don't like it here, you can leave," he said to me. "Not so fast," I answered. I pointed to my stripes. "I've signed up for twelve years," I said to him. "You'll need a court martial to take them off. But you can fight me in the ring, fair and square," I told him. Back in those days I was a rebel, I tell you.'

He paused. There, reflected in her eyes, was the champion boxer he had once been. He had represented his division in the army's featherweight category, holding his own in the ring against those Irish and Nepalese boys. Great boxers! Those were wonderful times. Not wanting her to see how pleased he was, he returned to his sandpapering, smoothing the edges of the wooden stool he was making for little Jason, rounding its corners. He moulded his palms over the wood and inhaled its sweet fragrance. His hands were still strong hands, used to dirt and grease, but of late they had found a new destiny.

'Didn't the sergeant give you trouble later?' he heard her ask, and without looking up he drawled, 'Nah,' closing his eyes as he cupped the piece of wood in his hands like a woman's breast.

'You would have been in big, big trouble, Uncle, if this had happened in the Philippines.'

She held out a mug of his favourite coffee, sweetened with condensed milk. As he took it he noticed how brown and thin her arms were. She was a slip of a girl, younger, much younger than his daughter. Still holding onto his piece of sandpaper, he took a grateful gulp of the hot brown brew and glanced at his watch. Nearly noon. He had been there all morning.

'Time for Jason's lunch soon, Uncle!'

When he turned round, she had already gone into the kitchen to prepare the boy's meal. He followed her with his mug of coffee, careful not to get in her way as he continued yarning while she cooked. He could tell that she was listening even as she clattered and washed and stirred, bustling between the fridge, the stove and the sink. Every now and then she glanced his way, nodded her head and smiled. Never once did she interrupt him. She just smiled and nodded to show that she was listening.

'You always go on and on. You think people are so interested in your stories, ah? You just don't know when to stop,' his wife had complained many times. Well, bull to her. If it wasn't his storytelling, it'd be something else that she'd find fault with. She was never happy with him. Never! If he were at home, she'd be complaining about the noise and mess he was making. "Why so much sawing and cutting? What are you making? Sawdust everywhere! What are you making, huh?" How would he know?

Let the wood answer her. The answer was in the wood. If he was out, she would complain that he was never home. If he stayed at home and read the papers, she would insist on talking to him. Talk, talk, talk. All day long he heard nothing but her grumbling about this neighbour and that neighbour. He was drowning in her voice. No one could edge in a word.

'Why don't you do *tai chi*? Good for health, you know. What about line dancing? Old Tan and that Eddie Lim join their wives for dancing and karaoke. Want to join them?'

'No, thank you.'

Walking with battalions of retired men and women, all chattering like mynahs and crows in trees, was not, as the Brits would say, his cuppa tea.

'What happened to the sergeant?' Maria broke his train of thought.

'Oh, the sergeant? That sergeant was eventually transferred out of our unit. The local corporals thought I had had a hand in it. They really looked up to me then, I tell you! So I kept quiet when some of them asked me.'

'Ah-ah! Uncle is not honest,' the girl giggled.

'Hey, I didn't lie. I just kept quiet. They thought I did it. I wasn't going to tell them they were wrong. Everyone in the unit hated that *ang moh* sergeant anyway. When the new sergeant took over, the chap was very polite to us. And all my friends said it was because I spoke up.'

'Interesting story, Uncle. You were very brave.'

'Nah!' He brushed her compliment aside and took a gulp of his coffee to hide his pleasure.

'Really, Uncle,' she insisted.

'Nah! My wife, she complains that I talk too much. She says I shouldn't open my mouth and tell people such things.'

'Why?'

'Oh, what's past is past. She says we're English speaking in Singapore now, and young people don't like to hear bad things about English people.'

'But the Philippines is not English. We were colonised by the Americans.'

She had studied history in high school and hoped to go to America to be a nurse some day, she told him. But first she had to save enough money to help her parents, who were poor farmers.

'Young people like you like America and Hollywood. So you see, that's why I should keep quiet about such things. My wife always says the world has changed. Singaporeans speak English, and we speak English at home so we shouldn't talk bad about the English.'

'But, Uncle, you say you were a rebel.'

'I was and I am,' he huffed.

'Am?'

'Yes! Am!' She was teasing him, but he couldn't let it pass.

'I always tell people that speaking English is one thing. Worshipping the English arse is another thing. Not the same. Not the same.'

He broke a chunk off the cheap French loaf he had bought from the Chinese bakery that morning, and dipped it into his coffee, slurping up the brown mush with relish. It was something he rarely had a chance to do these days. His wife disapproved of his working-class habits. Dipping bread into his coffee would drive her berserk. Had he become so soft that he minded what she thought? The question troubled him. He started to talk rapidly.

'I'm a rebel, I tell you! I've never let people push me around! Even in those days when I lost my job. You know how terrible it was for me when the British pulled out of Singapore? Overnight, we lost our homes and our jobs. My family was living in army quarters. We had to move out. And I had no job. Luckily I was in the technical wing so I could find work in a tractor company. But my first year was hell. Those Chinese fellas in the company called me English bootlicker, you know! Just because my Chinese was not so good, you know! Those Chinese-speaking fellows knew nothing about the likes of us Babas. They didn't know we spoke Malay and English at home. They wouldn't talk to me. Okay, I thought. You don't want to talk to me, never mind, I can still talk to you. I was very determined. I wanted to keep that job so I wasn't going to let their stupid attitude push me into leaving. Who would've suffered most if I'd left? Not them. It would've been my family.

'Sometimes those chaps answered me when I asked them a question. Sometimes they just walked away, you know. Many things they just kept quiet. Never said anything. Never told me. Called me English shit behind my back, you know. I had to find out things for myself or just make mistakes and let the boss correct me. I knew those buggers' tricks. They wanted to show me up. Prove to the boss that I was no good even though I had worked for the British army for a long time. But I kept quiet. I pretended I didn't notice anything. I needed the job. And they knew it, those buggers!

'All year I watched them, I watched my back and bided my time. Some nights I even went to their favourite *kopi tiam*, their neighbourhood coffee shop where a whole bunch of them used to gather. I'd have a beer and watch them play Chinese chess. I wanted to show them that their behaviour had no effect on me. I was not going to be cowed. Then one night one of the ringleaders challenged me to play. As a joke, you know. He thought I'd refuse but I accepted his challenge. "You pay for my beer and everybody else's if you lose," I said. "No problem, Uncle," he laughed. And his friends, they all laughed! They felt sure the old man was going to lose. But that night I got my chance. I really *hamtam* the fella, as the Malays say! Hammered him. Those jokers were shocked. Wah! Uncle, you can play Chinese chess, ah! "Pay for my beer," I told him, and straightaway I ordered Tiger stouts for everybody. That night I must have burnt a big hole in his pocket. There was a big crowd there. It was Saturday night. After that he never challenged me again. Then, slowly, the men in my workshop started talking to me. Now, even after my retirement, they come to see me and ask my advice.'

Maria clapped her hands like a child. Little Jason looked up from his building blocks on the floor and clapped too so that all three of them ended up clapping and laughing as Maria coaxed the two year old to finish his rice porridge and fish. Then later, as his grandson played with his blocks, he and Maria had their lunch, eating the rice and fish curry that he had bought from the market that morning. When the meal was over, he fished out a white plastic carrier from his canvas bag.

'Open it.' He pushed the parcel across the table.

She peered into the carrier and gasped.

'Try it on. I bought it in the market this morning.'

The girl ran into the bathroom. A few minutes later she came out wearing the pink blouse with tiny white flowers.

'Thank you, Uncle. I shall wear it to church on Sunday.'

'Good.'

Then he scooped up his grandson from the floor and made for the door.

'Uncle?'

'I'm taking Jason to the playground.'

'But it's so hot.'

He shut the door and headed for the lift.

Inside the lift he took a deep breath and hugged the little boy against his beating heart. It was beating a wee bit too fast. That girl was too bloody attractive for his old heart.

'*Koong-koong*!' his grandson cooed.

That night his daughter phoned.

'Pa! Did you buy a blouse for Maria?'

'Ye-es?' He was cautious. Pat's voice was shrill over the phone.

'Why? Why do you have to do that?'

'Why what? It's not a crime, is it?'

'I didn't say it's a crime.'

'Then why ask this and that?'

His wife came and sat in the armchair facing him. He didn't look at her. Pat was going on and on in her usual excited way. He could feel his temper rising from the pit of his belly, like a bull preparing to charge at the red cloth of a matador. Finally he said, 'Do you know that all the girl's clothes are old?'

'How do you know? Did Maria show you her clothes?'

'No.'

'So she didn't complain about her clothes? Did she *ask* you to buy her some clothes? *Hinted* that she had no clothes or something like that?'

'No! No! I have eyes! I can see!' he yelled into the phone. 'You think old people have no eyes? Did you take a look at her slippers? They're fit for the dustbin. The girl's got no shoes. And is she listening to all this?'

He had a vision of Maria crying in the kitchen, her shoulders hunched over the dirty dishes in the sink, listening to his daughter yelling over the phone.

'Did she ask you for shoes too, Pa? Did she?'

'No! She didn't ask for anything! And she didn't ask me for a new blouse.'

'Pa, these maids are not stupid. They know that retired old men have plenty of money to spend.'

'You dare to insult me like this? I'm still your father, you know!'

'I know, Pa!'

'The hell you know! You think my brain goes soft the minute I leave my job. And you worry about my money. Don't worry! Even if I lose every cent of my CPF, even if I have to beg, I won't come to you!'

'There you go again, Pa. I wasn't trying to insult you or anything like that.' Pat's tone softened, and she started talking to him as though she were placating a child throwing a tantrum. 'Pa, listen, I'm not worried. Why should I worry? It's your money. You earned it. I just want you to be careful. What you want for the maid, I can buy for her, you know. I just don't want you to spoil Maria and raise her expectations. Why don't you go travelling? Go with Mum. Join a tour group. Or go to JB or KL to shop and eat. Things are so cheap there. Find something to do that you and

Mum like.'

He banged down the phone. Damn it! Like mother, like daughter. Both of them have dirty minds. Did Pat think he was dense? He was sickened by his daughter's talk and what she'd left unsaid. Did Pat think ...? Did his wife think he was a dirty old man going after the maid? That he was a retiree with too much time dripping from his hands? Go on a tour with the old lady! What rot! What utter rot! Spend money and be nagged day and night in a foreign country? No, thank you. Couldn't they see who he really was?

He went out and stayed out. When he returned to their tiny three-room apartment around midnight, his wife had gone to bed. He pushed away the three pieces of white lace that covered the back rest of the sofa. They fell onto the floor and he kicked them aside. Why must she cover every darn thing in the flat with white lace? White was for weddings or mourning. He felt like tearing off the lace curtains that covered the windows. Lace doilies and lace tablecloths—he loathed the sight of them.

Their sitting room was a long narrow rectangle leading to the tiny kitchen at the back. On its right were the two bedrooms, one of which belonged to their daughters before the girls had got married.

'Give away their beds and cupboards,' he'd said.

'No. Can still use, what! *Sekali*, the room empty, you bring back rubbish and put inside. No, thank you,' she'd said.

And so the ugly furniture remained, kept scrupulously spotless, dustless and lifeless. He swept off her neat little cushions from the sofa and kicked them into a corner of the room. She'd fluffed and straightened, beaten and dusted every stick of furniture in the flat. The two armchairs looked as though they had never been sat on. They still had their plastic covers on, to keep out the dust she'd said when he complained about sitting on plastic. He kicked aside two pairs of slippers placed side by side by the door, slippers he would never wear at home.

'Ya, he's always like this—barefoot and half naked in a sarong,' she'd complained to her relatives. How could he do it in this flat then? So clean. So neat. So dead.

He poured himself a glass of cold water from the fridge, drank it and fell asleep on the couch.

He woke with a start. The phone was ringing. He picked it up.

'Pa.' It was Pat again. 'Pa, you don't have to come today. I'm bringing Jason and Maria over.'

'Hm.' He put down the phone. He wasn't born yesterday. He knew why Pat was doing this, and he didn't like it one bit. But that's how everybody thinks these days. A man is not allowed to be kind to a woman. What woman? Maria is a slip of a girl! The snort in his thoughts escaped him. His wife came out of their bedroom. He brushed past her and made for the bathroom.

'Was that Pat?' she hollered outside the bathroom door.

'Yes!' He turned on the shower, grateful for the cold rush of water over him.

'Is she bringing Jason over?'

'Yes! Yes!'

Then it struck him. The bitch had planned it and now she was pretending that she hadn't. Just as well. Pat's apartment would be empty today. They'd forgotten that he still had the keys to his daughter's apartment. This would be a perfect day to start then.

He hummed jauntily as he dressed, busily planning the day ahead of him. An empty apartment all to himself. The whole day. To do what he liked as he liked. All day long. They wouldn't be back till evening. By then he would have cleared up everything. No one would know. As long as he made sure that the front door was bolted and the windows closed. Ah, what a luxury privacy is to a man, especially to a man who has had to share his bedroom and his bed with a shrew for more than forty years. When did he get married? No matter. Since his wedding day he hadn't had a room to himself. No wonder the rich in England and China in the old days used to have separate rooms. The husband had his library, and the wife her boudoir. A man has to have a room of his own, especially after he's retired. He opened the bathroom door.

'Oi! Wipe your feet on the mat, lah! Whole morning since five I cleaned the house, you know! Just mopped the kitchen and you're dripping all over the floor! Here! Wipe your feet!' She pointed to the cloth.

Had she ordered him around like this when he'd been working? Or had he been too busy to notice it then? Anyway, when he'd been working he'd usually left the house by half past seven. These days, he had nowhere to go. But today would be different. Today, hm, hm, today ... he hummed and got dressed.

'Are you going out or staying in for lunch?'

'Out.'

'But Jason's coming today, and today you're going out. I thought you said every day you must go to Ocean View because you must see your grandson? Then grandson coming and you go out.'

'Cannot change my mind, is it? Go out, you grumble. I stay

in, you grumble. Today you have company, I go out, you also grumble.'

And people wonder why so many retired men sit in the *kopi tiam* and drink black coffee all day long! Those people should ask the wives!

With great effort, he gave her one final shove and she was in. Now careful. Don't leave any marks. No scratches. Now gently. Gently. He half pushed and half lifted till he had her on the rug. Then he half pushed and half dragged her out onto the balcony. She was a beauty. And he was lucky that the men from Public Works were cutting trees downstairs.

'Hey, Inche! Can I take this?' he'd asked.

'Take! Take!' They laughed at him, an old man wanting a bit of wood. He'd had to strip off her leaves and branches and leave her out in the sun and rain for weeks.

Sweat poured out of him and dripped onto the floor. He ran his hands across her rough surface, gazing intently at her shapely form. He had come to look at her every day under the pretext of visiting Jason.

He closed the apartment door behind him and bolted it. The moment the door closed he sensed that the Other was waiting. He shut his eyes and rested his head against the wall, allowing himself to be enveloped by the silence and emptiness inside the apartment. They were a welcome presence. The traffic on the expressway below was muted and seemed to be floating in from a great distance away. His eyes remained shut while he took deep breaths to still his excited heart. A light breeze blew in from the balcony and lifted the few remaining strands of grey on his head. The sea air smelt of freedom and solitude. Ah, blessed solitude.

Sweet solitude. Few, other than monks and nuns, understood his need to be alone on this noisy, crowded island where freedom ends at the tip of your nose. Six thousand bodies per square kilometre. More if you count the tourists and migrant labourers. Public places are littered with signs saying: DON'T and DO NOT. DON'T SPIT. DON'T SWIM. DON'T FISH. DO NOT LITTER. DO NOT ENTER. DO NOT CYCLE HERE. DO NOT WALK THERE. DO NOT BREATHE. DO NOT LIVE. Might as well die. Where can a retired man go to be alone other than the cemetery?

He looked out to the sea beyond. He was on the twenty-fifth floor. Alone. Ah, such a sense of space in an empty spacious apartment with a balcony and a view of the blue, blue sea. Even the very air smelt different from the air in his crowded, noisy Housing Board estate in Bukit Ho Swee. How tiny the cars looked on the road below. He marvelled at the view of distant islands and the tiny ships anchored in the bay. When would he pluck up enough courage to book a passage on one of the cargo ships and go sailing round the world? He would be sixty-two in a month's time. Would anyone say he was too old to work as a cargo hand? He used to think a long time ago that fifty was ancient, but at sixty-one going on sixty-two, there was still so much for him to learn in this world. An expansiveness in the air filled his lungs. He let out a happy sigh as he gazed at her body, such fullness of form. He could see her lines and curves. Strange that he should love wood when he used to repair trucks and tractors, and all he saw from morn till night were the undercarriages of vehicles. He didn't mind the smell of metal and steel, but he was obsessed with the smell of wood. He put his nose close to her and inhaled. Ah, the fragrance of angsana wood.

He picked up the watering can and went into the kitchen to fill it up. Then he went out onto the balcony again and started to water the plants. The ferns looked neglected and thirsty. He had read somewhere that the squishy brown centre of the bird's nest fern had to be kept moist. He gave it a few more drops. Then he sprinkled water all over the potted plants so that they would think it was raining. He watched the water drops gather, join and roll off the leaves, washing off the dust. When he had watered all the plants, he stood back and surveyed the results. Large diamond drops glistened on the leaves of the money plant and maidenhair ferns. The plants seemed happy, and a deep pleasure warmed and flowed through his veins. He felt energised. He had never noticed these plants when the women were around. But whenever he was alone he could pay attention to their presence as though they were silent, comforting companions. Palpable life forms that grew and died, they kept him in touch with the process of growing and dying that was going on inside him. Not that he wanted to talk about this to anyone, much less with his wife and two daughters. Jan was a stockbroker and had no time for him. He felt there was a hard practical edge in Singapore's young women these days; a certain hard logic that sees a leaf as a leaf and refuses to see that a rock is more than a rock and a leaf is not just a leaf. Ah, blessed are the literal minded in Singapore! For they are the makers of money, not art and beauty.

He put away the watering can. He could feel her waiting for him as he ran his hands lovingly across her rough surface. Pat wasn't going to like this one bit, but at least she wouldn't throw his things away. Unlike Jan. The men in the coffee shop would guffaw, and his wife and daughters would think he was going soft if they only knew what he was about to do. He touched the angsana log lovingly, like a man stroking his beloved cat or his mistress. If there was anybody he could talk to about this wood business, it was Maria. The girl had grown up on a farm. She knew about plants and trees. He imagined how she might cock her head and listen without interrupting him, how she might just nod; and that was all that he required of anyone, really.

He crouched on his haunches and gazed at the thick round log for a long while. What was happening to him? Here, in the quiet of the apartment, he could feel the presence of the stranger in him, his other self that had long been buried underneath years of work and the hours he had spent on the factory floor, crawling under dirty vehicles. At weekends, following his wife to markets and shopping malls, meeting relatives and his buddies on feast days, festival days and other public holidays, frittering his life away with mindless chatter and hours of inane activities. What was the sum total of his life? Eat, fuck, sleep, wake up, eat, work, eat, sleep. O God, let it not be too late. Not too late. Now that he was retired, he must get to know his Other. Who was this stranger who had been living under the skin of the tractor repairman? Through the calm steady gaze of this strange Other, he stared at the shape embedded in the wood. He marvelled at the grainy texture of the tree trunk, the shape of line and curve, the feel of grain and knots, the sensation of colours and patterns before him. He was the lover worshipping his beloved with the gaze of a man who could sit all day long studying what he'd loved all his life. He looked out at the empty sea and back again, alternating between wood and sea till all he saw were the lines and shape of his beloved in wood. Then he took his hammer and chisel and knelt before her, poised between fear and courage. Did he dare? This stranger, his Other, wanted above all else, after all those years of scrutinising grease-covered, dirt-encrusted engines and undercarriages of trucks, to chip at a block of wood and see beauty emerging from the chisel in his hands. How could his wife and daughters see this Other when they had branded 'retiree' on his forehead?

Heck them! He placed his chisel against the wood, and brought his hammer down.

USHA AND MY THIRD CHILD

Hae— hello, Auntie. C— can I help?'

'Hi, you must be Usha.'

I gave up the struggle with the video tape recorder, and straightened my back. Tired of processing bank loans, I'd signed up to do a counselling course. Twenty-nine years dealing with money, time to deal with the heart.

'Can you fix this? This machine won't obey me.'

'N— no problem, Auntie. Th— th— the plug is loose.'

'Oh.'

I recalled the notes in her case file. Usha Thiagarajah: age seventeen, stutters when nervous, excited or angry. Second of three daughters. Mother, forty-six; father, forty-eight; both parents are factory operators who work shifts. The three girls were looked after by their grandmother until they were in their teens. Usha's stuttering used to irritate her mother no end. She was slapped and hit whenever she stuttered during her primary school years. Her mother would send her to her room and not allow her to watch tv. Her father did not interfere. Her grandmother tried to protect her. There were frequent quarrels. Under her grandmother's protection, Usha did fairly well in school. In her last year in secondary school, a Chinese boy befriended her. Subsequently they went to the same church and polytechnic.

'It's ok— okay now.'

Usha adjusted the mike and the rest of the recording paraphernalia. She led the way into the counselling room. There were two armchairs with a table in between. The recording mike was on the table. Usha showed me to my seat. Then she sat down with a teddy bear resting on her belly, looking like any other teenage girl. Fresh-faced and innocent. You can't tell these days. They seem to get younger and younger, these girls in trouble.

'Hi, I'm Mrs Vivienne Chua. Is it okay if I video-tape our first interview? Sister Mary has explained things to you, am I right?' I handed her the interview consent form. 'A standard requirement. Please sign here.'

The girl looked fifteen, with her hair bunched up in a ponytail, held by a pink rubber band. A pair of heart-shaped gold studs in her ears. A gold stud in her nose. She was wearing an oversized tee shirt over a pair of blue shorts. She didn't look like she was ready to be a mum.

'Sister Mary said you've been staying at the centre for the past three months.'

'Th— three m— m— months and t— two days,' Usha corrected me.

I asked about her mother.

'Mm— my mother came to visit yesterday. Fir— first time.'

'You mean your mother didn't visit you for three months?'

'My ... my auntie came.'

'Do you know why your mother didn't want to come?'

Usha hugged her bear. Her voice dropped. I leant forward in my chair.

'Sh— she said I ... I shamed her. She got to h— h— hide from our re— relatives.'

'Do you keep in touch with your family?'

I shouldn't have asked that. She'd already said her aunt visited. Ask open-ended questions. Don't be interrogative, I reminded myself. I had to bring her round to talking about her feelings, perceptions, yearnings and expectations—a requirement of my course.

'I phoned ho— home every day. But my ... my mother cr— cr— cried and cried. Scolded and scolded. Talk— talked so long. The bat— bat— battery on my phone ran out.'

'Are you comfortable at the centre?'

'O— o— okay, lah. Four p— persons share one ... one room.'

I asked about sleeping arrangements, diet and how the work was shared out at the crisis centre, which took in abused foreign domestic workers, abused wives and children, and unmarried mothers. There were twenty-four women and six children staying at the centre. Four mothers and their children had run away from violent husbands and fathers. The rest were maids from India and Indonesia who had been beaten, scalded, molested or raped by their employers.

'Pe— people here he— he— help each other. S— sometimes the ... the mothers got to go to ... to ... to court. We ... we look after their children.'

'Breathe in slowly.' I encouraged her to relax. Her stuttering decreased.

'Padmini, my roommate, she was raped. I tell her, if I were the judge, I'd chop off that thing from all rapists! Make them rubbish collectors. For ... for life!'

I winced. 'Oh dear, I'm sure you're not that barbaric, Usha.'

'I wanted to make Padmini laugh. The women here, they cry all the time.'

'Maybe they need to cry. Do you cry sometimes?'

'I'm not like them. Don't want to be like them.'

My eyes rested on her already protruding belly. The girl had cheek. And arrogance. Didn't want to be lumped with foreign maids and runaway wives and mothers. 'But you're living here, Usha. You're one of them.'

'I ... I ... I not like them. I can ... can go home after my ... my baby is born. They ... they cannot go home.'

I bit my tongue. She didn't want to be seen as a helpless abused woman. I had been careless by not picking up on her clues.

'Would you like to tell me how you came to the crisis centre?'

'I took a ... a ... a bus and ca— came on my own.'

'Oh. You came alone. It must have been difficult.'

She was silent for a long while. I placed my hand on hers. She held the teddy bear tightly against her breast. Her eyes shut to block out the bright lights, switched on for the video taping.

'I ... I went to the ... the polyclinic. My boyfriend. He di— didn't want to go in. I wen— went in by myself. The nurse t— t— took my height, weight and all ... all ... all that and asked me to ... to go pass urine. When I came out, I ... I put the cup on the ... the counter. I went out to ... to tell my boyfriend. He didn't want to co— come in. The ... the doctor said ... said I was pregnant.'

'How did you feel then?'

Another long silence. Her eyes remained closed.

'My boyfriend. He ... he said his ... his family wouldn't accept. I got to ... to abort.' She opened her eyes. 'So I came here, lah!'

Her sudden change of tone threw me off balance. She smiled.

'The mothers here, they say I must think happy thoughts. Sad thoughts no good for my baby.' Her hand stroked her belly.

I didn't know how to respond to that so I said, 'I heard from Sister that you went for a scan at the hospital. Is it a girl or boy?'

'Boy.'

A dreamy look came into her eyes when she said 'boy' in a tone that was touchingly tender, her lips shaping the word, giving it a wholesome roundness. I could almost see the baby boy in her mind's eye. It upset me. Seventeen years old. No skill. No job. No husband. How was she going to look after her baby?

'Usha, have you thought about what you want to do after your baby is born?'

'Li— live one day at a ... a time, Sister said.'

She could say that as long as she was staying at the centre. What about after that? The interview wasn't going well. I was not able to probe her deeper. I needed to get her to talk about her feelings.

'Usha, do you want to talk about why you're feeling lousy today?'

Another long uncooperative silence.

'Usha, you seem to be remembering a lot of things inside you. I just want you to know that it's okay if you don't want to talk. We can just sit here quietly. It's all right.'

She hugged her bear tightly and closed her eyes. That was how our first interview ended.

The next day I slipped the tape into my video player. Yikes! My face loomed up on the screen. Usha's back was towards the camera. My voice was loud and clear. Hers was almost inaudible. I rang the crisis centre.

'You've been had!' Sister Mary giggled.

I wasn't amused. That girl had hijacked my interview. Idiot! How could I have been so naïve? She'd taken advantage of my dinosaur technical know-how, sat me in the seat facing the video cam. Humph! Got to be careful with her.

At our second interview Usha was upset. She'd shouted at her parents earlier, and had refused to say who the baby's father was.

'Not important, what! I must think of my ... my baby. They asked me to ... to ... to ... go home. I don't want. Home is ver— very noisy. So many people talk, talk, talking all the time. My grandmother talks. My mother talks. My fa— fa— father shouts. My au— aun— auntie shouts.'

'Take a deep breath, Usha. Breathe in slowly. Now breathe out slowly. Count to ten. One, two, three ...' Usha inhaled. Her breast heaved with the effort to calm herself.

'What did your parents say?' I asked.

'They asked me this, that, that! Mother asked. Father asked. Auntie asked. Till I got so ... so ... so confused.'

Since they'd found out the sex of the baby, Usha's parents had changed their minds. They'd stopped lamenting that she'd brought shame to the family by not going for an abortion. Now they were pressing her not to give the baby up for adoption. Her parents wanted to take the baby home.

'My ... my ... my father wants to put his name down as ... as the father. He ... he's mad. It's my ... my ... my baby. My baby. I

... I want to keep him. Do ... do what's best for him. If ... if giving him to other pe— pe— people is best, then I ... I ... I give him up.'

Tears filled her eyes. She closed them to shut out the noise in her head and heart.

'Yes, he's your baby. No one can take him away from you unless you want them to.'

Usha's dark youthful face stayed with me all week. When the third interview came round, I called the centre to say that I had a cold. My head was heavy. Seventeen years old. Shame tinged my cheeks. My face felt warm. Is this what counselling trainers called 'a trigger', a word or event that rakes up your suppressed memories?

At seventeen this girl was taking responsibility for another life. She wanted her baby. At forty-seven, fifteen years ago, I had refused to be responsible for another life.

A quarter to seven. I took a taxi to the General Hospital and checked in. I'd chosen this time so that Dave would think I was going to work early in the morning. I'd often leave the house before seven so that I could be at the bank by eight to clear my backlog of work. The nurse at the ward gave me some forms to sign. Under the heading 'Reasons for Termination of Pregnancy' I'd scribbled '*Obeying govt. orders to stop at two.*' The nurse smiled. For a brief moment, looking across the counter at each other, we were fellow conspirators who understood each other. Women tired of being told what to do—how many children to have and the penalties. Ah, the penalties! You would lose your place in the queue for public housing. If you had a third child, you were moved to the end of the housing queue and had to start all over again. And I had wanted then to move into a five-room flat as soon as possible. For the sake of peace. For the sake of my mother and two brothers living with us. Another penalty was that your third child was not allowed to go to the school of your choice even if his or her siblings were already in that school. A slew of such policies had hit us in the 1970s when Dave was unemployed.

'I'm between jobs! Is this how you support your husband? Telling your mother that your husband is jobless? Bloody hell.'

'Dave is freelancing,' I told my mother.

'*Sama-sama*, lah! *Dia tak kerja*! The same. He's got no work!'

'You tell your mother I was gracious enough to let her and her two sons live with us.'

'*Lu gasi dia tahu*! *Jangan lupa*! You tell him not to forget. I don't live here for free! I cook. I wash. I clean house. I look after his daughters. Go ask *lain orang*! Ask other people how much it costs to get a maid!'

Dave and my mother talked at each other. Their words in different tongues sliced through me. My widowed mother could not afford to live on her own with my teenage brothers. And I? I could not cope with another child.

My memory of that morning at the General Hospital is hazy. Lying in a room with pink walls. A fan whirring above me. By evening I was well enough to go home at the usual after-office hour. I told no one about my visit to the hospital. No one. Not even Dave whom I divorced two years later.

Today is Mother's Day.

Today, Usha Thiagarajah, aged twenty-one now, graduates as a nurse. She will work in Mt Alvernia Hospital. Her son, half Chinese, is in nursery school. His grandmother, Usha's mother, looks after him.

Tonight, my two daughters will take me out to dinner.

Tonight, alone in my room, I will remember my third child.

BIG WALL NEWSPAPER

In one minute's time, the electric bell will bong. The hungry horde will rush down the stairs and out through the school gates. But I'll be here, waiting for the Sengkang Kid. Thanks to the Auntie brigade this loo is clean and dry. That's how it is in our elite Saints' schools. We take pride in having a clean loo. And that's why the loo is the best place to have a fight. There's a clear space between the sinks and the urinals; and no teacher comes into the boys' loo. This block is deserted after school. There will be no spectators this evening. No smart-ass loudmouths to cheer him. It will be a clean fight between the Sengkang Kid and me. Not that I want to fight him. I don't like to fight. But that Kid tore up my Big Wall Newspaper.

I had written about the fight that the Kid lost after the soccer game last week. That got him so pissed he sent a fist towards my face, but I ducked. And all that punch and weight fell hard onto the floor. That got him madder. He swore to kick the hell out of my smart-ass face. This morning, he tore down our wall newspaper and showed it to the P.

Mr Harry Koh hit the roof when he saw the headline. Inside my pocket now is the P's note I've got to take home and show to my mom; my mom who pats her son on the shoulders each time he brings home a report card filled with A's and B's. These grades make her feel good. These grades make her feel her life is still worthwhile, and her divorce has not affected her boy. This note will make her cry tonight.

* * *

'You've got nothing better to do? So many other things happened in school. Why didn't you write about them?'

'This is news.'

That was his father's dictum: Dog bites man. Not news. Man bites dog. News. Of course, she understands why a young female teacher crying in front of her class is news in an all boys' school. But did he have to write about it and publish it in his Big Wall Newspaper, as he calls it?

'What happened in that Secondary Four class was none of your business! You didn't make this up, did you?'

'Mom!'

His eyes have that mix of fear and defiance that you see in a young dog when it's cornered. His tone is accusatory.

'You are the one who taught me to tell the truth.'

His face wears the look of a sullen mule. His voice is hoarse; it's changing fast. Soon he'll speak like a man. She wants to hug him and throttle him at the same time. Pride and annoyance surge through her. He's just fourteen and he's started a school newspaper. She reads his Principal's note again.

You are requested to attend an urgent meeting tomorrow at 8 a.m. sharp. Your son's abuse and violations of ... The note reels off a list of Wai Mun's offences: fighting, vandalism of the school's notice board, putting up notices without the Principal's permission, publishing a school newspaper without the Principal's permission, making a teacher cry. The punishment is a public caning. *Should his parents object, they are advised to take their son out of the school.*

Her hands are trembling a little, just a little. Her son is not a criminal. Her first impulse is to protect her boy. Her second is to seek 'damage control'. But what can she do? Vandals and errant students are caned in Singapore. But a public caning for a school boy? Even the most hardened vandal is caned in private in the prison. Not in front of an audience of a thousand students in the school hall! What will Richard say? For a fleeting second, she thinks of phoning him. But what's the point? He won't speak for his son. He can't even speak up for himself. O, God! What should she do?

'When did you start this stupid business?' she turns on the boy.

'Three weeks ago,' he growls.

'Haven't you anything better to do?' she screams at him.

'School's boring.'

'School's boring! So you fight and vandalise the school's notice board?'

'I didn't fight, Mom! That boy didn't turn up. I didn't vandalise the notice board! I pinned up *The Towgay News*.'

'What?' The surprise in her voice makes him smile.

'Rajiv said our Big Wall Newspaper should report bits of news about school. I said, ya, bits of news like bean sprouts. So we called it *Towgay News*.'

She wants to hug and slap him. The audacity of this boy. The pride in his voice is unmistakeable. He brings out the offending newspaper—an A3-sized broadsheet with a green and yellow computer-printed masthead of bean sprouts, and the date, July 1989. Below the masthead are the names of the two reporters, and their editor, John Wong Wai Mun. She was the one who named him, 'Wai Mun'. A Cantonese name meaning 'For the People'. She was young and idealistic then. She thought love could change the world.

Can it? Let's find out, Richard had whispered in her ear, his finger tracing the slight depression beneath her collarbone, sliding down the space between her breasts. She wants to scream at him now.

'Honestly, Mun! I don't know what to do with you. So tomorrow I've got to go and see the Principal about your vandalism.'

'I told you! It's not vandalism.'

'Don't you talk back to me like this! You're in deep shit already!'

'We only pinned up our newspaper on the board for everyone to read. We didn't want to print many copies. So we did one big wall newspaper. Like ... like the Chinese students in Tiananmen Square.'

'But you're not in China, Mun! You're in Singapore! In St Paul's! What's the matter with you?'

It's the top elite boys' school after Raffles' Institution (RI). 'We don't accept the rejects of RI. Is St Paul's your first choice?' That's how the Principal interrogates each poor sod who begs for a place for his son. Those whose sons are accepted will hear Harry Koh's sonorous voice booming through the loudspeakers. 'Parents! Give us your boys! We will return them to you as men! St Paul's results are exemplary. There are no failures in my school.'

'I'll have to take you out of that school.'

'No, Mom.'

'It's a public caning for God's sake! In the school hall! It's draconian and barbaric! You're only in Sec Two. You can start all over again in a new school.'

'No.'

She can't believe her ears, can't recognise this stubborn, mulish face in front of her. He looks just like Richard now. Just as stupid. Just as blind. The boy can't see that this is censorship of the worst kind. Not even the government would cane people for reporting a fact however unpalatable that fact. So. A young female teacher cried. So what? She's an adult and a professional who should be able to hold her own against a bunch of boys. Why should the school protect the adult against the child?

Her brain is ticking. She's marshalling all her arguments, lining them up against the school. Her boy and his friends had started a newspaper by themselves. A bunch of fourteen-year-olds. They should be applauded for their initiative. Not caned! *Forty pairs of male eyes stared in shock and wonder as tears rolled down Miss Tan's ...* Agreed! The report is a little sensational. The boys should apologise to the teacher, make amends, wash the school toilets, or pick up litter, or whatever! But not caned! Sensational reporting is not a crime punishable by caning. Starting a school newspaper without the Principal's permission is not a crime punishable by caning. What's the matter with this Principal? His school is not the state of Singapore. Does he think he's the Prime Minister?

She's raving and she knows it.

'I'll put you in a private school for now. Next year, I'll send you overseas.'

Her boy shakes his head.

'Why? Are you scared of leaving school?'

The boy stares resolutely at his feet, and refuses to answer her. His sulky silence infuriates her. She resists the temptation to shake him ... and hug him. She wants so much to protect him. But she knows he wants to be treated as a grown-up. Especially now that it's just the two of them in the family. But he's only fourteen. Oh, God! How can she let this stupid school destroy him?

'Mun, please,' she pleads.

He looks up, his eyes dark and accusing.

'You're the one who said we must accept the consequences of our action.'

* * *

My mom says school gives you an education. My mom is biased. She's a teacher. School is where you learn your life is over unless you mug and pass exams. School is where you learn to stand up and sing like a bloody idiot, 'Gooooood morrrrr-ning, teeeee-chur!' You find out at great cost to your dignity that you've got to take all the crap that grown-ups vomit out in front of your desk or else you fail. You learn not to challenge, not to argue with grown-ups. Unless. Unless you've a fatal attraction for insults or humiliation, or detention class, or standing outside the classroom until the grown-up is·satisfied with your guard duty. School is where you learn power is in the hands of one man—the P. The P's office is a great place to feel small. You can't enter it unless his female dragons say 'Mr Koh will see you now.'

We're here in the P's office, my mom and I, and Seng and Rajiv's parents. Six chairs are arranged in a semi-circle in front of the P's table. The parents sit down. Five parents and a vacant chair. That must be for Dad. They don't know that my parents have split. We boys are told to stand behind our parents. I want to take away the empty chair next to Mom. It's making her uncomfortable. Rajiv and Seng Huat's parents have come together. My mom is alone. I step forward. I stand between her and the vacant chair. This way, she can't see the chair. This way, she can see me standing beside her. She's not alone.

'Please wait.' The school clerk closes the door.

No one says a word. The parents sit like they're waiting for the funeral service to start. Mom is wearing her dark blue dress. Rajiv's mom is in a grey sari. Seng's mom wears a black pantsuit; and the two fathers are in dark trousers, long-sleeved white shirt and tie. This is how it is when the principal of your son's elite school tells you to come to his office. Rajiv, poor sod, looks like he's been bonked on his head. His father's face is grim. His back is ramrod straight, and his arms are folded in front of his chest. Not a good sign. Poor Rajiv's mom is staring at the floor. Seng Huat's fat face is the only one with a smile. But I know he's scared shit, like Raj and me.

I watch the hands of the clock above Mr Koh's black leather armchair. Its tick, tick, tick is the only sound in the room. Then the door opens. Mr Koh enters. The parents stand up. They introduce themselves.

'Sit down. Please. Sit down. Sorry to keep you waiting. I had some urgent matters to attend to. Thank you for coming. Boys!'

'Yes, sir!'

'You know why your parents are here, don't you?'

'Yes, sir!'

'Vandalism is a serious offence ...'

'Mr Koh, sorry, may I interrupt?'

That's my mom. She's not like other parents. She can't keep her gap shut.

'Yes, Mrs Wong.'

'Exactly what constitutes vandalism in St Paul's?'

'We have very strict rules governing the use of the school's notice boards in St Paul's. No teacher or student is allowed to put up anything without the Principal's prior permission. These boys broke that rule. They pinned up all sorts of papers without my knowledge and my permission. That constitutes vandalism. It's a serious violation. The school rules have been made known to all our boys from the day they joined this school. But these boys have flouted the rules.'

'Mr Koh, I agree that these boys have broken the school's rule regarding the use of the notice boards. But does this merit a public caning?'

'Mrs Wong, I cannot allow any Tom, Dick and Harry to pin up anything they wish without the Principal's expressed knowledge and permission. Such flagrant disregard of rules and regulations undermines the authority of the school and the principal. And I cannot allow it. This is a serious offence. And we cane boys for serious offences. Like smoking. They do harm to their own health. We cane them. These three boys have done harm not to themselves. Worse. They've done harm to a teacher's reputation and authority. They've destroyed my teacher's confidence. She's a young woman. New in the service. A scholar sent by the Ministry of Education. Now she wants to resign. Do you know how hard it is for me to retain teachers nowadays? A good teacher is hard to come by. Now if these boys had followed the rules, had come to me first, I wouldn't have let them publish this story. They should have gone to their teachers. Their teachers would've advised them. They would've vetted the boys' writing, corrected their mistakes, and sent them to see me in the office. But these boys went over their teachers' heads! Went over the principal's head! I'm the Principal of this school. I cannot let them go unpunished!'

'Mr Koh ...'

'Mrs Wong, I'm the Principal of this school. I set the rules. I'm in charge. When things go wrong, I'm responsible.'

He stares at Mom. I'm praying. I pray that Mom will keep her word. I place my hand on her shoulders to remind her of her promise. None of the other parents dare to say anything. Rajiv's father has unfolded his arms. His back is no longer ramrod straight. We watch in silence as Mr Koh opens the brown folder on his desk.

'If any of you wish to take your son out of my school, I will not stop you.'

Silence.

'Well then,' Mr Koh looks at us. 'If there's no objection to corporal punishment, please sign this document to give the school permission to cane your son. Rest assured. I will do the caning myself. Not the discipline master.'

* * *

That night, she can't sleep. She has failed her son. Where is her lively seven-year-old? Where's the little boy who had so bravely stood up for his friend in Primary Two? As an eight-year-old, her boy had refused to go for a class outing. *Because Miss Tan was unfair to Aziz, Mommy.* She was proud that he had insisted on staying back in school with his friend. At ten, he had written a note (with her help) to tell his class teacher why he and his friends hated Chinese. *Zhen Lao-shi brings a cane to class.* When did her boy change? How did the courageous little fellow turn into this compliant silent teenager who accepts a public caning? Has she been so absorbed in her own despair that she has failed to notice his change? Has he become like his father?

Last night, she looked through the three issues of his Big Wall Newspaper again. Full of typical schoolboy humour, but the reports were well written. There were no grammatical errors. The boy had edited the three issues himself. He's meticulous like his father. And like his father, he's gotten into trouble because of what he wrote. She frets about the caning. How will it affect him? Richard never recovered from that fiasco with the now defunct *Singapore Morning Herald*. His report had caught her attention. In clear, crisp English, he had written about a university students' group, critical of the Prime Minister and his cabinet. And he'd quoted her, and, based on something she had told him in confidence, he'd described her as one of the group's leaders. She stared at the report. There it was, her confidence purveyed and packed into a two-inch column of black print with a half-inch high headline. Below that was his byline: *I'm very sorry. Very very sorry. I had to break the news before* The Straits Times *does it.*

A single yellow rose and a box of Scottish nougat were proffered. She should have known better then. To think that her heart and forgiveness were so cheaply bought.

When the *Herald* was abruptly closed down by the government, he'd run like the rest of them to Malaysia, and then to Hong Kong before making his way back a year later after the fallout and debris had cleared, and he knew he wouldn't be detained again. Like a blind fool, she thought he had courage, and married him.

For god's sake! You're my wife! You can act for me. You're a teacher. You work only half a day. I don't have the time to meet these people.

You don't have the time or you don't have the guts?

He'd stormed out of their bedroom. He would rather pay fines, sometimes, heavy fines that they could barely afford, rather than deal with government authorities. She was the one who blundered through, argued, and fought with the Inland Revenue Authority, the Public Utilities Authority, the Housing Board Authority, the Property Tax Authority, the school authorities, the bank authorities, the hospital authorities—anyone and everyone in a position of authority. For years, she had refused to see it. Refused to see that he was cowering behind her. Perhaps *cowering* was too strong a word. But what else could she call it? Government officials unnerved him. But he wouldn't admit it. At home, he raved against the powers that be, the fools and tyrants who run this country. But put him in front of a government official, and he scraped and bowed.

Yes, yes, yes, I understand, sir. No problem, sir. Er... er ... I'll ... I'll wait. So sorry. So sorry to bother you, mister, er, mister. Sir.

She suspected that it was his brush with Internal Security that had so unnerved him. But he refused to talk about it.

You were in there two weeks. What did they do to you?

Please, Richard. You've got to talk it out.

Stop it, Joan.

He clammed up. She reckoned he was roughed up. She'd heard such stories whispered among friends. Sometimes, alone at night, she thought of him, imagining how they must've stripped him naked, made him sit on a block of ice or shone two hundred megawatt spotlights on him. Sleep deprived and stripped, he must have said or done things he was now ashamed of. For years, he'd suffered from insomnia and nightmares.

On the day of his release, his chief editor had told him to run. And so he ran. The next day, the chief editor himself was detained. The newspaper was closed down. Its publishing permit was withdrawn. Richard's parents told everyone they didn't know what their son had done, so they could not vouch for him, they said. His parents' reaction had shocked her. How could his parents wash their hands off their only son? But that was the madness of the sixties in Singapore when the air was choked with rumours of Black Ops CIA agents, and student activists as pawns of the Communist Front. Many fled the country in fear. Richard's father denounced them all, including his own son.

Why run if you've done nothing wrong? You say right or not?

But cowardice is in the Wong genes. It's in their bloody DNA. She fears her son will turn out to be like his father. Rave and rant in the safety of home. Cringe and shrink outside when authority appears. How could her son stay on in the school? He will not go against the school. He's refused to leave. Which mother wouldn't cry? She should stop it. She will call the school. Tell them she has changed her mind. She will rescind her agreement. She will withhold her consent. She will not let him become like his father.

'Mun! Where are you? Mun! Answer me! Open your door! Mun!'

* * *

1 October 2007. It's Mom's birthday. We're having dinner in a little shophouse restaurant along Upper Bukit Timah Road. Just the two of us, the way she likes it. All mothers are suckers for this mother and son thing. She's fifty-five today. So I indulge her. Call her Momsy the way I used to as a kid and make her smile.

'I felt such a failure then.'

'Don't be so melodramatic, Mom. You didn't fail.'

'What do you mean melodramatic? It was traumatic.'

'For you, Mom. You were always so worried about face.'

'Now that's not a fair statement.'

'But it's true. You made a big fuss. See, you're still thinking about it after all these years. It wasn't such a big deal. I wasn't the only one caned.'

'It was a big deal for me, son. How could I have known it wasn't a big deal for you? We never spoke about it after that. You were so moody and morose as a teenager. Remember? You stopped talking to me after that.'

The waiter brings us our food. I've ordered a white wine for us as well.

'To your health, Mom.'

A pause. Then she starts again. 'Can I ask …?'

'Must we do this? Is this your guilt or nostalgia? Oh, okay, okay.'

I give up. I relent. I haven't flown all the way back from New

York to quarrel with her on her birthday. She lives alone. Poor Mom. She's bound to think of the past. Old people do. I know her. She will ponder and fret. She will recall my silence and the long hours I spent in my room as a teenager. She will say I didn't talk to her for days, for weeks, even months. She exaggerates sometimes. She tells me that I'd locked her out of my life; that her divorce took a toll on her poor boy, and many other such things. Mothers love to talk about their children's childhood. Tonight it's the caning in school. She never forgot the caning. Still, it's her birthday today so I will indulge her.

'So what do you want to know, Mom?'

'Why didn't you talk to me about it?'

'I don't know. It really wasn't a big deal. Anyway we weren't caned in the school hall.'

'You mean Harry Koh didn't carry out his threat?'

'No. I was given two strokes in class. Rajiv and Seng Huat had one stroke each.'

'That's not fair. How come you had two?'

'I was the editor. I was the one who decided what to publish.'

'So he gave you one more stroke.'

'Something like that,' I laugh. 'Mr Koh said he had to show that he supported the teacher. Said he had to protect his staff.'

'What? Protect his staff but not his students?'

'I didn't need his protection, Mom. I could protect myself. I protected my future, didn't I? I stayed. I didn't quit.'

'Because you were afraid to change school.'

'Good grief, Mom. Did you think so little of me then?'

'No. You know I didn't mean that. I was proud of you, son. I wanted you to change school because I couldn't stand that bully of a principal.'

'I wanted to handle it myself. I didn't want to have it on my record that I'd to quit school. Like I was expelled. Besides, I reckoned that bullies die. Eventually. Like all of us. Dad said, 'All tyrants have to die some day. All that the young have to do is to stay put and wait'.'

'Did he say that?'

'He did. He even wrote about it in one of his articles. Write, he said. Write to keep the flame burning. It is Rajiv's mantra now. That guy's a bum but he's one of the best reporters in ST today.'

Mom is silent, thinking.

'Don't you see, Mom? Dad was right. Rajiv and I are still writing today. Huat's into internet publishing. Where's Mr Koh?'

Mom almost falls off her chair, laughing. 'Who was it who said, lose a battle, win a war?' she giggles. 'Oh, this is absolutely my best birthday dinner ever.'

But I take that with a pinch of salt. Mom's humour has always been a bit off tangent. She taught literature before her retirement, and her favourite Shakespearean character was the Fool in King Lear.

'So you did go and see your dad. How come I didn't know?'

'I didn't tell you.'

'Oh.'

'Another thing I didn't tell you. Mr Koh coached me in maths for my 'O' Level.'

'And you didn't you tell me that either?'

She wanted to know everything in those days. But she could only guess at what her son must have gone through during those difficult years. An only child torn between his parents. Was it her fault that he'd hidden from her his visits and consultations with his father and others? Was she too clingy? Too possessive? A divorced parent clinging to her child, afraid of losing him? I can see these thoughts racing through my mother's brain. To distract her I tell her about Dad.

'Dad said happy birthday to you. I spoke with him this morning.'

'How's he?'

'He's recovering from his op. He wants to continue his freelance writing. And he's learning to blog, he says.'

'Hmmm. Good for him. Did you tell him about Susannah?'

'Not yet. You're the first to know that your son's getting married.'

Mom's eyes light up at this. Although she will never admit it, she wants to come first in her son's life.

'I'm proud of you, son.'

'And I'm proud of you, Mom.'

THE TRAGEDY OF

MY THIRD EYE

My third eye popped open when Linda's father spat on me and robbed me of my childhood forever. That little tyrant lorded over us in Primary 1A because she could speak English so well. Standing in front of us, her proud little face tilted upwards, she tossed her curls, gave our teacher a sweet smile and recited, 'Humpty Dumpty sat on the wall ...'

Her voice, clear as a bell, held me spellbound as I sat in the back row of the class, my mouth a little open. Like the other little girls, I yearned to be like her. I, who couldn't speak a word of English, hoped some day to also be touched by magic and recite 'Humpty Dumpty' and a host of other nursery rhymes in English.

'Doesn't Linda sound just like little Alice in "Alice and the Toy Soldier"?' Miss Wang purred.

I looked at the floor and kept my eyes down. After the first few weeks of primary school, I quickly learnt never to look up when a teacher was talking. That was one sure way of avoiding punishment. If I had looked up, Miss Wang would have caught my eye and asked me a question. Then I would have been unable to answer her, and so she would have had to punish me. I couldn't say any of the English words which seemed to flow out of Linda like water from a tap. When Miss Wang pointed to the letters of the alphabet—say, the letter A—an entire repertoire of English sounds whooshed out of my head. How do I say it? Air? Aye? Arr? What?

Miss Wang waited and coaxed. Then she tapped her ruler and pointed to the little black squiggle on the chart.

'Come on. Say it. What is it? How does it sound?'

But my mouth refused to open. I looked down at my feet.

'Come on. Try. We don't have all day.'

And still no word came. My head was a dark emptiness even though the sun was shining outside the window. I shut my eyes. I didn't want my tears to seep out.

'Who can tell Ping-Ping what this word is?'

I remained standing for the rest of the reading period.

I hated school. It had turned me into a dumb mute. Except during recess. And I couldn't read. I couldn't sing. I couldn't spell, couldn't count and, worst of all, I couldn't recite those blasted English nursery rhymes which Miss Wang inflicted upon us each morning.

I wanted to run away. The grown-ups had cheated me. Mother had lied when she said school would make me clever. School made me stupid. I was a clever girl before I came to school. Grandma had said I was smart. My teacher in the Chinese kindergarten had also said I was smart. Why did Mother send me to a place where I became stupid? I asked myself this question each night when I lay in bed alone after Mother had locked me up in our bedroom. Am I clever only when I'm with Grandma and stupid when I'm not with her? Did Grandma lie? Did she cast a spell on me as

Mother claimed?

I could recite my *Three Character Classic* primer from page one to the last page, in Cantonese, without once looking at the book. I could sing arias from *The Patriotic Princess*, *Hua Mulan* and *Madam White Snake*. Everyone listened to me in Grandma's house when I sang. I could tell Auntie Jen what to do when I waved my sword and threatened to chop off her head. Grandma called me her clever little princess. But in Primary 1A of the Convent of the Holy Infant Jesus, Miss Wang called me 'stupido'. I brushed off my tears. I would not cry. I would fight. Princesses are brave and smart like Princess Chang Ping.

That night I shut my eyes tightly against the darkness and reached out to grasp the magic of the universe, like the Monkey King who journeyed with Tripitaka, the holy monk, in *Journey to the West*. He was the greatest fairy spirit, that Monkey King. He could change himself into anything and change his voice to speak any language. I prayed that I could change my voice from a Chinese voice to an English one.

'Pay attention in class. Learn to speak like Linda,' Miss Wang said.

Silly cow. How could we? Oops! Who was that? Who said silly cow inside my head? I quickly stopped the smile from spreading across my face and bent down, pretending to tie my shoelaces. Was that the Monkey King spirit in me?

My eyes followed Miss Wang all day. I saw how she asked Linda to answer questions or recite poems in class. Not only could Linda Tan recite English nursery rhymes, she could even sing English songs like *Down By the Station*. Miss Wang loved her. I knew that because I counted that she smiled at Linda more than ten times yesterday. She said, 'Thank you, Linda, that was very nice.' To the rest of us she yelled, 'Who's talking? If I catch anyone talking again, I'll send her out of the class!'

When Miss Wang was not in class, Linda took out her little blue book and pencil. She wrote our names in the book if we didn't listen to her. Then she would show it to Miss Wang and we would be punished. Because of this, everyone wanted to be Linda's friend—everyone wanted to be part of her gang.

Well, maybe not everyone, which was why, one day during recess, her minions made us stand in a line in front of their princess in class.

'We're playing slave and enemy. This big finger is for slave. This little finger is for enemy. Choose. Which finger?' Her Royal Highness looked at us.

We looked at one another. No one spoke. We waited to see who would have to choose first. Mugface, the biggest and ugliest girl in class and Linda's most devoted slave, singled out May Yin, my best friend.

'Touch this finger and you'll be Linda's slave. Touch this little finger and you'll be our enemy. Understand or not?' Mugface demanded.

I understood the words 'slave' and 'enemy'. Sister Josephine had told us stories about slaves in the Bible, like that slave, Daniel, who was thrown into the lion's den but the lion didn't eat him because, like the song said,

'He had faith in all good men,
and for that faith, he was willing to die.'

I didn't know what the words meant, but I could remember the music and the song, and I knew what a slave was. But why do I have to be a slave or an enemy? Why can't we be friends? I wanted to ask Linda but I didn't have the English words then and she couldn't understand my Cantonese.

'Which finger? Quick, choose, lah!'

May Yin looked as if she was going to cry.

'Choose!' Mugface barked at her.

Linda stood like a stone princess, with her two fingers pointed at my best friend's throat. Instinctively May Yin's hands were clasped in front of her chest. Her face was flushed.

'Quick, lah! Choose!'

Like the tongue of a snake, May Yin's finger darted out. It flicked Linda's forefinger and retreated. Desperately I tried to catch her eye, but May Yin refused to look at me.

'One slave!' Linda sang and moved on to the next girl.

'Two slaves!' she sang.

'Three slaves!' Mugface and the others added.

'Four slaves!'

And it went on. I began to edge away. Please Monkey King, please make the bell ring. Please, please, please, make recess over soon. My heart was pounding so fast that I almost couldn't breathe, but I dared not move away any further. Mugface had seen me. She walked to the door and stood at the doorway of the classroom. I looked out, hoping that a teacher would walk past, but no one did.

'Your turn.' One of Linda's slaves poked me in the ribs. Except for May Yin, who looked downcast and forlorn in the corner, the rest of the slaves were eager for me to join them. 'Your turn, Ping-Ping! Choose, choose!'

Linda stuck out her two fingers. 'Which one?'

I gazed at her two daggers.

'Quick, this one or this one?'

'If I be your slave then what?'

'Stupido, you didn't hear what I said? You go and line up and buy food for me during recess. Then you obey me and do what I tell you.'

The girls pressed forward.

'Quick! Choose!'

The gang closed in.

'Big or small finger?'

'Quick, lah! Choose!'

Linda glared at me. 'Choose!'

My little finger touched her little one.

The girls gasped.

The bell rang.

No one spoke to me after recess. May Yin, who sat next to me, was dumb. I knew we were being watched. I nudged May Yin. I played tap with my pencil when the teacher was not looking. I drew a funny face on a piece of paper and pushed it across my desk to May Yin. But she didn't even dare to look at it. After school, no one spoke to me.

I tried to catch a cold or fever the next day, but nothing happened, even though I had covered myself from head to toe with a blanket. I dared not tell Mother. I was afraid she might cane me.

The next day it was a little better. May Yin and I drew pictures and exchanged drawings under our desks. Linda had ordered everyone not to talk to me, so I was glad when we had to recite our nursery rhymes. That was the only time I could open my mouth and say something.

On the third day I couldn't bear it any longer. I ran off to play with the Indian girls. They were lucky. The two Indian girls in our class were not included in Linda's game because she didn't like them. They could speak English better than her, even though they didn't know how to sing English pop songs. Satvindar Kaur became my best friend. Together with that other girl, Param, we went out to the saga trees during recess to collect red saga seeds to play *kuti kuti*, and the wonderful thing was that Satvindar and Param talked to me in class.

They weren't bothered by what Linda said or what Linda did. Not even when Linda glared at them. When she saw us together, Linda's eyes grew dark. All day long her eyes followed us and got darker and angrier whenever she looked in my direction. Several times during the day, she shot poisonous darts at me. 'Don't look!' She even scolded those who looked at me. The Chinese girls in class, even my former best friend, pretended I wasn't there.

But I don't care! I don't care! My little heart sang. Playing *kuti kuti* during recess was so much better than queuing up to buy noodles for Linda Tan, or running back and forth to fetch things for her, or playing only those games that she wanted to play.

I might be only six and a half, and a 'stupido' in Primary 1A, but I would rather be an outcast than a slave.

Linda and I lived in the same neighbourhood, down the same row of town houses and dilapidated shop houses. Each evening our trishaws dropped us at the top of the lane, and we would walk home from there. One evening I was trailing Linda and her minions. They were giggling and glancing back at me every now and then, talking loudly about lice and cow dung. I pretended I couldn't hear them. They walked, four abreast, blocking my way whenever I tried to walk past them and move ahead.

'Something white is crawling in her hair.'

'And she smells!'

They giggled and held their noses.

'Ooh! She smells!'

I ignored them. We were approaching Linda's house. Their laughter grew louder. I saw Linda's father, a spindly man in a white shirt and striped pyjama bottoms, emerge from their house and stand in the middle of the pavement, waiting for her. Linda ran up to him. As he bent down to take her school bag, she whispered something in his ear.

He looked up and fixed his stern eyes on me.

Just as I was walking past him on the pavement, he spat.

'Pui! You! So proud for what? Why don't you friend my daughter?' he hissed in Hokkien. 'You know what kind of woman your mother is?'

I could only gaze at the dark patch on my convent blue uniform where his spittle had landed.

Out! Out! Out!

I scrubbed my thigh till the flesh was red and raw, but the spot where his spit had soaked through my school uniform and touched my flesh was still burning. I scrubbed harder and harder. In desperation I applied more soap, turned on the hose and pointed it at the contaminated spot. Little rivulets of red ran down my leg where my brush had broken the skin. Soon my socks and shoes were soaked and streaked pink. But I didn't care. His question was jangling inside my head. My ears were burning. I could feel that they had turned red and raw like the spot on my thigh.

I hated Linda's father, but I hated my mother even more. What kind of a woman was she to invite such comments from a man like Linda's father?

She became my mother just two months ago! It was she who had yanked me away from my grandma, the one and only person who loved me the most in the whole wide world! Before that she had always been Ah Koo, my aunt. Now she was my mother, but inside my six-year-old heart she was still the woman who'd forced me to live with her. Wicked witch! I vowed never ever to love her. Only my grandma was worthy of my love.

'Nooo! I don't want to go! I don't want to live with Ah Koo!'

'Mama. Call me Mama.'

'You're not my mama!'

She pushed me into the room and locked the door. I banged on it till she came in and caned me without mercy. She stopped only when I stopped yelling.

I never cried again, at least not when she could hear me or see me.

She made me empty the chamber pot every morning. I had to be careful not to spill any of the urine in it when I took it out to the communal toilet down the corridor of Kim Poh's tenement house. If she were really my mama, she'd be like Janet and John's mummy in my English storybook. Janet and John's mummy baked cakes for them, kissed them goodbye and good night and tucked them into bed. In the morning she helped them to put on their coats and took them to the baker's, the grocer's and the music school where John played the violin and Janet played the piano.

Mother never did any of these things. She slept till noon and was never awake when I got up to go to school. Every morning I could hear Mrs Lee in the room across the common passageway. I could hear the murmur of her children's excited voices as she made breakfast for them while in my room, dimly lit by a small bedside lamp, I climbed onto a chair to reach for the hot-water flask. I brought it down from the shelf and made myself a cup of Ovaltine, which I drank with a biscuit for company. After breakfast I took our chamber pot to the communal toilet, a hut, away from the main house where we lived. No one ever dared to go to the toilet in the middle of the night because a ghost lived there. After I had cleaned the chamber pot, I brushed my teeth in the communal bathroom before returning to our bedroom to dress for school. All these things I had to do as quietly as possible so as not to awaken the sleeping dragon, and every morning when I drank my Ovaltine, tears would inevitably fall because I missed my grandma so very very much.

'Ping! What *are* you doing? Turn off the tap! NOW! Are you stupid or what? Look at you! Dripping wet! Strip off that uniform!'

The urchins flew into the communal kitchen like flies to a dead cat. Watching other children being scolded or whacked was great entertainment in this house of a thousand lodgers. All the urchins loved it, which was why I despised them. I despised them all.

'What were you doing? Tell me! Did you fall down at school?'

When I remained silent, Mother yanked the blue pinafore over my head and unbuttoned my white blouse. She left me standing in my white panties. The hooligans hooted. 'Naked!'

'What's there to laugh about? Go away!' Mother yelled at them.

They fled, screaming, 'Naked! Ping's naked! Naked!'

At that moment I hated Mother more than I detested the hooligans.

'Take off your socks and shoes! Hurry!'

I pulled them off.

'Into the bathroom! Now!'

I went inside and closed the door, trembling in the dark. The sun had set by now. It was dark inside the bath hut, and I dared not open my eyes. What if they met the red eyes of the goblins which lived inside the water jar?

'Ping!'

I jumped. The light came on. I opened my eyes. A naked bulb was hanging from the ceiling. I could see the tiny strands of cobwebs clinging to it, but where were the spiders? I couldn't see any spiders.

'What are you gaping at?'

She threw a bucket of cold water over me. I gasped. I took off my panties.

'Soap.'

I scrubbed that spot again, and it started to bleed again.

'Did you fall at school? How many times do I have to tell you not to climb those rails at school, eh? Did you climb? Did you? Answer me.'

When I chose silence, she turned on the tap full blast and flung jugs of water at me. The water was cold. My teeth started to chatter. She rubbed me down with a large towel. Her hands with red painted fingernails went up and down my stiff little body.

Angry hands. Hands waiting for a chance to slap me if I were to answer back.

'Run to our room and stay there till I call you for dinner.'

Wrapped in a white towel, I raced down the corridor, past the hooting hooligans, stumbled against the stools they kicked into my path, then ran past the other rooms with their gaping lodgers till I plunged into the safety of our bedroom and shut the door. I was lying in bed in my pyjamas with my face to the wall when Mother came in.

'Get up and have your dinner. Now!'

Our dining table was outside our rented room, next to the cupboard which Mother used for storing her groceries. In Kim Poh's lodging house, all lodgers had to eat either in their rooms or in the common passageway. Mother's room was on the ground floor of the two-storey bungalow. Mrs Lee's room was opposite ours, and our dining tables were in the corridor.

'Ping! Don't just sit there! Eat! Must I feed you too? Look at her, Mrs Lee, just look at her. Food is on the table right in front of her and she just sits there waiting for me. Six years old coming to seven and she doesn't know how to feed herself! I look around at other people's children her age. Like your children. They're minding their baby brothers and sisters already. Look at Ah Peck. Same age as this one here but your daughter knows how to cook rice over a charcoal fire already. Not this one. Not that I expect her to cook. Oh no! I'm lucky if she can eat on her own. Every evening she sits and waits to be served. Like a helpless little princess! If this is how her grandma has brought her up, she hasn't done me any favours. That old witch can say what she likes but this wasn't how she brought me up.'

Mrs Lee shook a finger at me.

'Ping, you'd better be good, eh!'

Mother pushed a bowl of soup and a plate of rice under my nose. Then she chose the choicest part of the steamed fish and put it on my rice, together with some vegetables and a large piece of pork.

'Eat,' she ordered.

I cringed. My stomach had shrunk as though it had been tied and knotted up. There was no room for food. To appease Mother I spooned out some rice and put it in my mouth, hoping that she wouldn't notice that I had lost my appetite. The spot I had rubbed clean of spit still hurt. Mother had forgotten to give me any ointment for it. My left hand moved stealthily under the table, feeling for the spot on my thigh. That part of my pyjama bottoms felt damp, so I knew it was still bleeding.

'Look at her. Just look at her, Mrs Lee! A few grains of rice at a time, chewing like a toothless old woman! Eat the fish, ingrate!'

I crammed some fish into my mouth at once, trying to swallow as fast as I could. My throat was as dry as sand. I was afraid that I'd throw up again. If that happened, I would be caned. My stomach felt bloated and full, but Mother would never believe me if I told her. She always wanted me to eat more and more and more because she was fed up with Grandma always telling her that I was too skinny. 'What? Does she think she's the only one who can feed you? Am I so useless that I don't even know how to feed my daughter?' I dreaded meal times more than any other time with Mother. Every mouthful I ate was an acceptance of her and every grain of rice left on my plate was a rejection of her. I couldn't bear it. I just couldn't eat.

This evening, however, I had to try. Mother had been attacked and, even though I hated her with all my heart for yanking me away from Grandma, I still had to protect her against that spindly spider who had spat on me. I gazed at the scoop of white rice before me. Mother was watching to see what I would do. The hump was growing bigger and bigger, and higher and higher. First it was a mound, then a dune and still it grew. Even as I spooned bit by difficult bit and crammed it into my mouth, the hill of white grains still grew till I couldn't stuff any more rice into my mouth.

'Eat!'

I shoved another spoonful into my mouth. Grandma. I wanted my grandma.

'What are you crying for? I'm not dead yet. Stop it!'

Mother's eyes were like burning red-hot coals.

'Drink up!'

I forced myself to drink a spoonful of soup.

'Eat your fish! Now!'

Across the aisle Mrs Lee placed a big pot of rice and a big pot of soup on the table. Her five children pulled up their stools and held up their bowls. She ladled two large scoops of rice into each child's bowl, followed by a ladle of soup.

'More, Ma! More soup!'

'Finish what you have first.'

Mrs Lee waved away her pesky urchins, three boys and two girls. The baby was sleeping inside their room, otherwise one of the girls would be cradling him in one arm and eating with the other. The children wolfed down their rice, working their chopsticks at a furious pace, pushing the white grains into wide open mouths, slurping up their noodle soup noisily. I envied their hunger. They looked so happy.

I tried to smile at Mother but she barked, 'Swallow what's in your mouth. Eat your fish even if you can't finish your rice.'

I swallowed hard. I was afraid the lump in my mouth might choke me as it had done the night before.

'Is there a bone stuck in your throat?'

I shook my head vigorously.

'Mrs Lee! How I wish I'd no eyes to see her! I just can't stand the way she scoops up her fish. Little bit, little bit at a time! You think the fish will bite you, is it?' she screamed at me. 'If you think you're doing me a great favour by eating, don't eat! Starve!' Mother turned to Mrs Lee again. 'I know she's doing this deliberately to anger me!'

'Aiyah, Ah Lien! Children are like this. You don't care, they'll eat. You scold, they don't eat. Look at my brood. They know if they don't eat now, tonight, there'll be no more food.'

'I know, Mrs Lee, I'm impatient. She's the death of me. Am I going to let this six-year-old lump control me? I could've just left her with her wretched grandmother. Let her be brought up a prostitute like my sister. But my heart wouldn't let me do it.'

'Then blame your heart,' Mrs Lee laughed.

'Aye, I blame my heart.'

'Aiyah, Ah Lien, a few nights of going to bed hungry will cure her.'

Mother got up. She reached for the plates of fish and vegetables.

'Then I hope you don't mind leftovers. Your children can have these since this one here doesn't want them.'

'Thank you so much, thank you!'

'Ma, give me some fish, I want some!'

Her three boys plunged their chopsticks into my fish.

'Hey, no manners, ah! Say thank you to Auntie Ah Lien first!'

'Thank you, Auntie Ah Lien!'

I kept my eyes on my plate, pretending to be oblivious to the noise and laughter at the next table. I was hoping that Mother would leave me alone now. She cleared the table except for the hillock of rice still in front of me.

'Eat up!'

I was about to put some rice into my mouth when she grabbed my hand and took away my spoon.

'Open your mouth,' she hissed and shoved a spoonful of fish and rice into it. 'Now chew quickly. And don't you dare cry.'

She was staring at my lips which were threatening to tremble. I bit hard and tasted blood.

'Open your mouth! Now!'

She shoved another mouthful of fish and rice into me.

'Chew and swallow quickly!'

I thought I was going to faint. She grabbed my shoulders and shook me.

'Don't shut your eyes. Swallow your food.'

I swallowed but the lump was as hard and dry as stone.

'Drink some soup.'

She pushed the bowl towards me.

'Drink up!'

She held the bowl to my mouth.

'Open up! Wider! No! Wider! Now drink.'

I coughed and gasped for air. Warm soup splashed on my arm. Mother pushed me away from her.

'Don't you dare puke on me! Go to the bathroom, you little devil! I feel like smacking her hard, Mrs Lee! Just to wake her up!'

In the bathroom I splashed cold water on my face and tried to clean up my pyjamas as best as I could.

'You're not going to bed in those filthy pyjamas. Go and change!'

I looked at the time. Half past seven.

'Hurry! Get into bed.'

The phone in the hallway rang.

'Ah Lien! For you! It's the millionaire!'

'Coming!'

Mother's sweet dulcet voice floated up the stairs and down the passageway where Mrs Lee was helping me to mop up the spilt soup.

'Hm, darling, don't be like that! Just half an hour more, then I'll be with you. Give me half an hour. I'll be dressed and ready.'

CHRISTMAS MEMORIES OF A CHINESE STEPFATHER

For Seb & Ben

Not easy running a small real estate company in the outback of Hougang. But I survive. I was minding my own business that Saturday afternoon, Christmas Eve, when Alice George walked right into me on the stairs.

'Whoa!'

'Sorry! Sorry! Are you Mr Bob Lim?'

'Ya. You looking for a flat?'

'No, no! My father! He's in hospital. I'm Alice George, his daughter.'

'Mr George. How's he?'

Tears gushing, this Alice woman wailed, 'He's dying! My father! He's dying!'

Whát to do? I couldn't let her cry on the stairs.

'Please, please, come inside my office and talk.'

'Seb! Ben!'

That was when I noticed her two boys at the foot of the stairs.

'My sons. Sebastian! Benedict! Come up here! Say hello to Uncle Bob!'

She thrust her father's brown briefcase into my arms. 'Here.

Take them. All his clients' files and documents. He can't ...' She started to cry again.

'Please sit down. Er ... How old are your boys?'

'Seb's six. Ben's four.'

'Here, boys.' I handed Seb the bottle of fish food on my desk. 'Go feed the fish in the tank over there.'

The poor little buggers looked stunned. Like *kenna* bonked on the head. Their mother was sniffling and her eyes were red. All that crying and sobbing didn't make her look attractive, although I did notice her skin was a nice honey brown. Not dark like Mr George.

'Sorry, Mr Lim. I didn't mean to burden you with my problems.'

'Please call me Bob.'

She updated me on her father's illness and the progress of various pending sales. Her father was one of my housing agents.

'Very hardworking,' I told Alice.

'A workaholic. Work, work, work. He doesn't know when to stop. Everything's in his file. That Bedok North apartment. The owner is ready to bite—will sell for twenty grand less but wants some cash immediately. I can arrange that. I know the buyer. I recommended him to my dad before ... before ...' She was crying again.

I placed a box of tissues in front of her. How come women can cry so much?

She sobbed her way through half the box. Luckily the other agents were not in. She said she was tearing her hair out running between home, hospital and the Housing Board office.

'Got to close two sales. I need the commission, Mr Lim.'

'Call me Bob, please.'

'Thank you, Bob. My dad, he's got no savings.'

'Your mother?'

'My mum passed away. No, don't be sorry. I'm not sorry she went. Swear! I'm not sorry. She made his life hell. Wasted my dad's money. Gambled left, right and centre! I don't mind telling you. Gambling. She was addicted to gambling. Borrowed here, borrowed there. Our relatives avoided her like the plague. Treated her like a pariah. Can't blame them. My dad got to pay off the loan sharks who hounded us day and night. When she died, he was finally free. It's not fair. Not fair. God's not fair! She died last year. Now he's free. Free to do what he likes, and what did he get? Cancer! His liver and stomach. And he doesn't drink, doesn't even smoke! Three months! The doctor said three months! It's not bloody fair! Why only three months? My dad's a good man! O Mother of God!'

Once she'd started, she couldn't stop. All that afternoon she talked and cried over the injustice of life. She had moved back to live with her father. Had been helping him with the paperwork for the housing loans, transfer of ownership and such things.

'I've got to work harder now. Earn more. Help him out. Look after my two boys. But ... but how?' she wailed.

The two boys moved away from the fish tank. They stood beside their weeping mother. They looked at me. Yeah, like I could help. Seb, the older boy, was holding the hand of the younger one who started to suck his thumb.

'Don't!' Seb struck his little brother's hand.

'Mummy!'

'He was sucking his thumb, Mummy!'

'Stop it! Stop fighting you two! You're driving me crazy! I've got to clear Grandpa's desk. You hear me? Stop crying!'

She slapped the younger boy. He was just a chubby brown doughnut. So I scooped him into my arms.

'I'll take your boys downstairs for ice cream. Go ahead. Clear your father's desk.'

She didn't exactly ask me for her father's job, but in the end that was what I offered her. After all, as I tried to explain to Ma, 'She did do all her father's paperwork. She knows how to do the work. It's not like she faked it.'

Maybe I did it for her two boys. 'Their father's Chinese,' Alice said.

The poor mixed-up buggers. Lost their father. Now they were about to lose their grandpa. I didn't tell Ma, but those two doughnuts reminded me of Kit and I when our father left us. Overnight Ma turned into a raving mad woman.

'His heart is made of stone! Left us for his witch! If a car knocks him dead this very minute, not one tear will I shed! Merciful Kuan Yin, forgive me! You two! Grow up. Study hard. Work hard. You hear me? Don't depend on others! Never depend on others! Like that cad, your father!'

It was just before Christmas. My father didn't come home that year, or since. I was eight and Kit was six. The first time that our father was not around on Christmas Day. We're not Christians but we always celebrate Christmas Day. So Ma took us to visit her relatives. Some of them are Christians. We had to sit up straight. She made us wear white long-sleeved shirts, thick brown trousers, thick white socks and black leather shoes. Very painful. Very hot and stuffy. We couldn't move, couldn't run around, couldn't talk.

We sat like statues because Ma didn't want us to mess up our clothes and shame her in front of our relatives.

'Your father left us. So behave!'

We had to behave better than our cousins.

'Your cousins have fathers to teach them! Yours ran off to his witch!'

That was what she said. Over and over again throughout our years growing up, I could never see the logic of it. She caned us harder and more often. As if we were the ones to blame. I ended up hating her instead of Father. These days she no longer raves against the old man.

'What for? Dead or alive he's not my business any more. If he ends up begging in the streets, that's his fate! Brought it on himself. To tell the truth if I bump into him today, I won't recognise him. Who knows what he looks like now? But,' she dropped her voice, 'some people say he's gone to work in Batam. Maybe Bintan. His witch threw him out. No money. So she threw him out. Don't know if that's true. I pray that my sons will not be like him. I pray you and Kit will marry good wives.'

I kept my silence. I didn't tell her about Alice. I'd been going to the hospital to see Mr George. When Mr George passed away, I was beside Alice. Hours later Alice ran around like a headless chicken, arranging for the funeral, the cremation and calling all her relatives. Dishevelled and red-eyed, she yelled at her boys.

'You don't have to do everything,' I tried to tell her.

'But I've got to! My brother and his wife are paying for everything. They have money. They give money. I've no money so I've to give my labour. It's only fair!'

She was big on fairness, Alice. Her boys were left in my care.

'I must go and see the pastor. Phone the caterer. Order food for the mourners.'

Her family were Christians with their own customs and rituals. I took the two boys to my office. My colleagues—you know these jokers in the office—they started to kid me about being the boys' godfather.

'Uncle Bob, can you be my father?' Little Ben pulled my hand.

The whole office roared! 'Oi! You heard that or not? Call him Daddy! Or Papa!'

When word got back to Alice, she cuffed Ben's ears and apologised for putting me in a spot.

'Nah! He misses his father.'

At this, Alice started to cry. I held her tight, her breasts heaving against my chest. What else could I do? It was the same old story. Her guy had left her and the children for another woman. The divorce was followed by a bruising custody battle. Ben went to Alice and poor Seb had to live with his father and stepmother.

'But the stepmother hit him black and blue,' Alice sobbed. 'My son's body was covered with cane marks all over the place. Can you imagine how I felt when I saw him? That woman is a bloody racist. Called my son a dirty Indian. My son's half Chinese! She bloody well knows that her husband is Seb's father! So I didn't care! If I've to fight, I fight! I went back to court with a social worker and wrested Seb back from his father. He can't even protect his own son! His wife's a racist!'

'Sh! Hush!' I tried to calm her down.

'It's true! I'm not making this up. You Chinese are so bloody racist!'

I kissed her burning lips. Her back was stiff like a cat about to fight, and then suddenly she put her head on my shoulders and just cried. I kissed her again and again.

'Not all Chinese are racists.' She was smiling and crying at the same time but she let me kiss her again.

Her boys hungered for my attention. Every time I visited them they wanted to do things for me. Very eager to serve and please me. Too eager sometimes. Especially Seb, who polished my shoes and sharpened my pencils. The poor kid was starved of attention from a father. Ben clung to my hand. Just held my hand the whole time I was there. Never saying a word. The little fella just held my hand. He followed me everywhere. I told myself: never walk out on your wife and children if you marry. I knew what it was like to have your old man leave you. But, I told Alice, not all men are cads. Some of us are quite decent. I didn't know if she believed me or what, but six months after her father's death I was practically living in her flat. I took all my meals with her and the boys.

Her aunts and uncles didn't approve. In their eyes I was another bloody Chinese man and a non-Christian. A heathen with no faith, no God. Why was she making the same mistake again? her aunts and uncles asked her. Their large extended family— the Georges, the Jacobs and the Solomons—were staunch Tamil Christians in the Methodist Church. Their great grandparents were from Kerala in South India. Alice's cousins were teachers, professors and civil servants.

'My uncles don't think much of housing agents, insurance agents and car salesmen. They look down on my family. So I don't go near them.'

I knew exactly what she meant. These professional types with their fancy titles and university degrees. I only completed secondary school myself, but I could speak better English than some of them. I made sure I didn't speak Singlish with my clients. No hor, lor, walau and sibeh hor like the other housing agents. During my national service days I listened to the BBC on my radio and I learned.

'The world's my university,' I told Seb and Ben.

Their big dark eyes looked up. 'Dad!'

Wah! The first time they said it my heart felt like it wanted to burst. It sounded strange—Dad. Like something I'd heard long ago and forgotten. That was what Kit and I had called our father. I wondered where my old man had gone. He'd dropped out of our lives. Which hole did he fall into? Was he dead in some foreign country? But I didn't waste too much time thinking of the past. I had a future now and a headache—Ma.

'So you approve?' I had asked her before I married Alice.

'What's there to approve or disapprove? Son's grown up. It's the son's world, as the saying goes. Not my world.' Her Hokkien speech was tart and sharp.

'Ma, you don't mind that Alice is not Chinese?'

'You think I'm so narrow-minded, is it? Chinese or not Chinese, the same to me!'

'And she has two sons like you, Ma.'

'She is not like me!'

'I didn't mean like you exactly. She has two boys. And I ... er ... I thought we could live together. That is if you don't mind.' I held my breath.

'This is your home. Your flat. You can do what you like. If necessary, I can move out with Kit and they can move in.'

'Ma, it's not necessary. Alice and I will apply to buy a bigger flat for all of us. Kit included. But she's got to sell off her father's flat first to settle his medical bills before she can apply with me. Housing Board regulations. I can't explain everything to you. It's very complicated.'

'She's divorced, isn't she?'

'Yes, Ma.'

'As long as you don't mind ...'

'No, Ma, I don't mind. But I'm asking you if you'll let her and the two boys move in here first while we wait for our flat to be ready.'

'Why ask me? This is your apartment. As long as you people don't mind my altar and my gods. Did you tell her? I chant when I pray. I'm your ma. I can change everything for your sake, but my gods, I cannot change.'

The next day Ma surprised me. Actually she shocked me. She moved out of the master bedroom and moved into Kit's bedroom.

'What happened? Why are you sharing Kit's room?'

'I used my head. If I don't move out of the master bedroom, where are you and Alice going to sleep? You're going to marry her, right or not? You will need the master bedroom. There are only three bedrooms here. The two boys and the maid will sleep in one room. Kit has the other bedroom. Where am I going to sleep? In the kitchen, ah?'

'Ma, we've changed plans. We can live in Alice's three-room flat until she sells it. The flat is also her brother's flat so we must sell.'

'But I've already moved out of the master bedroom for you. Isn't this enough? You still want to move out?'

What could I do? Move out and break Ma's heart?

Luckily Alice didn't make a fuss. We didn't have the traditional rowdy costly Chinese wedding dinner. 'Better to save the money to buy a bigger flat,' I said. An executive flat with three bedrooms and a utility room that could be converted into another bedroom. All of us under one roof. That was my dream.

Six months later Alice and I went to the lawyer's office. Her ex-husband had agreed to sign the papers to give up his rights to the boys. He already had two children with his new wife. So the boys became Sebastian Lim and Benedict Lim. They called me Dad and called Ma, Nai-nai, the Mandarin term for granny.

'Nai-nai, eat.' Seb had learnt to speak a little Hokkien by then.

'Nai-nai, eat,' Ben followed.

Then the little *won ton* meatball jumped onto my lap.

'Oi! Let your father eat in peace!' Ma yelled at him.

Ben made a face but he slipped off my lap and sat on the chair next to me.

'Eat up, Ben. Eat, Seb. Eat as much as you want both of you so you won't act like hungry wolves afterwards,' Ma said.

She scooped two large pieces of stewed pork into the boys' bowls. Using her chopsticks, she picked up two large fried prawns and put them on a side plate for each boy.

'Eat now. Eat all you want so you don't have to dig into my biscuit tins looking for something to eat later. They're always so hungry. Don't know why!'

'Boys, say thank you to Nai-nai.' Alice's frown had come on. A bad sign.

'Thank you, Nai-nai!'

'Now say sorry to Nai-nai. How many times have I told you

not to be greedy little pigs? Say sorry! Why didn't you eat the biscuits in our room? How many times do I have to tell you not to touch Nai-nai's things in the kitchen? How dare you disobey me!'

'I didn't, Mummy! Seb did it!'

Alice slapped Ben who was nearer to her than Seb. The boy bawled holding his cheek. She slapped him again.

'Stop it! Stop crying!'

'For god's sake, it's Christmas Eve, Alice!' I yelled.

'Why don't you tell that to your mother? She hates my boys!'

'No, Alice, Mother was trying to teach them manners.'

'Oi! You two. Mother, mother! I might not understand English but I know you people are talking about me! What's that woman of yours saying?' Ma asked in her crisp sharp Hokkien voice. Of course that made it worse.

I don't know what else went wrong after that. One thing after the other. Small, small things. Just doing the laundry could lead to a big argument. Why are women like this? Alice said I was blind. Said that Ma was coming between us.

'How?'

'Use your eyes! Look! See for yourself.'

I did look, but I didn't see anything terrible. Maybe Ma was a little too strict. Like she wouldn't let Ben sit on my lap.

'Big boy already! Sit on your own chair!'

'It's just her way. She was like this with Kit and me too.' I tried to tell Alice.

But she took it hard. And sometimes Ma complained a little too much.

'Like monkeys, those two! Jump here. Jump there. No stop! Whatever they like, they eee-eat! Then at dinnertime, full already.

Can't eat. Then their mother gets angry. Scolds the maid for letting them eat too much. She dares not scold me! So she scolds the maid. Scolding the maid is for my ears.'

'What did Alice say?' I was exasperated.

'How do I know? I don't know what she says to the maid! All this *fee-lee-fee-leh* in English! One Indian, one Filipina! How do I know what they say in this house? This house is not my home any more. These days the maid doesn't listen to me any more! Her boys have no respect for me! They call me Nai-nai. What for? They've no respect for me. They eat what they want! I can't do anything. Cane them? Not my own grandchildren. I dare not touch them in case people say I abuse their children, then how?' Ma looked at me.

I walked away. I was tired.

'The older one tells lies. That Seb is a snake. Can tell a lie without blinking his eyes. And the younger one just eats like a dustbin with no bottom. He gobbled up a whole tin of my biscuits in two days! Didn't ask me. Didn't say a word to me. I opened the tin. Aiyoh! Not one biscuit left. It's not that I begrudge them the biscuits. But ask me. If you say I'm their granny, ask them to show me some respect! Ask permission.'

'Ma, the boys don't speak Hokkien that well. They're scared of you.'

'Scared of me? Where are your eyes? You turn your back and the boys are rude to me. They behave in front of you. Every afternoon they watch tv. Never do their school work. What do you and your wife know? You're both at work. And the maid doesn't tell you the truth!'

I checked Seb's schoolbag and books. There was a letter from his teacher. He hadn't handed in his homework for a week. I whacked him hard and proper.

'Good! Whack him harder! Harder! Show your mother you know how to discipline them!' Alice shouted from our bedroom. She had a soft spot for her elder boy; some sort of guilt like she'd let him down, blaming herself for what had happened to Seb in his father's house. 'Kill him! Why don't you kill him? After all he's only half Chinese!'

I felt guilty like hell. Maybe I would've acted differently if they were my flesh and blood, Alice said. That shook me up. Seb was just eight and in Primary Two, but already he'd learnt to hide things from us. I talked to him and explained why he must not lie. I promised myself that I wouldn't whack the boy again.

But when Ben was six he stole a classmate's pen. He'd lost his own pen in a betting game. I hit the roof. Betting at his age! I whacked him hard and proper too. Alice wailed. She wanted to move out that very night. I handed her the cane, left the flat, got into the car and went for a long drive. Had I become an abusive father? Then I wondered if the boys had inherited bad genes. Their genes were not mine. Maybe I'd made a mistake. Their grandmother was a gambler. Poor buggers. Their own father had given them up. They needed a father but they only had me. I wished I'd done better.

Two years had passed, and we were still stuck in the same apartment with Kit, Ma and the maid. Trouble every day. The maid and Ma. The maid and Alice. Alice and Ma. One chicken one duck. Hokkien and English. Neither could understand the other. I fired the Filipina maid and got a Sri Lankan maid. Even worse. Spoilt the washing machine. Then the fridge. Even cleaning the windows led to problems! Every day Alice screamed and yelled at the maid and the boys when she came home. Most days my head wanted to break and explode when I got home after work. Every day *kenna* listen to your mother and wife complain, complain, complain could drive a man to murder. I didn't know marriage could be like this.

It wasn't just language. There was Ma's altar and her pantheon of Chinese gods. Alice wanted the boys to go to church. When Ma took them to the temple to meet the priest, Alice screamed, 'I don't want my sons to worship idols!'

On some days I thought maybe Alice and I shouldn't have married. So many things came between Ma and her. In two years we sacked so many maids: Filipina, then Indonesian, then Sri Lankan. All didn't work out. *Wah-piah-ah*! English has no word for my kind of frustration. I didn't know whom to believe when they quarrelled: mother, wife or maid. 'Best thing, I don't listen to anybody,' I told Alice. She said I didn't love her. She refused to talk to me for days. Weeks sometimes. My nerves were frayed. *Koyak*! How do you say it in proper English? My heart aches?

I drove for hours that night after whacking Ben. When I reached home past midnight, Ben was asleep, slumped in the armchair that he must have placed near the doorway. I locked the front door. The soft click woke him.

'Ben, are you waiting for me?'

Without a word, he hugged me before padding off to bed.

Alice and I quarrelled every day. Sometimes it was over office matters. We got into each other's hair working in the same tiny office. At home she slammed doors and broke bowls. Three or four times in the past year Ma had threatened to jump out of the window so that Alice and I could see what we were doing to her. I stopped taking her threats seriously. Luckily Kit had a job which kept him out late. Sometimes he slept in his office. Who could blame him? I would've slept in the office too if I'd had to share a room with Ma. I'd enough problems already trying to keep the housing agency going. The economy had hit a slump. Business slowed down. Prices fell. But there were no buyers. Money was tight. Every day Alice wanted a divorce. Every morning and night Ma knelt before her gods and chanted prayers in a loud voice to pray for my business and prosperity. Her chanting drove me up the wall but I couldn't tell her not to pray.

Then one day Alice and the boys moved out. She had rented a flat in Serangoon.

'Her husband meets with hardship, and she leaves him,' I overheard Ma telling someone on the phone. I started to pack a few things. Kit, man of few words, said to me, 'If you don't join Alice and the boys, you'll lose them.'

I moved in with the boys in the new flat. Alice didn't say a word. I knew she felt I'd let her down because I hadn't moved out *with* her, at the same time. I hadn't put her and the boys first. I'd put my mother first.

I sighed. What else could I do? I had to focus on my business. Times were bad. Singapore was trapped in a recession. But life went on. We continued to work long hours. Alice and I. Housing agents in a recession. What to do? Recession or no recession, people only viewed flats after work or after dinner.

I could not spend much time with the boys.

Whenever I could I took them out during the school holidays. We went swimming. Sometimes we went to the community centre to watch Kit play badminton. The boys cheered him on, jumping up and down. 'Uncle Kit! Uncle Kit! Champion! Champion!' They loved to embarrass Kit. Sometimes the four of us went out for dinner. Nothing expensive. The boys, they didn't have expensive tastes. Burgers and fries. They were very happy already. I didn't have to spend much. Not that I had much. I had debts to clear. The closing of my company was a great blow. I'd let everybody down. Let myself down. Failed to give Alice and the boys a good life. Failed to make the grade, you know what I mean? Last year I had a business, was my own boss, drove a big car. This year I drive a small car and work for other people. And Alice still doesn't talk to me. I'm still sleeping in the boys' room.

And Christmas was here again. Yesterday. My first Christmas without Ma and Kit. He sent me an email: *So how, bro? How are things?*

I wrote back at once. The longest bit of writing I've done since school days:

The best present I received this year was from Ben. I don't know why but he always touches the softest spot in my heart. He acts as if he owes me, and his love for me is unconditional. I've been asking the two boys since January this year to think about what they want for Christmas. Seb, as usual, always knows what he wants. It's good 'cos I know he will have a direction in life, and his immediate request was for an MP3 player. When I ask Ben if he wants one too, he says no. I ask him why? since he also likes to listen to music. He says he can always listen to the radio or use the home PC, no point buying something just to put there and own just because everyone has one.

Since that day on every time we were free, we would discuss what he wants, and every time he would end up a bit frustrated. Then on the twenty-third night, while I was resting, he came to me, lay down on my tummy as usual and said, 'It's very hard for me to make a decision 'cos I already have everything that I need.'

All this while I was thinking that he is indecisive and slow in making decisions, that he will grow up as a worker and can never be a thinker, planner or decision maker. I was wrong—he is just an easily contented and practical type of person. He does not need the frills and fringes in life. He is happy with what he has now, and that means I have not failed him. Gratitude—the best present in life.

From Seb I learn persistence.

From Ben I learn simplicity.

My boys.

Shall I send it to Kit? Not the sort of thing you send your brother. But hey, what the heck? It's just a day after Christmas. It's still Christmas.

CHRISTMAS AT

SINGAPORE CASKET

Marley was dead—to begin with. There is no doubt whatever about that. The register of his burial was signed by the clergyman, the clerk, the undertaker and the chief mourner. Scrooge signed it: and Scrooge's name was good upon the Change, for anything he chose to put his hand to. Old Marley was as dead as a doornail ...'

'But mind you! He vowed that he would rise up from his coffin if anything were to happen to his company.'

'Imagine! To vow such a thing on his deathbed!'

'Aye, he was more Chinese than he thought he was. All his life the bugger claimed he was Irish.'

'My foot he was! He married a strange kettle of fish. Out in the Far East on that little tropical island conquered by the Japs because those fools had the battery guns facing the wrong direction. Out there, old Marley married a Chinese writer.'

'You don't say!'

I walked up to them and flashed my father's name card. The two old coots almost fell off their barstools in Heathrow Airport.

'Cripes! Are you a member of the family?'

'I'm Mah-Li's daughter.'

I might as well set them right about my parents. My mother is the Chinese writer, I tell them, but she writes in English. She left my father, Mah-Li O'Connor, years ago. There's no Scrooge in my father's company. He invented that when he started the company with my mother's savings. Why that name, you might ask? Because my father believed that his name, Mah-Li, was the Chinese version of the Irish name Marley. He had read Charles Dickens in school, and had been colonised by his English Literature teacher. As you can tell from his name, my father was what the racist Chinese in Singapore used to call *chap cheng* or mixed blood. He was half Chinese, but his Irish side disappeared when his father left his mother and returned to Ireland for good. His maternal grandmother gave him the name Mah-Li, (horse's strength), when he was born. Admittedly it was not an elegant name but a necessary one. My father was a sickly child. The Taoist priest said that he needed the strength of a horse to survive— *loong-ma qin shen* (dragon-horse vitality). It was something that my father turned to his advantage later in life. His business cards read: MARLEY O'CONNOR in English on one side, and MAH-LI O'CONNOR in Chinese on the other. Sometimes I wonder if it wasn't his name that gave him his troubled personality: Mah-Li, horse's strength, a name that only a peasant would give to his child. My father, the workhorse, worked himself to death. I'm flying home for the funeral.

Mother and Leonard will be waiting for me at Changi Airport. Waiting and reading—the two things I remember most about my childhood. I did a lot of reading then and still do, mostly legal books now. In my closet is a stack of Dr Seuss' books, grey and worn with use. I don't look at them any more. They are of no use

246 SUCHEN CHRISTINE LIM

to me. I should have given them away to some poor child except that inside each book my father had written, *For my darling daughter, Michelle*. Every year Leonard and I received a book from him for our birthday and Christmas. No money for child maintenance, just two books each year. My father was absolutely right when he told the divorce judge that Scrooge was not my mother's name and therefore she didn't own half of the company, Mah-Li & Scrooge.

My mother sobbed and raged. I can still see myself, a girl of ten, holding Leonard's hand. He's five, tired and irritable. We are waiting for our father. He is late again. He's always late. Sometimes hours late. Leonard is being tiresome again. He keeps pulling his hand away from me. He cries, so I smack him. And he cries harder. He's tired and hungry. It's eight o'clock. He wants his dinner. We've been waiting since two o'clock this afternoon. At such times I hated both my parents.

We spent weekends with my father and stayed every Saturday night in his apartment. The routine seldom changed. After dinner, while he worked on his computer, Leonard and I watched tv. Sometimes Marilyn, my father's Filipino maid, played with us. When I was ten, I didn't think it unusual that my father could afford a maid yet he couldn't afford to pay child maintenance. When Leonard went to bed, I stayed up to read or watched the late night movie on tv. Sometimes my father sat next to me, eating a bowl of ice cream.

'Is everything okay?' he asked.

I nodded but kept my eyes on the tv.

On Sundays he would take us to church. He was very insistent on that.

'Your mother is a heathen and writes rubbish.'

His opinions and pronouncements on Mother are popping into my head above the roar of the plane. I close my eyes and try to nap.

'Charles Dickens is the author for me. I make it a point not to read anything by a Singapore writer.'

My father waited for me to take his bait. Mother's third book had just been published. But I smiled. No comment. I'm just a lawyer. Who am I to stop a man from making a fool of himself? He used to hold forth and harangue Mother about how English should be taught in school, especially after Mother's friends had visited us.

'Call yourselves English teachers? Your colleagues couldn't even string a sentence together. Do they speak like this in class?'

'No, lah! Only among ourselves we speak like this.'

'Stop that! Don't bring the lah and walau into my house. I don't want Leonard and Michelle to pick up these expressions from you. You're an English language teacher. You should be a model of good speech. But you speak such rubbish.'

Mother was silent in those days. Was she cowed by his 'near native' English? Was that why she turned to writing? Because her spoken English could never measure up to my father's standard? He used to send me long emails about Mother when I was studying overseas. After reading them, I pressed delete.

'Brain haemorrhage, very sudden.'

Leonard sounds matter of fact when he tells me about the nature of our father's death. We are walking out of Changi Airport. I'm holding Mother's hand. She is glad to see me. I have not been home for four years.

'By the time his wife found him he was brain dead,' Mother adds. 'But they kept him on the machine for a few hours to make sure.'

'You were there?'

'Leonard wanted me there.'

I look at her but her face gives nothing away. Leonard is taking me straightaway to Singapore Casket. Mother is coming with us. I'm surprised, but I don't show it. I wouldn't go if I were her. By the time we reach the funeral parlour it is one o'clock in the morning. The place is deserted.

'Christmas Eve,' Leonard says. 'People are at midnight mass. Auntie Joan herself wanted to go.'

Auntie Joan is our father's wife. She will get everything he owned now. My mother will get nothing, even though it was her money that started the company. Leonard hands me a packet of fruit juice. I poke a straw into it and drink thirstily. On the table, covered with a white tablecloth, are plates of groundnuts and sweets and several lengths of red thread.

'Take a red thread when we go home later. Your grandma is still alive,' Mother says. 'A red thread, symbol of blood, of life, the red that links us, the living.'

Mother walks towards the casket in the middle of the room. I hold back, unsure of what I ought to do. Leonard stands beside me. We watch our mother, two children watching over her as she gazes down at the man she has not seen or spoken to for more than twenty years. She is dry-eyed.

'Why did you marry him, Mum?'

It is two in the morning when this question pops out of Leonard's mouth. There are just the three of us with my father's body. Leonard is standing on one side of Mother and I on the other side. We have sandwiched her between us—something we did throughout our childhood to shield her from my father's barbs. But now she takes our hands in her own, her two children, her sweet children, who want so much to protect her. She leads us to our father's casket. She bows her head. In death do us part, but here we are, the four of us, together at last after twenty years. A sudden intake of air rushes through me. My throat constricts. I try to breathe, but a sob escapes. Mother puts her arm around me.

'Your dad and I were very idealistic. We wanted to marry and volunteer to serve in a Third World country. But things didn't turn out that way. Life's like that, isn't it? He started a business, went to Ireland. Then things changed. He wanted to make his first million before thirty.'

'Half his company should be yours, Mum,' I say.

But she gives no sign that she has heard. And yet her phrase 'not a cent, not a single cent did he give' was a constant refrain in my teenage years when she taught during the day and wrote late into the night. We didn't lack anything except ... except joy, perhaps. Mother wrote her books while we studied. She would rather write than press our father or sue him for the child maintenance money. 'If I spend my time suing your father, I won't have the time and energy to write.' Hell, I remember thinking, she puts her writing first, before us. She should have sued the pants off him. I was a litigation lawyer even in my teens.

'He looks okay, doesn't he? Like he's asleep,' she says.

'The mortician did a good job,' Leonard adds.

I look from one to the other. Nothing they say makes sense.

'Dad donated his body to science. We found that out only at

the hospital.'

'Is that why they kept him on the life-support machine?'

'Ya, to keep him till they could get a team of surgeons to operate on him.'

'What did they take from him?'

'The cornea of his eyes, all his skin, the heart, the liver and other things. I can't remember. We were in a daze. We had to say goodbye to Dad in hospital because after that ...'

Leonard points to the casket.

'That's why it's closed up, sealed,' he says.

The casket is completely sealed, unlike at other wakes where the body of the dear departed lies in an open casket until the day of the funeral. In Dad's case only his face is visible through the glass.

'Shall we say a prayer for your father's soul?'

The three of us hold hands.

'It's Christmas Eve. Be generous, Michelle. He was a generous man in the end, your dad. I didn't expect him to donate all his organs away. I guess it's something you two can be proud of. People don't do such things in Singapore. In death, your father was the giving man I once loved.'

Leonard and I look at each other above our mother's bowed head. We must have thought of it at the same time. Mah-Li & Scrooge. Our father was Scrooge, after all. Generous in the end.

THE LIES THAT

BUILD A MARRIAGE

'Bring me a face towel, pleeease, somebody! This heat is killing meee.'

Mei plonked herself on the sofa next to me. She liked to act as though she was my mother's spoilt younger sister and part of our family. But she wasn't. She was Mother's prized lodger and the major source of her income. Desperate for money, my enterprising mother had rented out one of our three bedrooms to Miss Pak Mei, or White Beauty in Cantonese. She was a dance hostess at the Golden Swallow Cabaret.

The first thing that Mother did when Mei came to live with us was to tell me to address Miss Pak as Auntie Mei.

'And don't give me that look, I'm telling you,' she warned. 'I'm not running a guesthouse. I'm just letting out one room. Your father gives me peanuts each month. If he wants to eat well, drive a car and sleep in an air-con room, I've got to rent out to people like Miss Pak. Who else can pay me six hundred a month for board and lodging, eh?'

This was in the Sixties when I was fourteen and fifty dollars could buy enough food to last a family for a week. Mei's six hundred each month paid for Fah Chay, our *amah*, who did all the housework including making Mei's bed and tidying her room. Mei seldom woke up before noon. And because Mei paid Mother so handsomely, my mother didn't have to lift a finger to do any housework except to look after my precious younger brother, Boy Boy. Yet if you had heard my mother talk, you would've thought she was carrying a huge burden on her back. What annoyed me most was her constant worrying about money. She quarrelled with my father over money all the time.

My father was an irresponsible man. He had a car, a chauffeur and his own business. What business it was wasn't clear to me, but he was his own boss. So I couldn't understand why he didn't have enough money to pay our landlord, or why we had to live in a big house and then rent out a room to a dance hostess. As parents, they weren't the least bit concerned about the influence such a woman would have on me. Nor what our neighbours would think. They were laid-back parents. It didn't bother them, but it bothered me.

'If you want to follow blindly and become a dance hostess, I can't stop you. I sent you to a good school. My job's done. The rest is up to you. My own mother didn't even care whether I went to school or not. She had thirteen children. No time for any child. You don't know how lucky you are.'

Typical parent blather.

Our two-storey house was semidetached with a large garden. Our landlord was said to be rich but the old man, who walked with an obsequious stoop, behaved like a beggar. My father, on the other hand, acted as though he were a tycoon even though he couldn't pay his rent on time. When the landlord came to the house on the first of each month to collect his rent, my father would keep him waiting at the gate. Sometimes for two or three hours. We were not allowed to let him in.

'Who asked him to come so early? It's only seven. I'm not awake yet,' he retorted when Mother tried to pull him out of bed. 'I didn't go to the bank yesterday. Tell him to come back tomorrow.'

The following morning the old man would arrive promptly at seven. Again he was made to wait outside our gate. Our neighbours could see him, seated hunched on the stone bench, waiting outside the house he owned. But my father stayed in bed till ten or eleven o'clock. If he had the money that day, he would come down the stairs like a grand lord, hand the money to Mother who would then run out to pay the poor man. If he didn't have the money for the rent that day, my father would stride down the stairs as if he was late for a very important meeting, get into his car, slam the door and tell the chauffeur to drive off. Immediately after that, my poor mother would invite our landlord into the house, out of the hot sun, offer him coffee and breakfast and plead with him to be patient.

Yes, our landlord was a doormat. I couldn't understand why he accepted such shit from my father, and said so one day.

'Don't you be rude,' Mother chided me. 'Don't think our landlord is so pitiful! Poor thing! Appearances deceive. He was a loan shark in his younger days, an illegal moneylender who drove poor people to suicide. His interest rates were exorbitant. He did unspeakable things to those who couldn't pay back their loans. That's what people say about him, not I say, ah! These days he's paying for his ill-gotten wealth. I always believe the wicked will get their due. His wife was murdered. Stabbed outside their house. In front of his very eyes. To this day the killer has not been found. His only son and only daughter, both are mentally retarded. Men! Because of him his whole family suffers. So he acts humble now. Atoning for his crimes.'

Still, I didn't think it was right for Father to treat him like that. Fortunately, after Mei moved in, Father could pay the rent on time and the landlord stopped hounding us. So I began to appreciate Mei's presence in our house. But my father didn't. He disliked Mei. He took pains to ignore her. I never saw him nor heard him talk to Mei. Not even 'good morning' or 'how are you?' He pretended he didn't see her. Yet it was obvious to Mother and me that he noticed all that was going on.

'Aiyah! What shall I *dooo*?' Mei moaned.

My father looked up from his evening papers.

'Should I dress up or not? I don't know where Wong is taking me tonight.'

He put his head down again when Mother spoke.

'Can't you just wear your usual?'

'No, he doesn't like me to look like a cabaret dancer when we go out.'

'But he knows you work at the Golden Swallow.'

'But my darling's *sooo* old-fashioned!'

'Humph!' My father snorted and buried his head behind the papers again.

'Mr Wong is old-fashioned? Why, he visits bars and nightclubs,' Mother said.

'Aiyah, he's old-fashioned only when it's meee! Not old-fashioned when it's other wooo-men.' Mei giggled.

'Doesn't that mean Uncle Wong cares about you, Auntie

Mei?'

'How many times have I told you not to butt in when adults are talking? Run upstairs. Switch on the air-con for Auntie Mei!' Mother glared at me.

That was how she pampered her prize lodger. I had to run errands for Mei whenever she fretted about her boyfriends. And she had dozens. She was an attractive dance hostess. Had a slim waist and hair that reached her shoulders. Many men phoned to ask for her. I met two of them.

The first one was the boss of the furniture shop where Mei had bought her bedroom suite when she moved in. Like a fly caught in a spider's web, the poor sod was so besotted that he didn't charge Mei for the furniture. He even bought her a new air-con unit and paid for its installation. Can you beat that? The good thing was that it saved Mother some money because, as the landlady, she was supposed to have installed an air conditioner in Mei's room.

During the two years that Mei lived with us, Mother must have made a considerable sum as her landlady. Take Mr Khoo. He always paid Mother handsomely for a bowl of herbal chicken soup that she cooked specially for him.

Mr Khoo was an antique dealer who owned a shop in Orchard Road. He was a devout Catholic. Went to mass every Sunday with his family. But he also visited Mei every Saturday after dropping off his wife and daughters at the novena church service in Thomson Road. Mei liked him because he was very generous and he didn't stay long. He spent less than an hour in her bedroom at each visit, and left punctually at noon to pick up his family. Before he rushed off he would give Fah Chay ten dollars, sometimes twenty, because she had to make Mei's bed after he had messed it up. Sometimes he even gave me ten dollars when I brought him the soup that Mother had boiled for him.

'A strengthening soup. To build up your manly strength,' Mother said.

Mei's giggles and Mr Khoo's chuckles puzzled me. I couldn't see what was so funny about drinking black chicken and ginseng soup. It tasted horrible, but he gave Mother fifty dollars for it each week.

'Such a nice man,' my mother beamed.

But Fah Chay took a sterner view of things.

'He can't buy me with his dollars. I'm not so easily fooled,' she muttered in the kitchen. 'The old fox! Very clever to hide things from his wife. Lucky he's not a Buddhist. Thinks he can use money to pay for cheating on her. The Lord Buddha wouldn't hear of it.'

But I liked Mr Khoo. He was the one who introduced the novena to Mei and me. Before that I knew nothing about Our Lady and the novena, even though I went to a convent school.

'It's very good. Go for nine Saturdays. Don't stop. Must go all nine Saturdays. Pray to Mary, the mother of Jesus. You'll gain an indulgence, and your wish will be granted.'

'Mr Khoo, what's an indulgence?' I asked.

'Hm, I learnt that in catechism a long time ago. Can't remember what Father Paul said. In the Roman Catholic Church the pope can grant an indulgence. When we die, we go to purgatory because we're all sinners. But if you have an indulgence, your time in purgatory will be reduced. Something like that.'

'Ah so! An indulgence is like a special passport! Get you to heaven faster!' Mei laughed. She laughed a lot in those days before she met Mr Wong. 'That's why your wife goes to the novena every Saturday. You need a lot of indulgences!'

'Ya, ya, I need. I need.' Mr Khoo's face was flushed.

Now that Mei had fallen in love with Mr Wong, boyfriends like Mr Khoo had stopped coming to our house.

I switched on the air-con and bedside lamp. Mei's room was cool and perfumed. Thick maroon velvet curtains were kept drawn to keep out the sun during the day. Musk, rose and all sorts of mysterious scents emanated from the bottles lining her dressing table. There were jars of creams and lotions, boxes of powder, rouge and eye shadow, and lipsticks and hairbrushes. Her dressing table had three mirrors, with two side mirrors that folded towards the centre so that you could see not only your front but also your profile when you put on your make-up. Her drawers were crammed with boxes filled with rings, bracelets, trinkets, necklaces and earrings. All fakes, of course, except that these were not the cheap fakes sold in the *pasar malam* or night market. This was expensive costume jewellery that cost fifty or more dollars a piece. I opened another drawer. It held her scarves and shawls; a third was filled with her bras; and a fourth held her panties of satin, silk, lace and nylon so sheer that you could see through them. Red, black, purple, pink, green and blue panties with matching bras. Some were just itsy-bitsy pieces of silk. I couldn't see how they could cover anything. But, oh, I did adore those itsy-bitsy panties! Each was like a forbidden fruit—rich, ripe and luscious. How I loved the feel of cool silk against my warm skin.

I locked her bedroom door. Then I did an unspeakable thing.

I wore one of Mei's red panties. A flaming red pair. I pulled it over my dull white cotton, and lay down on Mei's king-size bed. Her peach-coloured satin bedsheet was smooth and cool against my body. I looked at myself in the mirrors. There I was, lying on my back, reflected in the three mirrors of the dressing table on my right. On my left, the full-length mirrors of Mei's wardrobe displayed my reflection. A thrill coursed through my lanky body. I felt heady and reckless. Like I had drunk a shot of whisky. What with the perfumes and the red satin sheen on my butt, I watched myself preen and stretch out a languid arm as I lay supine among the satin sheets. A seductive flat-chested Cleopatra reaching out to her Caesar. Each reflection in the mirror was a fragment of my body.

Is this how Mei sees herself with a man? In disembodied fragments?

I jumped out of bed, pulled off the red panties, unlocked the door and dashed into the bathroom across the landing. I stripped and threw off all my clothes. Turned on the tap. I didn't know what I was washing off but I needed a shower.

To this day I can't bear the sight of red panties or sleep on satin bedsheets. They smell of moral decadence.

One night—no, one morning—it must have been after three o'clock when a taxi drew up outside our gate. Our porch light came on. From my window upstairs I watched Fah Chay run out to help a dishevelled Mei out of the taxi.

'Todaaay ... I'm not com-ing hooome!'

'Shush! Shush! You'll wake up the whole neighbourhood, Miss Mei!'

'Wake up! Wake up, worrrld!'

I saw my father march out to give Fah Chay a hand.

'Nooo! You leave me alone! I want to walk! Walking alooone is meee!'

Mei belted out the lyrics of a Mandarin pop song as Father hauled her into the house. I hurried downstairs. My father's face was angry and grim.

'The taxi picked her up near the Chinese cemetery.'

'What was she doing there?' Mother asked him.

'Why don't you ask her yourself?' Father looked as if he would explode when Mei suddenly threw up all over him. 'Ugh! Take her away! Take her!'

He stomped upstairs and I heard the sound of running water as he washed himself. Fah Chay crushed some newspapers and started to mop up the mess. Vomit was everywhere. Mother made Mei sit down.

'Here! Drink this. Thick black coffee. People go to the cemetery to get lucky numbers from the dead. What were you doing there? We were worried sick. Mr Wong called so many times. "Where's she? Where's she?" I kept telling him I didn't know. You should've told me. He was very sorry for what he said. You shouldn't have forced his hand like that. Are you going to get drunk each time you quarrel with him? This is no way to carry on. If he could marry you now, he would. That's what he said. Believe you me! I want you to marry him. He's good for you. But you've got to give him time to talk to his mother. He's her only son. Why did you go to the cemetery at night? Anything could've happened.'

'I went there to scold my bloody ma!'

'What's this got to do with her? She's dead.'

'She abandoned *meee*! If she hadn't, I might've gone to school and become *somebodiii*! Now I'm *nobodiii*! Wong's mother doesn't want a nobody as her daughter-in-law. If I were somebody ...!' She threw up again.

'You're drunk.'

'Who says? I not drunk! I die!'

Mei slumped into the armchair, tears streaming down her cheeks.

'I die.'

'Fah Chay, make her a cup of ginger tea.'

'I'll do it, Mother.'

'You! What are you doing here? Go back to bed. *Kaypoh*. Busybody!'

A week later Mei asked me to accompany her to the novena service at the Thomson Road Catholic Church.

'But Auntie Mei, you don't understand English. The service is in English.'

I wasn't keen, you see. At fourteen I was acutely self-conscious and fearful of what my friends would say. How could I go to church with a dance hostess who wanted to ask the mother of Jesus to help her catch a man? It wasn't right.

'You don't know English, how are you going to pray to Mother Mary?'

'I pray to her in Cantonese, lor! She's a god, what! She should know all languages. Kuan Yin, Goddess of Mercy, is from India.

She understands us Chinese.'

What else could I say?

On Saturday morning I watched her put the finishing touches to her well-made-up face. Her red lips were a contrast to the green eyeshadow above her eyes. As she brushed her shoulder-length hair, I was suddenly reminded of another Mary in the Bible, the woman (was she a prostitute?) who washed Jesus' feet with her tears, dried them with her hair and anointed them with fragrant oil. An extravagant gesture that earned her the disapproval of the righteous men around Jesus. I didn't want to be judgemental like the men. I was determined to be nice. But it was hard work being nice.

'Squeeze, girl. Push ahead. Push.'

The church was packed. Mei bulldozed her way through the crowd, her bouquet of pink roses held high above her head.

'To the front! I want the holy water to fall on me when the priest does the blessing.' To my horror she hissed in broken English, 'Exicue me! Exicue me!'

I didn't know where to hide my face.

There was standing room only. Those who could not find a seat stood in the aisles between the pews, fanning themselves with their hymn books and blocking the way. The ceiling fans were whirring furiously above the crowd that had squeezed into the church, but it was impossible to disperse the heat and humidity rising from this mass of humanity. My tee shirt was soaked. I hoped no one would recognise me. If they did, I would pretend that Mei was my aunt. But I would not introduce her. She was not the kind of woman you could introduce to your classmates and say, 'Meet my aunt. She's a lawyer' or 'My aunt, she's a teacher.' I wanted to turn back, but Mei refused to give up.

'Exicue me, exicue me!' she pushed down the crowded aisle.

Like a hapless sampan, I was towed along.

'This is even worse than the Kuan Yin Temple in Waterloo Street, I tell you! But at least no burning joss sticks here. In the temple the women don't care if their joss sticks singe your hair. Church is better. We just bring flowers.'

She placed her bouquet of roses reverentially at the foot of the statue of Our Lady of Perpetual Succour.

'Look at all these baskets of flowers. She must have answered many prayers. A very powerful goddess, this mother of Jesus!'

We squeezed ourselves into a pew, forcing those already seated to make room for us. Then Mei fished out her rosary beads with a silver cross dangling at the end of a silver chain. She held the glass beads in both hands and bowed her head like the old lady next to us. I couldn't resist asking, 'Auntie Mei, you pray to Kuan Yin. Now you pray to Mary. Is this okay?'

'Why not? Mother Mary and Kuan Yin, both are merciful, what.'

The front of the church was like a stage. Four boys came out in their red and white vestments. They lighted the candles on the altar, genuflected and stood at the side.

'So cute! They look like girls. Are they boy priests?'

'No!' I was horrified at her ignorance. 'They're altar boys. They help the priest.'

'Oh, I thought like in Thailand where boys become monks for a while.'

'No, not like that. What are you praying for?' I asked so that she would stop making stupid remarks. The woman next to me was smiling. She must've overheard what Mei had said.

'I'm praying for marriage, what else?'

The choir burst into song.

I was relieved. Then the priest entered, resplendent in his green and white robes. The congregation stood up. Mei and I followed. I tried to pray, but I was distracted. Mei was holding her rosary and hymn book, pretending to follow the singing, pretending to the people around us that she could read the English words. Her hymn book was open at the same page as mine. She could read numbers, but not words. A grown woman unable to read. How sad. My finger traced the words of the hymn we were singing. I too pretended that she could read. Not because I was kind. More because I didn't want her to embarrass me. I felt exposed. Like I had worn the wrong dress for church. One that showed too much flesh. Any minute now someone might point at me and say that I was a fraud. I was hot under the collar. I felt the piercing glance of the woman behind us.

The next Saturday we went again. Every Saturday, rain or shine, I had to go to the novena service with Mei. The moment the service began, Mei's eyes never left the altar. She was held spellbound by the priest and his colourful robes.

'Last week a Chinese priest in white and red. This Saturday it's an *ang moh* priest in green and white.'

'He's Irish,' I said, appalled that she didn't know.

'So you like church?' Mother asked her.

'Yes, I like. Two more Saturdays. Then my wish will be granted.'

'Not *will* be, Aunti Mei. It's *may* be,' I stressed. 'Wishes aren't granted that easily. If that were so, every student would pass their exams with flying colours.'

'But I have faith,' Mei declared.

She enjoyed the hymn singing, the genuflections and the ritual blessing at the end of each service. When we sang, she glanced at my hymn book. She turned a page when I turned. Her mouth opened and closed like a goldfish when the congregation sang. Looking at her, no one would've guessed that she couldn't follow the service, which was conducted entirely in English.

On the ninth and last Saturday Mei surprised me. She sang the hymns with great gusto. Her voice was louder than the rest. When we sang the chorus of the *Ave Maria*, her 'áve, áve, áve Mariaaa' crescendoed. Her voice trilled and fell with the music of the organ as her eyes swept upwards to Our Lady in the stained glass window above the altar.

Such devotional pretence! I was irritated. I didn't like the way she was drawing attention to us. People turned to look at her. Could she have memorised the English sounds without understanding their meaning? Watching her, I teetered between admiration and condescension. She was bold. She believed. And she was singing as if she knew the words.

When the service ended, Mei genuflected. She daubed a copious amount of holy water on her forehead before we left the church.

'Now I will wait for my sweetheart's mother to accept me. I've been to church. I've been to the temple. I've prayed to Eastern and Western gods.'

'Won't they clash?' Mother teased her.

'Clash? What clash? Can you explain, my dear sister? What clash?'

Mother was stumped. She was a devout Taoist who prayed diligently to the Jade Emperor in heaven, the Goddess of Mercy, the God of Prosperity, the Earth God of Longevity, the Kitchen God and the entire pantheon of ancestral gods in the religion of our forefathers. She believed that the just would be rewarded and the wicked punished in the eighteen layers of Chinese hell. 'Don't lie. If you lie, the horse-headed guard will cut off your tongue when you die!' That about summed up my mother's religious faith.

When I was five or six, she punished me with the force of the Thunder God. Her justice oozed out of the end of a cane which she had bought for one dollar at the market. When I was eight, she said I was too old to be caned. I had to kneel under the table instead. For hours I knelt under the dining table till my legs were numb. No, I would not apologise. I would rather kneel and die under the table, which was covered with a tablecloth that reached to the floor. In that dark space underneath, I learnt to escape my mother's threats of Chinese hell.

She had sent my eight-year-old soul plummeting down its eighteen levels. Each level was like one of those depicted in the garden of Haw Par Villa. When I closed my eyes under the table, the horse-headed guards came. They took me to the level where liars, pretenders and hypocrites had their tongues cut off. Next, we descended to a lower level where murderers had their bellies slit open. Then the bull-headed guards removed their guts and intestines. Further down another level cheats, loan sharks and charlatans were flung into a cauldron of boiling oil. Then wife-beaters were whipped. Next level. Robbers had their hands chopped off. Level by level, the horse-headed guards guided me till we reached the level where the ungrateful child was judged. I opened my eyes. I could not go on. It was too terrible to contemplate.

I sought for ways to escape my mother's hell. At age eight I did the smartest thing that a child of my intelligence could do, a child who studied in the Convent of the Holy Infant Jesus. I ran into the school chapel. I beseeched Michael, the archangel, the slayer of the serpent and Satan, to save me. I became a Catholic at age eight. I told no one about it. It was my secret. I pledged loyalty to the Christian god and Michael, his archangel. My powerful archangel, my guardian angel and all the other angels in Christian heaven could now be summoned to fight against my mother's horse-headed guards and bull-headed guards in Chinese hell. Hail Mary, full of grace ...

'Mother Mary can understand *meee*! Both Mother Mary and the Goddess of Mercy will understand! Now I'll just wait for Wong's old ma to accept me, lor!'

How simplistic, I thought. At age fourteen I was proud of my ability to think and reason logically and objectively. School had trained me well. I knew where to draw boundaries between Eastern gods and Western gods, and I knew such out-of-bounds markers like 'don't have sex before marriage'. Mei had mixed up her gods and boundaries. She'd failed to distinguish between true gods and false gods. My mother, on the other hand, was very clear about what was what.

'Taoist heaven is different from Christian heaven. If you die a Taoist, you go to Taoist heaven. If you die a Christian, you go to Christian heaven. It's logical. You cannot mix. You're my daughter, girl. If you convert and become a Catholic, you'll never see me again when we die. I'll be in one heaven and you'll be in another heaven.'

'So there are boundaries even after we die, ha? Like borders between countries?' Mei laughed.

'Why not?' My mother was very firm. 'Heaven must have borders. If not, how to keep out the bad souls?'

'Sometimes I ask myself, you know, is there an English heaven? Where is the Chinese or Malay heaven? What do you think, girl?' Mei turned to me.

I was stuck. In catechism class we were taught that heaven belongs to the believer. The division between the believer and the nonbeliever was very clear. Nonbelievers with good hearts burn in purgatory until they accept Christ or until God takes pity on them. Of course, this doesn't make sense to me now but in those days, when I was fourteen, I was peeved when Mei challenged me.

'How would I know if there are boundaries or not?' I hated it when I was put in a spot. 'Do *you* know, Auntie Mei? Do you?'

'I know.'

The certainty in her voice caught me by surprise. 'You know what?'

'I know there's only one boundary in heaven. The boundary between a good heart and a bad heart.'

'Yeah, like you know everything!'

I was not only peeved, but also jealous. That answer should have come from me. It was brilliant.

'How do you know?'

Mei pointed to her head. 'Got brain.'

'Pity you didn't go to school.'

That silenced her. She stopped smiling. I was ashamed of

myself. I had hit her below the belt. I apologised.

'Who needs school anyway?' She laughed and dismissed my apology. 'I need oysters. Have you ever eaten fresh oysters?'

'No.'

'Come, I'll take you out for an oyster lunch. Your reward for nine weeks of novena friendship!'

I knew then that our friendship would last more than nine weeks.

'Go on. Eat as much as you like.'

'They look expensive, Auntie Mei.'

I felt very grown up. The waiter at the restaurant in the Grand Ocean Hotel had brought us a silver platter of grey shells shimmering with translucent jelly, topped with slices of fresh lemon. I was ecstatic. Fresh oysters were a rare delicacy in Singapore in the Sixties. Ordinarily, we ate tiny oysters fried in *oh-luak* with egg and spring onions.

'Relax. I earned three hundred dollars last night.'

'Wow! You dance only and you get three hundred dollars.'

'Hey, girl. You think it's so easy, is it? Try it. Make some fatso with gold teeth dance. He lumbers like a water buffalo. But you've got to make him think he's dancing like a prince! Then glue a smile on your face. Laugh. Laugh at his silly jokes. One ear in, one ear out. But, ah! When he greases my palm ...'

Mei's laugh had the tingle of cut glass. Sharp and brittle.

'What if you don't like to dance with him?'

I seized the chance to ask about her work.

'Don't like, also must pretend to like. If I say no I don't want to dance, word will get around. Soon people won't ask me anymore. In my line of work if you don't dance, others will. They cut in. You'll lose business. Then what do you eat?'

'So it is a business?'

'More or less. Profit and loss. I lose if people don't pay. Sometimes these men, they refuse to pay! Pretend only. They act drunk. So I got to let them go.'

'But why? It's not fair.'

'Life's not fair, girl. Cannot offend these guys. If they make trouble, then how? Worse, they might scar my face. Pour acid on me. Yeah, such things happen in the nightclubs.' She smiled when she saw that I was shocked. 'That's why I want to marry Mr Wong. Then I'll be safe, lor!'

She squeezed lemon juice onto the oysters. I did the same. She showed me how to use a tiny fork to pick the oyster out of its shell in the proper way. The cool jellied flesh slipped down my throat. I felt decadent, and troubled. I was gorging on oysters, paid for with money earned dangerously. I wanted to ask her why she didn't try to work as a maid, a salesgirl or a ticket seller in the cinema. Such respectable jobs were open to those with little or no schooling. But Mother had drummed into my head never to be rude, and that meant not asking adults such awkward questions.

The waiter brought us tall glasses of fresh lime juice and ice. I'd finished the half a dozen shells. Mei asked him to bring us more oysters despite my protests.

'Aiyah! My work is not that bad, lah! Eat!'

The blue sea shone and sparkled beyond the wide bay windows of the hotel. Splinters of sunlight danced on the bonnets of the cars parked outside. The tarmac in the car park steamed in the hot humid afternoon. Inside, the restaurant was cool and air-conditioned. I relaxed, pleased that Mei had brought me to a classy restaurant with tables covered with a starched white tablecloth and plush red velvet seats. Mother said one could always tell whether a restaurant was classy or not by its tablecloths. Cheap restaurants use plastic or leave their tables uncovered.

'A glass of water, please,' I said to the waiter hovering attentively near us. Mei's eyes twinkled. My Cantonese was imitative of the rich well-bred girls in the Hong Kong movies. 'Thank you so much.'

I held my glass delicately with my little finger sticking out. An affected gesture. It was my take on upper class gentility— just stick your little pinkie out when holding your glass. I was imagining what rich girls would do in a classy joint when Mei hissed, 'Psst! Mr Wong has just come in. On your right. Carry on talking but tell me what you see. Keep talking. Can you see him?' Mei lowered her eyes. 'Tell me who's with him.'

'A man and a woman.'

'Are they holding hands? He must be seeing some other woman.'

'Oops! Uncle Wong has seen me. He's waving.'

I raised my hand in a tentative greeting.

'He's walking over. They're all walking over.'

'Hello, hello!'

'Hello! What wind blows you here?' Mei pretended to be surprised.

'The lunch wind! Meet my sister, Anne, and her fiancé, George. Miss Pak Mei.'

They asked us about the oysters.

'Oh, very fresh. Sea fresh, straight from the sea, the waiter told us. You must order and try some, Miss Wong.'

'Oh really? They do look fresh, don't they, George?' Mr Wong's sister had a soft nasal voice but, although her Cantonese speech was well modulated, it was spoken in an English-educated voice. I disliked her at once. She sounded patronising.

'Do you like oysters, Miss Pak?'

'Oh, ya, ya! Oysters! I'm crazy about oysters, Miss Wong. Can I call you Anne?'

She glanced at her brother.

'Please do, Miss Pak.'

'Just before you came, Anne, I was teaching my niece here how to eat oysters with a fork. She's never had oysters before so I thought I'd show her. Show her how to eat them without using her hands. So important in good society not to use one's hands for oysters, you say right or not? So important to know these things if you want to eat in good restaurants that serve Western food, right or not? Can't use chopsticks all the time. Ha-ha!'

Mei was talking too much and too fast. Anne and George nodded and listened; they were courteous and polite, but they stuck stubbornly to bland comments on the food and the hot humid weather. I wished Mei would stop talking. She was too loud for the quiet restaurant. Heads had turned to look at her.

'Did you know that these oysters are flown in daily from Australia?' Anne turned to me.

But before I could answer Mei said, 'No wonder they cost a bomb! And this girl ate more than a dozen!'

'Please, it's my treat,' Mr Wong laughed. He turned to the waiter. 'Put it on my bill. Anne and George have just returned from Australia. They were in Melbourne. They graduated from the university there.'

'Wah! Are you doctors or lawyers? No wonder you can pay for our lunch!' Mei giggled.

I looked at my shoes and wished there was a hole I could sink into.

'No, Miss Pak,' George corrected her. 'We're opticians. I'm working in my father's shop, Bright & Clear.'

'Oh my! I know that shop! I must go there and make my sunglasses. You must recommend me a good pair and don't charge me a bomb! What about you, Anne? Are you working too?'

Anne's eyes appealed to her fiancé and her brother. I could tell that she was appalled by Mei's familiarity.

'Anne is going to work with me after our marriage,' George said.

'Oh, when? When are you marrying? You must let me know. I must come and wish you happiness! Congratulations! Congratulations! Big wedding dinner, eh?'

'No, no, my sister and George want a quiet wedding.'

'Oh, when? Where?'

'We really mustn't keep you and your niece from your lunch.' Anne put an abrupt end to Mei's questions. 'Goodbye, Miss Pak.' She turned and walked back to their table.

'See you later.'

Mr Wong gave me a wink and patted me on my shoulder. But he must have meant it for Mei who was overjoyed that she had met Anne. When we reached home, she told Mother all about the meeting.

'I made a very favourable impression on his sister. Very lucky, ah. I know that Wong usually takes his family to the Grand Ocean

Hotel for lunch on Saturdays. I was hoping to bump into them. Maybe meet his mother, you know. But the old lady didn't go. Just his sister and her boyfriend. But never mind. Wong brought them over to our table. That gave me a lot of face.'

I felt used. So Mei had more on her mind than just giving me a treat.

'If his sister accepts me, it'll be easier to bring his mother round. Let's see what my darling Wong-wong says when he comes tonight. His mother is called Wong Tai. I shall be called Mrs Wong. How does that sound to you?'

Mei's eyes were bright like a child's.

'It sounds very good, Mrs Wong!' Mother teased her.

Mei handed her an envelope.

'What's this? Why so much?' Mother counted the fifty-dollar notes. 'More than six hundred here. It's ... why, it's a thousand. Mei!'

'Just to thank you, Sister. I'm giving Fah Chay something too. I gave all of you a lot of trouble that night I was so drunk.'

'Aiyah, Mei, we're family.'

Mother stuffed the envelope into her handbag.

I was glad to get out of the sun and into the shade when I returned from school. I stopped in the doorway to allow my eyes to adjust to the sudden dimness. The three lethargic shapes in the living room barely noticed my entrance. The Rediffusion was switched on. Mei, Mother and Fah Chay were engrossed in another episode of *Wuthering Heights* retold in Cantonese.

Mother, pen in hand, had stopped tallying her accounts as she listened. She had started a tontine group recently to help my father because one of his businesses had failed yet again. Mei was lying on the sofa with a wet towel over her eyes while Fah Chay, eyes half-closed, was seated on the cool tiled floor with her back against the wall. Her face carried the scars of smallpox. A peasant from the Tung-Koon District near Canton, she had big hands and feet. She was not the sort of *amah* who was prized for her good looks, but for her willingness to work hard. Her favourite saying was, 'With two hands and two feet, I won't starve.' When her parents arranged for her to marry the idiot son of their landlord, Fah Chay eloped with the help of an aunt. She was eighteen at the time. Since then she had opted for the single life in Singapore.

'No need to depend on others. I depend on myself. One life. One journey. One step at a time to the next life.'

The voice of the housekeeper in *Wuthering Heights* sounded like Fah Chay's voice, the voice of a plain-speaking Cantonese peasant woman. Looking back on that afternoon, I realise now what I didn't at age fourteen: female independence comes in different shapes and sizes. Our *amah* had a mind of her own.

I tiptoed past the three of them, and sat down at the table to have my lunch. As I ate I listened to the Bronte story of love and passion with two ears. My English ear remembered the accents of the Yorkshire moors while my Chinese ear heard the Cantonese voices coming from a secluded mansion somewhere in the depths of rural China. There was no Singapore voice. It hadn't emerged yet. It was still enmeshed with the voices of traditional China, the China that taught and demanded unquestioning obedience and filial piety. Mother switched off the Rediffusion when the programme ended.

'Mei, aren't you going to call him yet?'

'What for? He's still his mother's filial son. She says sit, he sits. She says run, he runs.'

'Aiyah, Mei! You've got to see it from Wong's point of view too. His old ma owns all the family assets. His hands are tied. Unless you don't mind marrying a pauper. Can't you just wait? Listen to what he has to say first before you quarrel with him, can or not?'

'Can! You keep asking me to marry him, but his mother said no. What's there to quarrel about any more? That filial son should please his mother. Go and marry a virgin. Not me. I'm a lump of dirt! People pick me up and put me down. He picked me up from the roadside. That's what he said. Why do you think I went to the cemetery, eh? If my witch of a mother had had a heart, I wouldn't be the shit I am today! She sold me, her own flesh and blood, to a prostitute. Why do you think I ran away? I ran away before they could do anything to me. I ran away. At least give me some credit for that! I lived on the streets for months. How else could I live? Yet I've learnt to sing and dance. I made my own way from that miserable hole, Telok Anson, to this city, Sing-gah-pore! Wong knows all that. Why doesn't he have the guts to tell his mother? Oh damn it! I said I'm not going to cry! I will not! I will not cry!'

She ran upstairs and shut herself in her room. That night Father had to call the ambulance. Mei had taken an overdose of sleeping pills. She was rushed to the General Hospital.

'That's when she found out that she's expecting. She's had so many abortions and miscarriages she never thought that she would conceive.'

'She's sure it's Wong's?' Father asked.

'If not Wong's, whose? Who else has been sleeping here these past six months?' Mother retorted.

My father was silenced.

Ming Li was born in August, just before National Day. Mr Wong took his mother to the hospital to look at his newborn daughter. When Old Mrs Wong saw the baby, she said, 'Bring them home. Mother and child.'

But there was no wedding. No wedding dinner, no white gown or wedding cake. Only a few friends and relatives were invited. We went as Mei's family. My father was strangely quiet. He held my six-year-old brother's hand when we went in to see the baby.

'Aiyah! No wedding dinner, never mind. More important is the tea ceremony,' Mother consoled Mei. 'When you kneel in front of Old Mrs Wong and she accepts your cup of tea, she's accepting you as her daughter-in-law. That's the custom and tradition. Even the court accepts this tea ceremony as a sign that you're married. Right or not?' She turned to my father.

'Humph!'

That night my father went out and came home drunk. I heard Mother berating him in their bedroom. Oh god, they're at it again. I glanced at my watch: 3.15 a.m.

Our house was strangely quiet without Mei. Money was in short supply again. One morning I looked out of my window and my heart sank. Our landlord was back, waiting at the gate. Mother was furious.

'Must we always rent out rooms to cabaret girls to make ends meet? Don't you ever marry a rich man's son!' she yelled at me as though it was my fault that Father couldn't pay the rent. 'Rich men's sons are useless! Spineless!'

'Shut your gap!'

Father marched downstairs, got into his car and drove off. He had dismissed his chauffeur a month before.

'Useless! Helpless! Spineless!' Mother screeched after him.

I went outside to tell the landlord to come back another day. He handed me an eviction notice instead. My father owed him six months' rent.

Mother hit the roof. Sobbing into the phone, she managed to extract six months' rent as a personal loan from Mei. I don't know what my father said that night when Mother told him about it. They had a huge row.

I was preparing for my O levels that year, so I ignored the comings and goings of my parents. Some days my mother's eyes were red and swollen. She phoned Mei each time we needed money to tide us over to the following month. Father started coming home later and later. My brother and I hardly ever saw him.

Then one day Fah Chay resigned. Mother could no longer pay her.

'I'm very sorry to go, but I've got to think of my old age. I have to work and save for the day I cannot work. Take care of yourself, girl. Study hard. Your mother has a hard life. She comes from a poor family like me. Your father's family was very rich in Malacca. His parents didn't like your mother's family. They disowned your father when he insisted on marrying your mother. So they left Malacca and came to Singapore. When you were born, your grandaunt on your father's side sent them money regularly. Then she passed away, and there was no more money. That was when they rented out the room to Miss Pak Mei. So study hard, girl. Look after your brother.'

In 1969 Father's business collapsed.

'Got to go to Jakarta. Urgent business,' he'd told Mother.

He didn't come back. He went missing for months, hiding from his creditors. When the landlord evicted us, Mother called Mei several times but with no success. Either she wasn't in or she wasn't taking Mother's calls any more. One day when she called again, Mother discovered that the line had been cut.

'That's gratitude for you! After all that I've done for her, what thanks do I get?'

'A few thousand dollars,' I wanted to say but didn't.

Mother cried when we moved into a tiny three-room flat in Queenstown. Our world had suddenly shrunk to three small rooms. I missed our garden and trees.

We kept to ourselves. Father, who had returned by then, was listless, thin and worn out. His dreams of opening a nightclub and a grand restaurant—no, a chain of restaurants—had crashed. The odour of failure and bankruptcy clung to him. His friends and colleagues avoided him. No one seemed to have any work for him. Not even a clerical job.

'With two hands and two feet, we won't starve. That's what Fah Chay said.'

Mother pawned off her jewellery. She bought an oven and started to bake cakes. She hawked them door to door. My brother and I learnt to take orders over the phone. The work of baking, packing and delivering was backbreaking, especially during the festive seasons like Christmas and Chinese New Year. But we had food on the table. One day Mother came home and shouted at Father.

'Oi! I got you a job!'

'What job?' My father hadn't worked for a long time.

'Never mind what job! You know how to drive, right or not?'

Mother arched her brow, a sign that she would not brook any excuses from him. She was now the de facto head of the family. Her *kueh-kueh* and cakes were bringing in a small but steady income.

'The bus company is recruiting drivers. I asked the men at the bus interchange. "Very easy to apply," they said. Just bring your driver's licence and identity card. Driving is better than sitting at home. You'll rot if you don't work! Right or not?'

So my father became a bus driver. If he had any regrets about the work, he kept them to himself. He was a sad, silent man who sat in front of the tv when he was not working. My mother's temper had a short fuse in those days. She nagged and scolded and made him work even on his rest days.

'Oi! Help me. I've only one pair of hands. Pack these cakes in the boxes and take them over to Mrs Lim in Tiong Bahru! And take the bus, not taxi. All that I make will not pay for the taxis you take every time you deliver my cakes!'

My father did as he was told. I felt sorry for him then, and hated my mother for her harsh words.

We lost touch with Mei. And it would be more than forty years before I knew the rest of her story. In the meantime my parents continued to row and bicker but they stayed together, and I suppose my brother and I were grateful for that. In an age when married couples with more money divorced like flies, our bickering parents hung in there. I would like to think they did it for our sakes. Perhaps it was my father who did it for our sakes.

He smoked and drank but he did not leave us, and he kept his bus driver's job till he retired.

My brother was a gem; he grew up fast. Did well in school and got a scholarship to the polytechnic. I finished my A levels, worked for a few years, took the night school private university route, managed to acquire a degree in accountancy and got married.

Today my parents are still living in Queenstown. My father drives a Comfort taxi part time these days, and Mother does some home sewing and baking when she's not fussing over her grandchildren—my brother's two boys and my two girls.

Last year my father paid off all his debts. That was the first day he and Mother had gone out together since we'd left the house in Watten Estate, more than twenty years before. They had lived such angry separate lives that it seemed a miracle to me when Mother said she and Father were going to the Kuan Yin Temple in Waterloo Street to offer thanksgiving prayers.

'And that was where I saw Mei,' Mother reported when I dropped in for dinner. 'I waved and waved and called out to her but she walked away. Very fast. Disappeared into the crowd outside the temple. Right or not, Pa?'

She turned to my father but he was strangely reticent.

'Mother, maybe she didn't recognise you,' I said.

'Can't be. I saw her looking at your pa and me.

'Ah, well! She's gone, she's gone. Where's my dinner? Eat! Let's eat!' Father stopped all talk about Mei. 'Why bring up unhappy things on my happy day?'

'Yes, Ma. Let's celebrate!'

My brother opened a bottle of cold beer and handed it to our father.

'Come children! Sing "Happy Birthday" to Grandpa!'

I watched the deep lines on my father's face crinkle in a toothy smile. That day he promised his grandchildren that he would stop smoking.

'Yeah! Three cheers for Grandpa!'

'Humph! Let's see how long that will last!' Mother snorted.

I almost snapped at her. She had a knack for putting my father down. She'd been browbeating him ever since he'd become a bankrupt. She held it against him. He had failed her. Failed us. And she would not let him forget it.

In December James and I were at the wedding dinner of a colleague's daughter at Mandarin Court. To my surprise I found us seated next to Anne Wong and her husband, George. Naturally I asked about Mei.

'My brother divorced her years ago.'

'Oh, how's her daughter?'

'Ming Li's fine.'

'Who's she with? Father or mother?'

'Neither. She's overseas.'

My husband tapped my hand. I stopped being so darn inquisitive. Other guests joined us at the table. Anne and George praised the shark's fin soup, and we talked about the bride and groom.

I didn't tell my parents about bumping into Anne and George, but my curiosity was aroused. One evening after work I looked up the address of Bright & Clear. The shop had moved from its humble beginnings in South Bridge Road to The Orchard Grand. But to my dismay Anne and George had retired and the shop had changed hands.

'More than two years now,' the mother of the new proprietor said. She was a chatty woman in her sixties. 'I come to the shop every day to help my son. Sit at home, so boring.'

I asked if she knew the Wongs.

'I knew Anne's mother. She passed away some years ago.'

I asked her if she knew Mei. There was a long pause.

'Ah, the woman that the son brought home. That affair ended a long time ago. The son remarried. His wife is a doctor, I heard.'

I asked about Mei's daughter.

'Actually Old Mrs Wong was very kind. She kept the child even though the little girl wasn't her son's. She brought up the little girl. Now what's her name? Ming Li. Yes, that's her name. Spoilt her rotten, but the girl's quite smart. Now studying overseas, I hear.'

'You mean Ming Li is not Mr Wong's daughter?'

'Aye, he was a naïve young man in those days. Believed everything that woman said. He should've asked her to go for tests before taking her home. If not for her later miscarriages and the blood tests and everything, he wouldn't have known that the girl wasn't his. When he found out,' she dropped her voice, 'aiyoh, he hit the woman so bad that she had to wear a cast for weeks. I'm not exaggerating. He broke her bones. And then, to cut a long story short, he kicked her out of the house. So Old Mrs Wong gave the woman a large sum of money. Actually, if you ask me, it was to buy the little girl. Had a lawyer make the woman sign an agreement. She'd to give up her little girl. Old Mrs Wong doted on the girl. Said the woman wouldn't be a good mother to her.'

I said I was sorry for Mei.

'She brought it on herself. Cheated on so many fronts. Old Mrs Wong said the daughter could be her former landlord's. Her landlord's wife kept calling and asking for money. It was blackmail, I tell you. It was terrible. The landlord's wife knew that the Wongs were rich. They're still a very rich family today. The Wongs had to change their phone, and even moved house because of that.'

I couldn't sleep that night. My head was filled with all sorts of rubbish caught in a gale. I began to see my parents through new eyes.

Whenever I visited them, Mei came to mind. That my father had women friends did not surprise me. What shocked me was my own imagination. I kept thinking of Mei's bedroom with the dark maroon velvet curtains, satin bedsheets, the large mirrors and drawers stuffed with black, red and purple panties. And my father had gone in there.

I glanced at him. His hair, styled in a crew cut, had turned completely white. He wore dentures. He was already seventy-eight. What right have I to probe into his past? Disturb his peace? Would my mother want to know what I know? Should I tell her? And would she benefit from my telling? What good would it do her?

A part of me clung to the status quo. The other part sought knowledge and justice. I smelt the faint odour of exploitation somewhere. The truth was I was curious. But curiosity was not reason enough to destroy the truce that my parents had so painfully built between them. And so I dithered that whole year, and did nothing in the end.

If Mother hadn't found out that Fah Chay, our former *amah*, was in the home of the Little Sisters of the Poor in Thomson Road, I wouldn't have thought about Mei again. We visited Fah Chay who was delighted to see us. She sat in a wheelchair, frail and thin but as chirpy as a sparrow.

'And how are you?' I asked.

'Very blessed. They're very good to me here.'

Then she broke the news to us. Mei had hung herself.

'Died alone in a rented room in Kuala Lumpur's Chinatown. Very sad. Died on Chinese New Year's Eve. Couldn't accept her son's death. The boy had water in his brain. No cure. Five years old. She had him very late, you know. Very late in life.'

Fah Chay's cousin had worked for Mei in Kuala Lumpur. According to the cousin, Mei had gone there after she'd left Mr Wong. She used the money given to her to set herself up in Kuala Lumpur, and had returned to work in the nightclubs, first as a dance hostess then later as a *mamasan*, introducing women younger than herself to the nightclub's male clientele. Then she'd met a businessman who'd eventually married her.

'Grand wedding, ah! All paid for by her. Not the man. White wedding gown. Grand wedding feast. People said she was already over the hill. An old hen. More than forty years old and still wanted to wear white. But she didn't care. She'd never married properly before. For once in her life she wanted a proper wedding, she said. In the living room of her house in Kuala Lumpur, before she sold it, she hung a large wedding photo of herself and the groom. Boasted that she'd finally achieved what she'd always wanted—a husband and family. Then she suffered three miscarriages, one after the other. The son that was eventually born had a very large head. Full of water inside. The doctors said no cure. Poor Miss

Mei. She brought the boy to Singapore hoping to find a cure here. Because of my cousin, I saw her a few times. Back and forth. Back and forth she travelled. Very sad. Visited so many temples. Even went to church again. Also no use. By then that man, her husband, had taken all her money. He travelled very often. 'Sometimes gone for months,' my cousin said. Then Miss Mei found out he already had a wife and family in Sabah. Then her boy died. She was all alone. The husband didn't even come back for the funeral. The boy died a week before Chinese New Year. The husband didn't come back for New Year. Mei hung herself on New Year's Eve in a room she rented above the coffee shop. No one knew. On the third day her landlord broke down her door and discovered her body.'

Mother was very quiet on the way home. So was I, for different reasons. I was very sorry that as a self-righteous fourteen year old I had once judged her as frivolous and lacking in morals when all she wanted was to marry and have a family.

My father died in his sleep a few days before his eightieth birthday. According to Chinese tradition this called for celebration, not mourning. My father had lived to a ripe old age. His wake was held on the ground floor of their apartment block in Queenstown. On the second night, after our friends and relatives had left, I found Mother standing near my father's casket, gazing down at his body. When she saw me she said, 'There lies a rake.'

'Ma!' I was shocked.

'I wouldn't say it if it wasn't true. Ask him. I'm saying it in front of him.'

'Ma.'

'He was a rake. I'm not lying or slandering him. What didn't

I suffer as his wife? He fooled around with women. I even had to bring one of his women home to live with us.'

I gazed at my mother's white hair, curled in a short frizzy perm. The lines around her eyes and lips followed the downward curve of her mouth. Why hadn't she divorced him? I thought.

'Was it Pak Mei?' I asked her gently.

'Who else? I knew what they were up to behind my back. I was no fool. But I treated her well. Never let on that I knew. I squeezed my heart and taped shut my mouth. I let our room to her so she could see him for what he is—a lazy, arrogant layabout. Not a cent in his pocket. He talked big only. So she married Mr Wong.'

'Ma.'

'To be fair to your father, he left his family for me. I never forgot that. His family was rich. Mine was dirt poor. But he left his family to marry me. And we stayed married. To the end.'

I heard the note of pride in her voice, a woman's pride—he had loved her first and last. By venting her anger at last, she was getting rid of the bitterness in between. I took my mother's hand and squeezed it hard.

'That is love, Ma.'

Her thin frame shook in my arms. I held my seventy-six-year-old mother. I held her tight. She's all I have. Pa's gone. Did she love him? Did he love her? Does it matter now? What is love? Is it fidelity? The act of staying together till death do us part? In the end, everything must end in death and forgiveness. If not, how do we live?